HUGWHORE

DANiEL WILL-HARRIS

COPYRIGHT

THANKS

To my friends and family—both biological and logical —with love. You know who you are.

I'd also like to thank the characters who told me their stories. *Writing is about getting out of your own way and listening.*

A note about the fonts in the printed edition:
The body copy is *Georgia,* by Matthew Carter. It's designed for maximum readability. The headlines are *Autorich Sans* by \rief Setyo Wahyudi for his foundry Typia Nesia in Malang, ﹞onesia. It's designed for stylish fun!

THE 45

This is painful but it must be said. I am a forty... five year old man. There, I said it. I read that *the truth will set you free*—so why don't I feel better yet? I guess I have to spill *all* the tea.

Turning 40 didn't bother me—after all I'd enjoyed being 39 for three years. More importantly, I could still pass for a man of thirtysomething. But 45? You *know* you're aging—starting to look a little bit like your father —or worse—your mother, and there's no turning back.

I've drifted into *almost* middle age without a career, boyfriend, sugar-daddy, husband, alimony, retirement savings, sensible shoes, or a plan to get any of them.

I'm *not* unlovable. I've had a number of boyfriends— each for at least a month too long—well past the point where I knew that I couldn't really stand them anymore. I just didn't want to hurt their feelings or be alone—a bad combination.

I'm *not* incompetent. I'm good at so many different things. Like flower arranging. And decorating. And baking. And organizing. I *could* hold a job... if I wanted to. But I'd rather find a less tedious and more fulfilling way to get people to hand me stacks of cash.

I'm *not* stupid. I read somewhere that you don't pay a hooker to come to you—you pay them to leave.

So how do I get someone to pay *me* to go away? Or simply hand me money for being a good person: I never steal someone's parking space or tell them they have a bad haircut.

That kind of kindness doesn't come naturally. My mother couldn't stop herself from criticizing the hair and clothing of complete strangers. Those are genes she gave me, so, *not* talking shit to strangers merits some kind of compensation. Right?

What else could people pay me to do? Binging Netflix. Fine dining. Napping. *Cuddling!* I'm sure Type-A personalities would find these valuable traits because they don't know how to relax.

I am an expert relaxer! Type-A people might be better at going to work every day and bringing home a paycheck, but other than being poor and lonely I like to think I'm the happier one.

At least that's what I tell my best-friend and roommate, Esme, which is short for Esmeralda. None of her friends call her that because it makes her sound like a fortune teller. It doesn't help that she has a habit of wearing turbans with large rhinestone brooches in the center.

When I tell my tale of woe to Esme she rolls her eyes, "Yeah, so what's new?"

To which I reply, "Nothing. That's the problem!"

Esme is busy cooking for her food cart. She originally called it "Cupcakes for dinner," a questionable concept featuring savory cupcakes. *No,* this was *not* my idea, and *yes,* I think it's a bad idea, but Esme is my best friend and I support her, no matter what.

Besides, a "beef stroganoff brioche with sour cream frosting," doesn't sound entirely revolting. We bake all this stuff in our apartment kitchen which is wildly illegal and therefore exciting—pirate bakers! I even took to wearing a patch over one eye, but only after I'd accidentally hit my face with a spatula and was afraid of blinding myself.

Not surprisingly the cart hasn't done that well yet, even launching at pride in West Hollywood. Buff gays love cupcakes, but they only take a single bite then hand it to their other buff friends for a bite. Eventually the majority of the cupcake lands in the hands of their chubby bearish friend who they adore because he's no competition, so they make sure he's always well fed.

The truth is, pretty gays don't ever admit they're hungry or eat actual meals. When they think of food they imagine untouched Instagrammable plates. What they eat are bite sized portions of fancy food at exorbitant prices. So I first suggested naming the cart "tiny portions of fabulous food you otherwise wouldn't allow yourself to eat." But then I came up with *"Tiny Dinners: What's Lunch Got to Do with it?"* which instantly made her business jump by 250%. I am something of a marketing genius, but is anyone clamoring to hire me? Don't make me laugh.

Just like: is anybody clamoring to bring me home to their mother? Don't make me gag. Which remembering that I'm 45 does.

As luck would have it, I don't have wrinkles. It's called "the magic of fat." I used to fight it, but now I look at it as a blessing hidden under the curse of love handles. At least I don't need Botox or filler. There's only so much plastic surgery and filler a person can get without running the risk of looking injection molded, like Stallone and Schwarzenegger. Or completely unrecognizable like... I can't even remember her name anymore because after the nose job I couldn't recognize her... Jennifer Gray. That's who. She had her nose done and even her best friends didn't know who she was. That new nose put Baby in the corner.

Same with the actress who played a singer gays love... Why can't I remember names? Am I losing my mind at 45 or is this normal? Squinty eyed actress... I am not going to Google, I am going to remember, dammit! Bridget Jones... Judy Garland... I can think all around it until I figure it out. Renee Zelwegger! She got her eyes done so they were no longer squinty and the world thought, "Who dat?" Sad part was she swore she didn't have anything done, I mean, why not just come out and say, "I could hardly see through my squinty eyes so I got some work done and now I look like a stranger."

All that said, if I had the money I'd pull, stretch and inject 'till I looked like Ryan Reynolds (who, by the way, is my age!) Like that'd even be possible. What usually happens is you turn into something akin to the terrifying wax figures at Madame Tussaud's.

The new poster boy for "I've had too much work done," is Tom Ford who was, for many years, my dream boyfriend, but now he looks plasticized which I find less appealing than wrinkles. Or so I tell myself since I can't afford plastic surgery or injections. I also have a deathly fear of Botox which, little known to the people who shoot it into their face, is actually the deadline botulism poison that leads to paralysis and death. Who *wouldn't* want that *in their face?*

It helps that I don't have any mirrors in my apartment, except the one in the bathroom I can't rip off the wall without losing my security deposit. It must be hell to have to look at yourself all the time. Nobody should have to endure that.

At least my apartment is beautifully decorated—because I have exquisite taste. I don't need to be modest, I do. All my friends say, "It's amazing what you can do with thrift store crap, Charlie." I *am* amazing that way. A $30 can of paint can zhuzh up a room if you can paint the room yourself or have a friend who will do it for you for a pizza.

My friends come over, crying, "Please, please, please, Charlie, please help me before my mother visits and sees my shithole." And I do. For more than the price of a pizza, because, yes, we're friends, but still, this is work. Not work I can live on, because when the entire budget is $250, and I need to buy paint and some vintage patterned bed sheets to use like wallpaper, the most I can reasonably pocket is $50. But, still, you'd think from the dramatic before and after pics on my Instagram that I'd get some clients. Sometimes I do, but $50 for two days work does not a profession make.

50... I'll be that old in only five years! The number *45* is floating in front of my eyes like it's burned into my retina—which it is because I've been looking at bright animated GIF birthday cards on my phone so even when I shut my eyes I can see that number.

I hate being vain. I was never good looking enough to warrant it. One of the good things about *not* being cute when I was young is that I had this epiphany when I was about 18 — "I'm not that cute now—but that means I'm not going to lose my looks as I get older!"

In fact, I've been told by reliable sources who would tell me *the whole stinkin' truth,* that I am looking better as I get older—my proportions look less odd. As Esme herself said, "You're growing into your face, Chaz." She always calls me Chaz which is how I introduce myself to new people, hoping it will stick. It never does. Esme is the only one who calls me Chaz, and only at my insistence and even then she rolls her eyes almost every time she says it.

I simply wasn't a "Charles," even though that was my birth name. *Charles* is a *King Charles—spaniel*. I'm Charlie, which is cute, but Chaz is *cool*. Occasionally someone will call me "Chuck" which is quell horrible! I can never forgive my mother for naming me Charles *Junior!* Then again, I can never forgive her, period. Even as a child I never told anybody about the "Jr." because that was too, too mortifying. Even worse than anyone over 40 wearing Vans skater shoes and calf length white socks with shorts. Nooo.

So I sit on my bed covered with an elegant chocolate brown satin throw I found at the bottom of a pile at the Rose Bowl Flea Market, along with a gaggle of delightful vintage pillows with maps of various places I've never gone—like Paris and Rome or basically anywhere outside the country, unless you count Tijuana, which I certainly don't.

Tonight I don't even have the energy to watch Netflix which requires at least some concentration even for reality shows where you only have to guess which object is real and which one is made of cake. Now I want cake. There's a 7-11 at the end of the block that's open 24-hours a day and has frozen *Sara Lee Lemon Dream* cake... or so I've heard. Don't judge and don't lie. Nobody doesn't like her.

I judge but I don't lie, for the most part, because I find it too confusing to remember what I've said and things get messy. So I always tell the truth—my truth at any rate.

I lie here in bed (the only lying I do!), and look out my window at the scrap of sky where stars would be if this wasn't Los Angeles and wonder what to do with my life.

My friends get me actual jobs and I do them all well. I can work in a law office. I can work in a bakery. I can work in a vet's office, but not with the cute animals because they're sick and that makes me too sad. I can work retail, though customers are assholes.

And in each case, I do an excellent job because I don't want to reflect badly on the friend who recommended me. But after a few months (or weeks... OK, *days*), I am so bored out of my mind that I have no choice but to tearfully tell the boss that I have learned I only have three months to live and am going to spend it on the beach in Hawaii. I know, that sounds like a lie, but nobody knows how long they're going to live, so it's just a... *existentialist explanation*.

Besides, they usually say, "Oh my God, that's what I would do!" and give me a bonus which tides me over for a month or so while I do not go to Hawaii because that would be expensive and take a lot of effort. Besides, I am not planning on dying. Eventually, sure, but not at the moment, anyway. For fuck's sake, I'm only 45!

So why don't I go to Hawaii? It would be lovely, sure, but then I'd have to come back and live the rest of my life feeling disappointed, comparing it to that beautiful time when I was going to die in Hawaii.

Since I don't want to think about death, I fire up my favorite "dating" app, *Boink*. There are the usual suspects. I've met a few of them. They rarely look as good as their photos, but then I don't look as good as mine, either, having carefully curated it from literally thousands of selfies.

Wait, there's fresh meat... and he's unusual. Profiles of older men often say "not generous," which at first I thought was horrific. Like really, who wants to date you if you're not a generous human being? Then I realized it was because there are so many guys who are looking for a sugar daddy.

I, myself, would be thrilled to have a sugar daddy—if I thought I could be considered remotely sweet. But I figure I wasn't cute enough for that when I was young, so that ship has sailed. Still, I inspect this man's profile. He lives in Encino. He looks rather desiccated and the corners of his mouth turn down—but the living room furniture behind him is gorgeous!

I always notice the background of people's profile pics. So many men take pictures in their cars and I've even become a master of recognizing the make and model, like, "Who's this schmuck is in his wretched 2005 Pontiac Aztek? I am *so* not interested!" I'm not a gold digger but please, people, have some sense of style, even a 20-year-old salvaged Lexus like mine which I've named *Goldie* because she used to be gold but now she's brownish... She still has cream leather seats!

I recognize that this guy took a selfie in his Mercedes E Class while in the middle of a car wash. That shows some taste, refinement, cleanliness and maybe a sense of humor. The selfies he took at home were well-lit. Home selfies are always an important reflection of a person's value... I mean "values." For example, if they

have no art on the walls they're transient or artless—
nope. If they have piles of clothes on furniture, or
worse, the bed, I'm like "no, I'm not going over to your
house and have to deal with piles of possibly dirty
laundry before we get to it, that's not going to happen."

But this somewhat unhappy looking man has a very
beautiful house. There is the requisite Eames chair and
floor to ceiling windows and I can even see light
reflecting from a pool onto the mid-century beamed
ceiling. Definite possibility. I mean, just for afternoon
tea and the occasional skinny dip.

His profile says he's retired from finance. This all
sounds terribly dull. But then the last line of his profile
read, *"I'm very generous to my friends."*

I instantly think, "I could be your friend!" What's
more—miracle of miracles—he's not looking for twinks
or muscle guys but "younger polar bears," basically me!

To the rest of the world, "polar bear" means "old, fat
and gray." I don't think of it that way. I think of myself
as "*mature, substantial and silver!*" At least that's what
I tell myself every time the words "old fat and gray" pop
into my head.

I might be 45, but his profile says he's 62 and his
picture says, "I'm 70 if I'm a day," so to him I'll be (air
quotes) young (Closing air quotes). Bingo!

I reply to his profile with a simple, "I think we could
be friends." I no longer sweat over clicking *send,*
because 9 out of 10 times I'll hear nothing. More like 99
out of 100! I send men thoughtful notes after reading
their entire profile and picking something out that we
have in common, like "Wow, what a coincidence. I love
pizza too!" Or "I'm also interested in Studebakers from

the 1950s" which isn't really true, but at least I know Studebaker was a car. I'm sure the young 'uns think it has something to do with a studly baker.

I'm surprised when almost immediately I receive a reply saying "Hello Chaz, let me take you out to dinner." Well, this man has said the magic words right off the bat, "Let *me* take *you* out to dinner." Not "let's *go* out to dinner," which means anything from "we're going Dutch" to "I will forget my wallet at home and then you can pay for both of us." But in this case, he is very clearly inviting me to be his guest!

I take a few minutes to reply because I don't want to seem too eager or desperate. Both of which I am. I write, "That sounds lovely. Where do you suggest?" Right after I hit *send* I think, "That was a mistake! I should have suggested something like Mozza or another expensive restaurant I've wanted to go to but I *can't* afford." It would have been a test because if he suggests something like "In-n-out" which I actually do like but *can* afford myself, I would be less inclined.

Oh—I feel bad about thinking that because it sounds cheap and mercenary and while I don't mind being cheap, mercenary is an ugly word.

About 15 seconds later he writes back, "YAY!!!!!!" with six exclamation points which looks desperate but I can relate to that. He writes, "How about 8pm Saturday at Spago?" Hmm, Wolfgang Puck's classic restaurant in Beverly Hills where I'd never dreamed of going because the cheapest thing on the menu was a single baguette for $12 and that's more than I usually spend on an entire dinner.

This being Tuesday and I having nothing on my calendar for Saturday that sounds great. But first I Google "parking at Spago," which is $22, *with validation,* more than I would spend for an entire meal... Then I remember that Beverly Hills, being a super rich city, has a number of free parking structures. Yes, I'll be wearing my metallic Doc Marten wingtips which hurt like hell, but it will be worth the pain of walking two blocks to save $22.

I reply with, "That sounds fantastic. I'm so excited!!!!!" I am honestly excited to have something to do on Saturday night and to go for a nice dinner and maybe meet a nice man with good furniture.

30 seconds later he replies with, "Excellent! I've made reservations and it's on my calendar. I'm so looking forward to meeting you!"

Now I start to worry because, 1) he's too eager, which makes me wonder what's wrong with him, and 2) I only have five days to choose an outfit. Wait—Wednesday, Thursday, Friday, actually only four days, I'll be cutting it close.

I want to present myself in the best possible light— like I am worthy of his generosity. I talk with Esme about this and she is not very positive, "Sounds like you're setting yourself up for disappointment again."

Honestly, in this case, her snarkiness feels completely unwarranted because the worst that could happen is that I'll get a nice dinner and be bored and my feet will hurt and that's better than most of my Saturday nights.

I start working on what to wear. A sport coat—no, that's old-mannish—but this guy had been in finance and he was wearing a sport coat in his Mercedes so I could wear a sport coat and a shirt and some slacks. That isn't me, I never even call pants *slacks*, but I could wear them.

But I want to be myself so I don't have to pretend to be someone for months until I'm forced to reveal who I really am and have the other person drop me like a hot potato (you say pot-aw-to).

Let's just say it happened once with a guy named Rod (his real name) who I convinced that I loved hiking. Again, not a complete lie, as I like *urban hiking*, which means on flat, paved surfaces with charming shop windows and the occasional patisserie.

After meeting online, I met Rod in person at Starbucks. I wore an unfashionable hiking outfit I'd borrowed from my friend Bruce, who, for some unknown reason, actually likes hiking. I managed to avoid any actual hiking with Rod for three full months, during which we became intimate in his Subaru and elsewhere. One day he annoyingly insisted we hike Runyon Canyon and I literally almost died. That kind of exertion is simply not healthy, especially given LA's air quality.

After that I was determined to always be myself, but *not so much* myself that my date might find me outrageous or annoying or unworthy of generosity.

I settled on a pinkish *Liberty of London* flowered shirt, a heathered gray Ralph Lauren cardigan I found at a thrift store, and a pair of red chinos, the color of the accent pillows in the background of his living room photo. I checked out pictures of the restaurant on Yelp and saw that the lighting was dark and thought "this will give off colorful vibes in a semi traditional package."

Thinking about the outfit like this was not completely random because I've been a stylist on and off occasionally professionally for my friends when they were freaking out about what to wear for a job interview or a hookup. I always choose the right thing for them.

So I'm pretty confident in my choice and the week goes by very fast especially since I have no job at the moment (I'm technically "in Hawaii waiting to die") and I am in the middle of watching Downton Abbey which has 52 episodes which means I can watch nonstop for two full days, except that I will sleep and eat and nap so it'll take me at least three.

Still, Saturday arrives with a shock so I quickly clean out my car on the off-chance he sees it. I spritz it with Febreze so it doesn't smell like a cheeseburger on wheels.

I drive by Spago and park two blocks away for the free parking. I hobble down Beverly to Canon in my uncomfortably chic shoes and finally limp up to the door. The valets shake their heads, they know what I've done—taken money out of their red polyester pockets. I'd feel sorry for them except I don't—I'm sure they're swimming in tips from Bentley drivers.

I tried to be a valet when I was younger but 1) It involved too much walking (the other valets actually ran, which is against my religion), and 2) It was hard not to take the fancy cars on joy rides... or cruising—a man always looks sexier in a Lamborghini. I mean, why not? The owners had good insurance so they could get a new car... But the valet boss found out and suggested I could be arrested, so I quit. While I wasn't too pretty for jail, I still wanted to avoid incarceration as I imagined it would wreak havoc on my skincare routine.

The doorman gives me the eye too, as if to hiss, "Nobody walks, you must have parked your car at a free lot, cheapskate, good luck inside with $12 bread." But I hold my head up high and breeze in like I own the place, which I don't want to because, as I learned with Esme's food cart, the restaurant biz is brutal.

THE DATE

The restaurant is *very* nice. Not spectacular—just *very* nice, still that's a full "very" more than the restaurants I'm used to where I usually end up spending all my money drinking with friends and then not having money for dinner. On the way out I stuff myself with free bread (taken from empty tables) to sop up some of the alcohol so I won't feel sick in the morning. Doesn't work, but it's still a good excuse to eat bread. On those nights I take a taxi to the bar... I mean restaurant... and home so I don't have to drive drunk because nobody should do that! I'm so responsible!

Tonight, since I have to drive myself home and want to make a good impression—I'm limiting my drinking to one glass of wine at the beginning of the evening... maybe two... I know about alcohol safety because I got a moving violation for driving through a red light on Mulholland at midnight. It had *just* turned red and was one of those lights that would have been red for a full five minutes. I didn't want to be a sitting duck, rear-ended by a wealthy Chinese or Arabian 18-year-old whose money-laundering father bought them a Ferrari.

They're hell-on-wheels, racing through the hills, burning rubber and smashing into unsuspecting drivers stopped at a stop light.

I check in with the maître d' but don't know my date's name. I feel a tap on my shoulder and there he is—standing right next to me with what I guess passes for a smile. I mean, the corners of his lips turn up before they turn down. At least he looks like his picture. I wonder if I still look like mine which was taken… I don't remember.

He's wearing a gray suit, white shirt and a gray tie. He's one of those guys that's so skinny his skin kind of hangs off. As luck would have it, being too skinny isn't a problem I will ever have to deal with.

He reaches out and shakes my hand limply. I think "oh, you poor man," put my arms around him and give him a big hug—more than a hug—a tight squeeze. I hear him sigh which either means I've pushed all the air out of his lungs, endangering his life, or it's been a long time since he's had a hug

I don't want to hug for too long because that can be misconstrued, especially since I didn't ask for consent, so I pat him on the back a few times and pull myself back and he's smiling even more.

He has very good teeth—a bit long, very white, and they all match perfectly so I can't imagine he was born with them but good for him. If there's one thing I cannot abide, it is bad teeth, poor hygiene or anyone who's boring.

At least he knows how to get a good table! We're sitting in just the right spot so we can watch everyone come in and make rude comments about them. At least that's what I'll do if he seems at all amenable to catty comments. Otherwise I'll... be bored, I don't know.

He says, "This is my favorite restaurant."

This pricks up my ears because if he comes here often maybe he will want to take his new friend, *me*, here often. I will decide whether that works for me once I find out if being bored is a reasonable price to pay for a fancy meal.

Then he starts to talk. I am not expecting this at all because usually the boring ones just sit there and look at me and expect me to hold the conversation, which I can do single-handedly. But if you want me to do a monologue then I either want to be on stage or be paid —I'm not here for *your* entertainment. I'm here for *mine*.

This guy, whose name I still don't don't know, is surprisingly entertaining. For one thing, when we met in the lobby I hadn't noticed the red white and blue ribbon at the cuff of his sleeve which tells the world, "Yes, I'm conforming but in a trendy and expensive Thom Browne suit." I can dig that.

Then the real shocker—when he was standing next to me he was too close to see his shoes. But now, he gracefully lifts his right foot to table height to show me he's wearing bright red high heels with red soles which mean they're *Louboutin,* the trademarked red soles inspired by the shoes in Louie the 14th Court. I know important trivia like this from reading too many fashion magazines—though, truth, I don't read, I mostly just look at the ads.

This man is a sartorial mullet: Business on top and party down below. "Party down below" has always been the watchword of my people, so now I'm the one gasping. He explains, seriously but with a hint of instability, that during the day he wears men's cordovan wingtips but at night heels are his shoe of choice.

I know "cordovan" is a rich shade of burgundy often found in fine men's footwear because it supposedly goes with both brown and black. "Cordovan" reminds me of when Ricardo Montalban was doing TV ads for the Chrysler's Cordoba featuring the "rich Corinthian leather," which was an entirely made up marketing term.

But it was the phrase "fine men's footwear" that made my mind jump back to the time I was forced to go to a mysterious "consciousness training" weekend by my crazy boss, famous greeting card writer, Pieter (yes, just one name). He'd previously forced the entire office staff to take lie detector tests when the petty cash went missing, even though the obvious thief never returned to the office. The guy giving the lie detector test told me how to cheat (either because I looked guilty or it was his way of flirting): just cough or clear your throat a lot, which I did, because I didn't want it known I'd taken home an office computer. So I didn't even have to lie!

Not content with our positive lie detector scores, Pieter forced us all to go to his guru's training—the kind where they don't let you out, even to pee. Fuck that. At one point I simply insisted I had to throw up and they escorted me out. I sensed, correctly, that the guru-like leader, Ron Jodger, would have cameras in the bathroom, so I turned off the light and made puking noises while I peed.

When I got back we did an exercise I called "Porsche Training" where we learned that "if you want a Porsche, you will get a Porsche." This, sadly, has still not worked for me, but maybe I just don't want one bad enough to actually work for it.

For this exercise I was matched with a disgustingly handsome young man who Pieter was fucking or the other way around. Mr. Handsome's dream in life was to "import fine men's footwear," which I thought was hilarious although I kept a straight face because I didn't want to hurt his feelings. I needn't have bothered: Pieter hurt his feelings a few weeks later when he flew the future footwear guy to Paris, found him lacking, and sent him home the next day. At last, someone handsome I could feel sorry for if not superior to.

>>>

Oh, my God, I just snapped back to reality and my date is talking and I wonder how long I've been in my own little world and whether I've missed anything important, like his name!

Probably not, as he holds out his very well manicured hands and shows me how his nails are buffed, semi-matte, not shiny. He reaches his hand across the table and whispers, "Feel it!" a line I've heard many times before but always in a radically different context.

So, we're already at the touchy-feely portion of the date. Will wonders never cease. His fingernails are as smooth as the glass on my phone, only warmer.

I tell him I want my fingernails to feel like this, and he says, "Oh fun! I'll take you to my manicurist, Olga Moat." Her name sounds like a baroque Bavarian castle —a fine thing for a manicurist. More than that, he says,

"I'll take you," which once again more than implies he'll pay.

"I'm so there..." I trill (maybe not actual *trilling* but something akin to it). I want to say his name at the end of the sentence but I still don't know what it is.

The waiter materializes like an apparition. Damned good waitering. "Good evening, Rober, would you like the usual?"

Aha! Rober! Fancy!

My date smiles at the waiter, "Not tonight, Jiles,"

I think, "Jiles, like an English butler!" and now I've instantly forgotten my date's name. Shit!

"What can I bring you then, Rober," the waiter winks, which I guess is what they do in expensive restaurants. How would I know? Oh, wait, I'm going to repeat my date's name in my head so I can remember it later, "Rober, Rober, Rober, Rober... Rober, like Robot, but crossed with a bear, Ro-bear," good, I can remember that even if I can't spell it.

Ro-bear says, "Tonight is a special occasion as I am escorted by a new beau."

"Beau?" Am I suddenly in a Tennessee Williams play? Cool!

"What is the chef's off-menu special?" Robot Bear.. no, Ro-ber, asks.

The waiter proceeds to say something in French I don't understand, and Rober replies in what sounds like perfect French, then turns to me and says, in perfect English, "Oh, I'm sorry. How rude of me. Do you mind my ordering for you?"

I am too stunned to say "as long as it's not raw fish," so I just nod, then realize I'm saying "yes" and I mean "no" so I shake my head. The waiter silently disappears like a hologram.

Rober says, "It's so nice to have such a handsome companion."

I look around wondering who he's referring to, then realize it might be me and give him a tentative, "Thank you?"

Rober's shoes are exquisite—and he has shapely ankles so it's a good look for him. But it also feels like he's two different people which makes me wonder what he'll be like without anything on. I wonder in an oddly platonic way because I'm not really physically attracted to him. But now at least, I'm intrigued.

He folds his hands on the table, "What should we talk about?"

I'm relieved that he didn't just expect me to talk and the first thing that comes into my mind is "butter," which I say aloud.

He gets very excited and says, "How did you know butter is one of my favorite topics? It's criminal how commercialized butter has lost all of its earthiness. That's why I only eat *Rodolphe Le Meunier's* butter from the Loire Valley made from pasture fed cows and slow wood-churned by hand for extra richness."

I am simultaneously fascinated and ashamed. All I've ever eaten is supermarket butter, which tastes pretty damned good—but, really, what I keep in my fridge is something in a tub called "light butter" that's "infused" with water so it only has ½ the calories, meaning I can eat three times as much.

Rober picks up the butter knife—gallantly as if it's a scabbard—and butters a piece of bread with a flourish.

He holds it close to my mouth—butter side down. I open my mouth and he presses it in gently on my tongue.

I feel the butter melting and spreading across my mouth with a flavor I can only describe as *pasture in the sun,* which is odd because I've never been in a pasture—and I don't like being in direct sun.

Still, I am almost completely certain this is what it would smell and taste like if I lounged in a sunny pasture—*ambrosial.*

I hope my eyes haven't rolled back to my head like a snake biting its victim because I am just so damn happy. Then I notice Rober is staring intently at me—either like I'm some creature in the zoo, or as if he's actually *interested* in me. This is another new experience.

I take a sip of the water which has tiny bubbles—not like anything carbonated I had ever had—but like they were designed to tickle my taste buds. I let out a sigh.

He says, "Ambrosial, isn't it?"

Coincidence or fate? Now I'm frantically wondering, "Oh my God, he may have to be my boyfriend, and I'll end up in love. I don't know what to do about that." My leg muscles instinctively twitch to get me to run away, but I'm kept in place by the monogrammed medallion of butter I am not about to leave!

"I've never tasted anything like this," I say to him, and he nods vigorously.

"I know, most people haven't, but this is how butter is *supposed* to taste."

I tell him about the time I went to a friend's house and they had heirloom tomato salad. I didn't like tomatoes or at least I didn't think I liked tomatoes, but I didn't want to be rude because they made it and it looked beautiful—all those different colors: purple, orange, red, green. I took one bite and said, "I didn't know this is what tomatoes were supposed to taste like!"

He nods again and explains now that he's retired, his goal is to reintroduce real food to children so that they will know what it's supposed to taste like. Then they'll know what they're missing when they eat commercial processed foods.

I think, "Oh my god, this man is a saint!" and at the same time, "Oh, you motherfucker, if I can never eat regular butter again, imagine what you are doing to these poor children? Once they get a taste of real food they'll know what they're missing!"

The thought is cut short by a shock—what feels like a rat crawling up my leg! I hold my breath to keep from shrieking, then look down and see a hint of shiny red— it's his shoe. I have completely misjudged this man. I take a deep breath, sit back and enjoy the sensation of his foot against my inner thigh.

But also I feel bad because while the *fantasy* of this would make me so turned on I just couldn't hold it together—the *reality* is shocking. overwhelming, confusing... embarrassing... and annoying. Luckily the waiter makes another surprise appearance and Rober's foot returns from whence it came, only to reappear between courses.

First up are appetizers that look like tiny ice cream cones! I use my best manners to pick one up slowly, pinkie out, and place the entire thing in my mouth. Oh. Mmm. Eh? Oh no. Spicy. I can feel my face turning red.

"Spicy Big Eye Tuna Tartare—Delightful, isn't it?"

Raw fish? My eyes are watering and now that I know what it is I don't want to swallow it. I hear my grandma saying, "Shut up, you've had worse things in your mouth." I know, lots of people love eating raw animals but I am not one of them. I consider the old "spit it out into the napkin" bit, but he's still staring at me so I can't get away with that. Maybe I'll pull a "nod and excuse myself for the bathroom," but the waiter incarnates by my side and asks, "Is everything satisfactory?"

I automatically want to answer, so I swallow quickly and reply, "Yes, lovely," and only then realize I have raw fish in my stomach. I wonder how long it'll be there. Rober lifts another fishy cone and again tries to feed me, which is both intimate and icky, only this time I take it out of his hand and press it to his lips.

Luckily there were only three on the plate (I remember seeing the dish online and it was $34!) and before he can try to feed me the third, I give it to him. I sigh with relief, which he takes to mean I'm satisfied, but really I'm wondering if there's more raw stuff on the menu. I don't even like raw vegetables because I feel bad for everything I eat until I know it's cooked and therefore completely dead to the point where there's no risk of retaliation.

Next, pizza and black truffle—yum! I've never eaten truffles, which mostly taste like mushrooms which are fine, though I always think they have a secret plan to make me part of their network. I'd be OK with this if they made me their queen, but who can trust a fungus?

Veal chop. OMG, so good that I can make myself forget it's come from a baby cow... shit, I just remembered it. I don't care, it's cooked. Besides, it was already dead and I didn't kill it, I just happened to be here when it was served and it's spectacular. It's given its life for a good cause.

I believe that, if given the option, most people would choose to have a few perfect years living by the sea, eating whatever they wanted with no stigma about getting fat—even knowing that at the end of their time they'd be killed in their sleep and used for organ transplants. I'd sign up for that. It's not like I have anything better to do. Remembering this makes me feel better about the cow.

>>>

...I'm snapped back to reality by Rober's roving *Louboutin,* which is getting less annoying the more he does it. That said, it makes conversation difficult, if not awkward.

"I can see you're a man who enjoys the sensual," Rober says, buttering another piece of bread for me. Really, I could come here just for that little loaf of bread and magical butter. Everything is else wonderful (well, not the raw fish), but I would mainline this butter.

Rober leans towards me, "I'm a very sensual soul."

"I can see that. I am, too. Do you have this butter at home?"

"Exclusively. I'm monogamous when it comes to Rodolphe Le Meunier butter."

Two waiters clear the table and a third wheels a cart with a Matterhorn of meringue which he lights on fire! The flames dance until they fade away, leaving a golden brown mountain which the waiter deftly slices, plates and places in front of me. I wait until he's given a slice to Rober then I dig in like a child at a birthday party—cake and ice cream! I pause only when I notice Rober once again watching me like an anthropologist.

I'm trying to be cool and elegant but this food is all too good. He looks happy so at least I'm providing entertainment without really trying.

"Have another slice of baked Alaska," he suggests, having hardly touched his. It's only now that I realize he's hardly eaten at all, he's taken bites but not cleaned his plate like I did (though, to be fair to myself, I never once licked the plates, despite the strong desire to do so).

"Yes, thank you," I say and the waiter slides another plate in front of me.

"Do you not like yours?" I ask Rober.

"It's sheer heaven, but I've already eaten too much. A few years ago I had half my stomach removed so I could fit into Thom Browne suits."

I am almost dumbfounded enough to stop eating, but not quite, because if I stop eating I'll have to figure out how to reply to that crazy statement. Clearly, if I have to decide between chocolate brown and Mr. Browne, chocolate wins.

I finish the second slice of Alaska. "How interesting," I say, which is honest, because it's interesting if insane.

"More baked Alaska?" Rober asks. "I have to say I enjoy your unrestrained appetite."

Normally I'd take offense at this statement and hold a grudge to the point that, three years later while eating the last M&M in the bowl, I would say to Esme, "I must apologize for my *unrestrained appetite"* at which point we'd both laugh but I'd secretly still be mad.

Now I merely say "Thank you. I have many unrestrained appetites," I find myself saying it seductively more out of habit than actual desire and because it sounds like something from a Noel Coward play, which is what I've always dreamed life should, or at least, could be.

"How charming," he replies, his foot now conspicuously absent from my leg.

"Shall we retire to your abode?" I ask, again trying to sound sophisticated but the word "abode" makes me think of "adobe" and I have to stifle a giggle.

"Absolutely not," he says, as nicely as he possibly could so it takes me a few seconds to feel embarrassed and rejected. "I never sleep with friends, and I hope we shall be friends."

Suddenly the room is silent, or maybe I've gone temporarily deaf. His words are, at once, a relief, a rejection, and, when I stop and replay his entire sentence in my brain, an acceptance. *Friends.* The noise returns to the room and I say, "I'd like that very much," even though I wasn't sure that was true. I hadn't really wanted to sleep with him, I was just being nice and I wanted to swim in his pool.

Rober must have noticed the confusion on my face and offered, "I should be open with you and explain that I don't like sex. I'm not asexual, I simply find it messy and complicated. I prefer cuddling, and then only with licensed professionals."

I signal to the waiter for another slice of Alaska. I mean, why the fuck not, it's not like we're going to fuck?

A therapist I once had, but left when I noticed food between his teeth, told me that I needed to be a better listener, to repeat, in my head, what had actually been said rather than what I'd heard. So I remembered, "I hope we shall be friends," and thought "dinner friends." That would be OK as long as there was this butter.

I slide my third slice of Alaska down my throat and say, "I love cuddling, but also understand where you're coming from."

"Do you? Do you really?" he asks, hopefully, as if nobody before ever had.

"I do. I need physical contact and I love to cuddle, but don't want any emotional messiness."

"Exactly!" he says louder than he's said anything all night. "The LGBTQIA+ community preaches inclusivity but a lot of those bitches can be fucking judgmental."

"I know that all too well," I say, wondering if there is any more Alaska. I am very full. Too full, actually, but I don't want to leave any cake and ice cream.

Rober beams and eats the part of his baked Alaska that isn't melted. Suddenly he looks stricken, his breathing short and fast. "Excuse me..." he pants before rushing away from the table.

Oh no. Am I going to be stuck with the bill again, like that time at El Torito when my handsome Latino date excused himself and never returned? And this after he ordered three cocktails!

I am not going to be stuck with this crazy ass bill, so I eye my possible escape routes. Maybe there's a bathroom window I can crawl through, or maybe I can slip into the kitchen and out the back door... I feel like a trapped animal.

Rober appears, slightly sweaty and apologetic. "I'm so sorry. I simply ate too much and when that happens I..." he trails off. I remember his half-a-stomach and figured he had to throw up.

What a waste. Years ago I tried to be bulimic, thinking it sounded like the best of both worlds: eat all I wanted and lose weight. But it turned out to be horrible, made my voice raspy and worse than that, every time I ate, I thought about what it would look like coming back up, so I lost my appetite. Luckily this period only lasted 5 days, after which I realized wanting to be skinny, like wanting a Porsche, wasn't something I wanted badly enough to do anything about.

A few of my female friends actually were bulimic and it was a sad situation. I took one to a rehab clinic where all the other inmates looked sickly. I picked her up a month later and the color had returned to her cheeks and she seemed so relaxed and happy. In the next three months she not only gained 50 pounds but also started to do plus-size porn. It worked out *for her,* she made a lot of money, bought a big house in the Hollywood Hills and forgot all her old friends, like me.

>>>

"Are you OK?" I ask Rober when my brain returned to my body.

"Yes, don't worry, dear. Next time I'll let you do all the eating." Ah, now I understood why he stared at me while I ate.

"What do you eat when you come here by yourself?" I wonder.

"Just a bit of the wonderful bread, butter, and a sliver of Wagyu beef with a port reduction. I take the rest home and eat it for a week."

"You're surprising," I tell him honestly.

"That's nice of you to say. I'd like to see you again for another dinner, but I'll understand if you don't want to see me again."

Oh, it hurts to hear that. "Yes, I'd like that—you're an interesting man."

"And you were afraid I'd be boring!" he laughs.

This time he's the one hugging me—thankfully not too hard because I am too full—the kind of full where it starts to be hard to breathe. After that all-you-can-eat-buffet at the naked bear pool party I promised myself I'd never be this full again (first world problems), but here I am.

I waddle to the parking garage where I can't find my car. I was so excited about dinner I forgot to take a picture of where I'd parked. I painfully schlep up the ramp for six floors until I find my car. At least I'm getting some exercise.

THE DRIVE

I drive home, thinking about Rober wanting to be skinny bad enough to have half his stomach removed. Have I ever wanted anything that bad? Is this the problem with my life? I just float along, doing the bare minimum necessary to pay the rent and afford drinks with friends and Trader Joe's Pound Plus 60% Belgian chocolate bars.

Why don't I have... I can't remember the word for when you have the kind of drive that makes you successful... Yes, I've literally blocked that word from my brain. It starts with an "a." Some of my friends have it—they will literally do anything to get ahead, even giving head, not bad in itself, but in this case to men they'd otherwise shun for not being buff enough.

Like Jake, who is always working his network, always working out, always working. After 6 years of this Jake is finally the first assistant to an A-list talent agent at the Endeavor Agency. If he can suffer through a few more years, or kill his boss, or fuck his boss' boss, then he might finally realize his dream of being an agent.

Jake came over after his birthday party at BayGar, a club with $1,000 table service bottles. He was literally crying because he was so tired and wired from coke. He admitted he had no personal life and now he didn't even want to be an agent.

He *thought* his life would be full of fucking his of A-list actor clients, but, in reality, it was the hard, dirty work of cajoling, outfoxing, if not downright lying. You were only as good as your last deal, after which, it didn't matter what you'd done, only what you were going to do. He fell asleep on my sofa and if I hadn't been the total gentleman that I am, I could have felt up his 8-pack, but I did not.

In the morning he pretended as if he hadn't said what he said and acted excited to go back to work, helping to package a deal for a new Jennifer Aniston series on HBO, where she'd play Mother Theresa. "Lots of buzz, lots of buzz," he told me, feeling bold enough to eat an entire banana.

Now, if Jake, who couldn't have been better looking, smarter, or harder working, was unhappy with life, what chance was there for me?

At the time I'd been working as a receptionist in the Life|Art gallery in Santa Monica. That was when I thought I wanted to own my own gallery. I'd start as a receptionist, learn the biz, find a rich boyfriend (that being the key to most of the gallerists I'd met), and be on my way selling *real* art.

But Life|Art focused on performance artists. This meant that the gallery walls were usually blank, unless they happened to be spattered with blood or piss from yet another tiresome performance, each so-called artist trying to outdo the last, all trying to outdo Marina Abramović.

I'd seen Abramović at MoMA and she was transcendent, a true artist. But the so-called-artists at this gallery were more like failed models who thought it was edgy to crawl naked between patrons' legs, then take a shit in the corner while everyone watched in disgust. Honestly, that's what *more* than one did during the opening cocktail party where well-dressed people (including me) were trying to enjoy their martinis.

I watched one otherwise-normal-looking young man, sporting a pitiful attempt at a mustache and goatee, squat, his face straining. I thought about slipping him a note that simply said, "More fiber, dear" but he had no pockets and besides he was trying so hard, poor thing. It was painful to watch, yet somehow I couldn't look away. Still, I wouldn't call that *art*.

Afterwards the gallery owner, who shall remain nameless because I swore to myself never again to utter

Ula's name... damn, I just did... expected *me* to clean up. Dealbreaker. Next morning when she came in and the shit was still there, I explained (not lied, *ass*umed since it came from their asses) this is what the artist would have wanted. The artist was dropped. I was fired —and greatly relieved.

...Oh, shit! I got lost in my thoughts and forgot to turn on Coldwater to drive home to Noho. Now I'll have to drive through *Boy's Town* (aka West Hollywood) where, as a 45 year old non-muscular man, I am basically invisible. I drive by the bars with their flashing lights and music so loud it rocks my car even with the windows up.

Inside I see the writhing shirtless bodies of boys with nothing better to do than gym and tan so they can look pretty for other boys who do the same thing. It's so empty, meaningless and attractive that I pity and envy them. They will grow old, their best days behind them. While I, having yet to be beautiful or successful, still have hope I'll magically become both.

I get home and Esme is too asleep for me to regale her about Rober. I sit on the sofa, still too full to lie down, and look out the window at the yellow street lights and the occasional Orthodox Jew walking their dog. I like those orthodox outfits but they seem awfully heavy for Los Angeles. Orthodox Jews don't even consider me a Jew, which I am, but only in a cultural sense... like I love Canter's Deli but never order cheesecake after midnight after that food poisoning incident.

I fall asleep for what feels like five minutes and am awakened by Esme banging pots and pans in the kitchen to prep her *Tiny Dinners* food cart she'll schlep to *Smorgasburg Sunday* downtown.

I hate downtown LA. Talk about "no there there," other than the Music Center for theater, really, why does anyone venture down there. It always feels dusty, dirty and vaguely vacant.

Despite this, I offer to help Esme because I am a fucking saint, but she says, "it's just easier if I do it myself." Now—there's something I could take personally, but, knowing Esme, she'd actually *rather* do it herself. At least that's what I tell myself as I take a poop the size of the Loch Ness Monster, followed by a bath.

THE BATH

I love taking baths, especially since, as a tenant, we don't pay for the hot water. I used to feel bad about using hot water because of global warming. For several years I only took cool, or maybe lukewarm showers. Then I saw a movie about Tokyo where the millions of people there *all* had bathtubs (and air conditioners!) and I thought, "If they can take baths there, I can take a bath here."

A bath is like returning to the womb, only in this case it smells like lavender, not something I remember from my mother's womb. Then again, if you looked at my mother you would wonder how anything human could have emerged from her skinny bitch hips. That explains why I was a cesarean, but it doesn't explain why, when the nurse came with me for her to hold, my mother said, "I'll pass."

Dad held me, and was always there for me while she was... I don't know where she was. She left dad when I was three and usually the only time I think of her is when I smell Chanel #5 which makes me retch.

She went on to marry a very rich man and live in an estate just six point five miles away in Beverly Hills but I never saw it, or her.

I hate her so much it still hurts. I need to stop thinking of her as "Mom" and use her real adult almost-human name, *Narcissa*. Ha! That alone should have warned dad away as a Narcissa flower is a daffodil and they're poisonous! But no. He was a romantic and she was a heartless cunt (a word I never use except for her because she's a cunt).

Dad was a landscape architect who specialized in high-end corporate offices—flowery contemplation gardens for the CEOs and atriums full of prickly low cacti for the staff so they could be watched from all sides if they dared to sit and try to enjoy the flora.

Dad was never happier than when he was in the backyard fussing with flowers. He loved arranging flowers and taught me how. He was so artistic I now wonder whether he was gay, but I never saw him with a boyfriend or girlfriend. When I went to the Art Institute school in Chicago, he sold our little house in Sherman Oaks and moved to 50 acres in Montana where he started the only organic tulip farm in the entire country. I hoped he had a secret boyfriend, or, yes, even a girlfriend.

I visited him for school holidays and he was happier than I'd ever seen him. A year later he dropped dead while tending the fields. At least I knew he'd died happy.

Meanwhile, the bank repossessed his farm and I felt alone in the world.

>>>

...Wow, all this from lavender in the bath.

Esme shouts, "I'm off, have a good Sunday, Charlie."

I come back to reality and the water is cold. I forgot it's Sunday. Does it even matter? I eat Fage plain yogurt with fig jam for breakfast and call Debbie LaPlant (she swears it's her real last name) to see if she needs any help at the florist shop.

THE FLOWERS

Sundays are usually busy, being the day when men and women relax before realizing in terror they've forgotten their mother's birthday. Then they're in a mad rush to send flowers to try to make up for it and blame the florist for delivering it late!

I actively try to forget my mother's birthday but remember every November 11th, because it's 11/11 and the skinny bitch "1's" remind me of her in profile.

Debbie croons, "I'm glad you called, Doll, I could sure use your help, but I didn't know if you'd be conscious yet." She has a suspiciously heavy Southern accent. She claims to be from Tallahassee, but then, everybody in LA claims to be from somewhere else to make themselves seem more interesting. Debbie's been here for a good 40 years so you'd think the accent would have worn off, but I think she keeps it because people in Los Angeles find it charming and it's part of her brand "Southern Fried Flowers." Once a month she does, in fact, serve fried flowers, zucchini blossoms like they do in Venice, Italy, but she serves them with pimento cheese and BBQ sauce claiming they're "Just like mama used to make!" at $75 a plate.

This is LA—it doesn't have to make sense.

I never admit to being born in the Valley, except to another "native" (which we're not allowed to call ourselves anymore, since we're not from *native American ancestry*, my family having dragged their sorry asses from Eastern Europe where the poor Jews came from).

When people ask me where I grew up, I tell them about Montana and make up stories about how my father had pushed me out of the house at 12 to do a "walkabout," and how I spent weeks in the wild, eventually making friends with a mountain lion.

It's a good story, and if they show any signs of doubt, I explain that before I befriended the lion, he ate my pinky toe, which isn't a lie but a "story." And, in fact, I did lose my pinky toe in a childish bicycle accident which didn't involve riding, just me wondering why I couldn't see the spokes of a spinning wheel and sticking my toe in to feel it... It doesn't look bad now, in fact, I feel free to wear flip flops because people rarely notice it, and, if they do, I get to tell them about Myron, a mountain lion.

This also explains why I hate bicycles, not to mention that so few people look good in spandex.

I dress in comfy sweats and a hoodie because it's always cold in the floral area to keep the flowers fresh, and I wasn't going to be out front in the store so it wasn't as if I'd be seen by anybody who was anybody.

I actually didn't hate working for Debbie. I was amused by her accent, delighted by her dedicated free parking and hankered for her hugs. She was a fine hugger even if she was skinny—she'd grab me, tight, like she really cared about me (except she even did this with the clients she hated and later told me it was a power move—but it always felt genuine) and then rock me side to side while making a happy humming sound. I know, that makes her sound a bit unhinged, but no, she'd developed it over many years and it even worked with celebrities and they've had to train themselves to be dead inside so the endless global criticism doesn't kill them.

Debbie's big break was doing flower arrangements for Julie Andrews' on-set trailer. The regular florist had a tragic laurel hedge accident (which I take to mean Debbie locked him in a little room with a lot of laurel hedges—they're toxic and the smell can make you crazy dizzy), so she stepped in. Julie loved Debbie's arrangements so much (she should, Debbie used flowers that cost twice as much as the "just-get-her-some-damned-cheap-flowers-because-it's-in-her-contract" the regular florist had been giving her).

Julie started using Debbie for her home where she had a weekly flower budget of $750. A week. In the 80s. Which is like, I don't really know, but I remember my dad saying he bought our little Sherman Oaks house in 1982 (three years before I was born) for $47,000 and now that house is worth like $2.5 million. While I still love him with all my heart I wish he'd kept that house for me so I could sell it and retire.

Back to Julie's flower budget... Let's just say that in today's money that's like $15,000 a week in flowers.

Julie recommended Debbie to her friends, so Debbie and *Southern Fried Flowers* were set. Of course, that was decades ago, all those movie stars are dead or living in Switzerland (basically the same thing), so now Debbie has to live on her past glory as "Florist to the Stars," with rows of signed photos from once-famous, now mostly unknown actors. Even Esme, who's my age, has never heard of Joan Collins. Joan Collins, people! How can you not know her? Charlene Tilton, maybe, but Miss Collins?

Sometimes, just to see if I'm sane, I'll quiz anybody under 40 who comes into the shop. I point to Joan, at her most glamorous in her fabulous Nolan Miller Ultrasuede and furs and announce, "Look, it's Joan Collins!" 9 out of 10 times they stare blankly at me, like I've pointed to a little known medieval saint who died trying to save Paris from rats. Occasionally they'll say, "Yeah, my mom keeps trying to give me a tacky QVC necklace from her line... Die-nasty, is that the thing she was on?"

I roll my eyes and hope she'll give me her mother's address so I can deliver the flowers (which I otherwise never do), see the necklace and cajole her into giving it to me since I appreciate it when her daughter so obviously does not. I once got a Joan Rivers QVC pendant that way—a genuine copy of a fake Faberge—I still love it!

>>>

Oh, damn, I come back to reality and Debbie is saying something about chrysanthemums. I look in at my arrangement. I have tastelessly combined them with roses in a display only a mother could hopefully love, but I hated.

"Sorry," I say to Debbie, who looks at me like I've peed in a vase again. I only ever did that once and it was because her toilet was backed up (not my fault that time) and I didn't want to cross the street to McDonald's where their bathroom was literally one of the circles of hell. Not figuratively, literally. So I peed in a vase, thinking I'd pour it down the work sink and rinse it with bleach, but Debbie saw it before I could and I've never lived it down.

"Come on, hun," she says affectionately, which means nothing because she *always* sounds nice, I mean, really nice, I mean Southern Hospitality nice. In fact, the nicer she sounds the less sincere she is.

"I didn't pee in anything," I explain.

"Not *today*, doll."

"My mind wandered a bit. I know this arrangement is ugly, I'll fix it..." I admit. I know what she's going to say next.

"...Dear Lord—get out the baby's breath!" she cries like the water in the crick is risin' again!

Debbie always believed, as I have come to, that anything can be improved with enough baby's breath—those darling little white flowers that look like clouds. In Debbie's case she means literally *anything*, so she'll stick a little in her hair, her decolletage, in the hat of ladies of a certain age, even in an electrical socket she called "unsightly," causing a fire, something I would occasionally remind her of when she'd bring up the vase. But she ended up getting a big check from the insurance company so she could remodel which made me think it might not have been a complete accident.

She throws me a bunch of baby's breath, probably harder than she needed to—it smacks me in the face. I have an impulse to yank out the roses and throw them at her, but I always remember she was a pitcher for the "Ladies League of Tallahassee" which she used to say was the inspiration for the movie *A League of Their Own,* whispering conspiratorially "I was the Madonna character." Today almost nobody knows what that means.

We actually did the backstage flowers for a Madonna tour when she was at the Wiltern Theater. I said, "I'll deliver them," or I might have said, "If you don't let me deliver them there might just be another fire here." I got to go backstage and see how her dressing room was painted violet—not mauve or orchid or, God forbid, heliotrope. I hung around, using my clipboard to pretend to be someone important (that trick used to work everywhere, now you have to use an iPad but that's not the same because everybody has one).

I saw her sweep in, shout obscenities, then smash something against the door. Water dripped out from under the sill... along with some baby's breath. Well, I never! What a bitch! I went home and snapped all her CDs in half, which was mostly an empty gesture as I'd already ripped them to MP3s, but still!

>>>

Debbie claps her hands in front of my face, "Oh, my Lord, honeychild! Ya know I love you to bits and pieces, but I simply can't afford to have another Tori Spelling incident!"

Now, to be fair—to me—the Tori in question was wearing a baseball cap and sunglasses (the uniform of celebs who don't want to be recognized except they really do) and I didn't recognize her because I'd just broken up with Jason and was texting him incessantly, as one does.

"Don't you know who I am?" she asked, all haughty, so I assumed she was a nobody, because real celebs just don't say that—I mean, if you don't recognize them then either they're not famous enough or you're brain-dead.

"I'm sorry, miss…"

"Miss Spelling!" she cried, whipping off her sunglasses so dramatically I was sure she'd practiced in front of a mirror.

"You look kinda like her," I said, still distracted because Jason had just sent me a dick pic by mistake. I took it to be a sign of reconciliation, then he wrote, "Oh Juan, my pecker misses you," and I simultaneously laughed and wanted to throw the phone across the room except whenever I do that I have to pay $100 to fix the screen.

"How dare you!" Tori said, "I will speak to your boss about your insubordinate behavior!"

Now the odd part of the story is that she never did complain to Debbie, and in the end I wasn't fully convinced it was actually Tori, who I've since heard is very nice. It was most likely her stand-in or body-double or a random impersonator trying to get attention.

But Debbie overheard the end of the conversation and, being a worrier, was afraid Tori might tell her mother to get her flowers elsewhere, and her mother had the biggest house in Beverly Hills, literally the size of the Cairo Hilton hotel, and that required a lot of flowers.

I explained, "Tori and her mother aren't on speaking terms," which was true. But years later it's still *a thing*.

I relayed the entire story to Esme who said, "What's a Tori Spelling?" Now, if Tori had been K.D. Lang you can bet your grandmother's ass Esme'd have known who she was.

God, those references are old. I'm old. I'm never going to have sex again. I'm going to die alone.

>>>

Why am I thinking about this? Oh, right, because Debbie said... Now I have to remember what she said. "What did you say?" I ask her so I don't have to rack my brain.

"Sweetie, sweetie, sweetie," she drawls. *"Focus on the fucking flowers."*

Yes, right, flowers. They remind me of my dad, and I start to drift off remembering him in the backyard watering the geraniums with one of those old fashioned galvanized steel watering cans. One time I asked him to water me and... NO! I am going to be in the present and focus on the fucking flowers!

I actually can focus when I put my mind to it, but normally it feels unnecessary. I know I wander off but I never seem to miss anything important, and if it is important, someone will surely say it again, or yell it again, and then I won't have missed anything!

I focus on the fucking flowers—on their shapes and colors and scents. I make a yellow-and-white arrangement of mums for a man who said his mother loves those colors *and* Maltese dogs. For the puppy part I glue two googly eyes to a white mum, with a shiny black half olive from a leftover Subway sandwich for the nose. It looks like one of those yappy little white dogs who always have dark stains around their eyes and mouth, making them look slightly Satanic. People *love* those dogs.

"Ke-ute, baby! Look what you can do, boy, when your brain is in the same room as your body!"

She is right—but my brain doesn't love being in my body—it longs to be in someone else's, like a ballerino, gymnast, or professional ice skater. I know this will never, ever happen, but I still hold out hope for some sci-fi miracle that will allow my beloved brain to be transplanted into the recently deceased but still completely intact body it deserves.

I focus for the rest of the day—creating one stand out: The order says, "My mother is very sophisticated and loathes baby's breath. This must be couture or I'll Yelp you into oblivion."

I take it as a challenge and use the Ikebana skills my father taught me to create a stunning, I mean *stun-ning* globe of dried bamboo. Delicately placed inside are a fiddlehead and fern leaf placed so as to make a single perfect purple orchid appear to float in space. Exquisite.

It is so good I have to take multiple photos for Instagram. I post them and immediately get 258 likes, including one from an assistant to an assistant to Martha Stewart who I'd slept with a couple of years ago when I was at my skinniest and didn't even need stretch jeans.

Debbie looks up from her baby's breath and more baby's breath concoction and gasps. "Love, love, love!" She takes a picture (not as well composed as mine) and posts it to her Instagram, with a @ link to my page, which is nice. "Eric Butterbaugh eat your heart out!"

I'd met Eric. He was truly the "new florist to the stars" and even had his own line of fragrances. He tried to pick me up at a party once but I was holding out for Kerr Smith, an actor I'd seen kiss another boy on Dawson's Creek when I was 15. Kerr didn't even glance at me, but I was redeemed later when I found out he married a woman and enjoyed motocross—Ick!

>>>

The rest of the orders are from men who've forgotten their wife's birthday. Lesson: never get married. Most of these ungrateful assholes don't even know their wife's favorite flowers if you can believe that, which, even after years of doing this I still can't.

What's wrong with these men? What's wrong with men in general? What's wrong with me that even these thoughtless men aren't knocking on my door with red roses, which I hate, because they can't be bothered to know my favorite flower?

Since they don't know, I turn to a zip code database which shows the most-ordered flower in each zip code. This is generally safe, but how am I supposed to know if one of these so-called mothers is secretly into S&M, wears latex under her yoga clothes and only gets turned on by black tulips?

I usually just go with my gut which means my own favorite flowers, which means sunflowers. I never met a sunflower I didn't like. Sunflowers genuinely look happy, plus, their smiling faces grow tall on a rough hairy stem—I mean, how sexy is that!

Roses can look funeral and sad. In Japan, chrysanthemums, bless them, symbolize death. But nobody's ever seen a sunflower at a funeral, except perhaps for an old hippie and those people are happy to die and become fertilizer.

When I make an arrangement of sunflowers, I handwrite a little note explaining that if you dry the sunflower you can remove the seeds, plant them in your yard and grow your own! You can't touch this! Cue M.C. Hammer, if anyone still remembers him. I do—I begged my dad for a pair of Hammer's big harem pants!

Of course, I like pansies being a pansy myself—we're fabulous! The flowers look and feel like velvet and bloom all year long. What's not to love?

My hands are flying now—tossing flowers hither and yon and gently guiding them into romantic relationships. I love when I get into this groove because I can turn off my brain. What a relief not to have so much chatter in my head.

Calm.

Peace.

Pansies.

I am so in the zone I don't realize it's 7pm. Debbie gives me her trademark rocking hug and hands me $140 in cash. I should probably ask her for a raise but honestly, I'd do this for free.

She kindly invites me to her deep fried zucchini blossom dinner tonight and doesn't even suggest I help her cook. But I've had them. I hate them. Still, they're free food. Tis a puzzlement.

I kiss her face and feel the cheekbone implants she insists make her look not unlike Michelle Pfeiffer.

I drive through Taco Bell and get a *Quesarito* which I wolf down while driving. Despite what Rober might teach poor unsuspecting children, there is beauty in fake cheese sauce and meat from unknown sources... damn, I just thought about how meat comes from animals and it always makes me sad but it's too late, I ate half and am still hungry.

I love LA at night. It's when the city actually looks beautiful. In the summer, it's the time when the weather is bearable. If I take off my glasses, something I normally avoid while driving, the lights melt into each other like a psychedelic film set.

Everything here is fake, but at least we don't make a pretense of reality.

I mean, look at Steamer Cleaners on Ventura, a dry cleaner that looks like a set from *Hello Dolly*—and might be, since Streisand's costume budget bankrupted *20th Century Fox*. They had to sell off most of the backlot to create what today is Century City. The cleaner's facade is covered with lights that run through a rainbow of colors, which is clearly a sign that should I ever buy anything "dry clean only" again, I must go to this cleaner.

>>>

Crap, the people behind me are honking because I didn't notice the light turn green. Fuck you, bad LA drivers!

Debbie gave me a box full of past-their-sell-date sunflowers that'll only last a day or two. That's OK, I'll hang them upside down and pretend I'm living in

Provence. I can plant a few seeds in pots near the windows, but the others I'll dry and roast and salt and eat—delish!

I park in the carport below my apartment. It's a "dingbat" building built in the 50's, which means it's precariously perched on stilts above the parked cars. The skinny metal poles that hold up the place look like they could fall over in an earthquake, but there've been many quakes since it was built. As far as I can tell only the front part of the building collapsed in the 70s which doesn't concern me as I live in the back.

I take the sunflowers to my room and arrange them in the infamous vase which Debbie said could never be used again. Her loss, it's a lovely round one that reminds me of an astronaut helmet turned upside down (I wore it on my head one Halloween and got light-headed from the lack of oxygen which was fun).

The flowers really pop against my chocolate brown walls. I painted pretty much everything in my room chocolate brown—the walls, ceiling, furniture, even the old vinyl flooring which, when I moved in, looked like a gas station.

Now it feels like living in a high end chocolate box, which of course is a dream come true.

As a child, I watched *I Dream of Jeannie* reruns every day... Do people under 30 even know what a rerun is? Or Jeannie? Anyway, I dreamed of living in a genie's bottle and decorated my first apartment to look like Jeannie's, all pink and gold and walls studded with big plastic jewels from Michael's craft store. Everything was patterned and tufted and the end result was spectacular if claustrophobic. A lot of my so-called suitors were put off by this, but I didn't care! I'd put on my best crop top and Hammer pants and dance around to the show's theme music! Alone. But even the best genie needs a master, or all they can do is masturbate.

So for this place, I painted everything Sherwin Williams Bitter Chocolate SW 6013. I rubbed the edges of the furniture and baseboards with gold gilding wax by Barnabas Blattgold (I did not make up that name), giving them a glimmer—of hope!

I bought brown satin sheets and made chocolate bonbon shaped pillows, complete with crinkled edges that looked like those little paper cups caressing each piece. It's a bed fit for a king, queen, or chocoholic.

I lay in bed, looking at the golden sunflowers against the brown walls, smelling the slightly sweet earthy smell... of the seven, $20 bills and feeling all is right with the world.

I listen to dogs barking, Orthodox men bickering in Yiddish, my stomach digesting a *Quesarito*, my upstairs neighbor taking a shower (I pretend it's rain, which we otherwise so rarely get in LA), and my eyes grow heavy.

Now I do the one thing guaranteed to put me to sleep, I pick up my phone, go to the Cameo website and look at all the formerly famous people who now sell videos of themselves wishing anyone who remembers them a happy birthday, bar mitzvah, or death of a not-so-loved one, for a fee.

My favorite section is for the former boy band members I jacked off over when I was a teen. They all so cute and had great hair and could harmonize their perky little asses off. Now they look like they work at a car wash (though, actually, there's one super cute guy who works at the nearby Fashion Square Car Wash—he always throws in a free Hot Turtle Wax which I'm pretty sure is flirting, but he wears polo shirts which is a total turnoff).

I find it deeply encouraging that these formerly super-adorable boys have become slightly-repulsive men, whereas I, having never been burdened with cuteness, could still conceivably become one of those men who looks distinguished like that guy who played the "most interesting man in the world" to sell some kind of liquor. His real name was Goldsmith and he was Jewish. There's hope for me.

I know I'm actually ready for sleep when my phone slips out of my hand. My eyes close and I go to my favorite place in the world—my dreams.

THE DREAM

I am walking down a long hallway. It's all white with unflattering fluorescent lights above. It's getting narrower and narrower, the walls are getting closer together. I can hear water running.

I see someone at the far far end of the hallway—he's a debonair older man with a white beard. Could it be "future me?" I think about running to meet him but then think better of it and continue to walk, albeit a bit faster.

I feel water rising up to my ankles and keep walking. The water gets higher, knocks me off my feet, and drags me down the hallway like one of those delightful yet disgusting water rides where you know all the kids have peed into the pool so you desperately try not to get water in your mouth or nose, but to no avail.

I am being pulled deeper and deeper into an ever-narrowing tube where I fear I won't fit, then I'll stop the plumbing up like I've done all too many times in too many toilets.

The pipe takes a 90 degree turn—straight down, and I'm falling, falling, falling into the darkness.

I end up in a dark space that smells like a gym. I hate that smell. I float in a smelly fog. I want to get out but it will involve exercise, so I am at first, unwilling, then unable to move.

I feel myself being pushed out of the darkness into a very bright place, like being born, except I'm watching from above as I lie on a slab of tasteless grocery-store butter that's slowly moving... towards a cremation chamber.

I hate this fucking dream! Why am I unable to fly? Why is Oscar Issac not my husband? Where are the flowers and rivers made of chocolate like in Willy Wonka? Where is my *Bloomie*, the Oscar for florists? And, oh yeah, why am I going to be burned alive?

I struggle to scream but I'm paralyzed.

My body slides into the cremation chamber and the heavy door closes behind me. Yet there are no flames, just the knowledge that, day by day, there will be less oxygen until I suffocate.

"WOAAAA OHH!" I'm finally able to scream and wake myself.

The yellow light from the street is creeping into the room, making the brown look like bile.

There's a knock at my bedroom door. I assume it's Esme, either that or a very polite burglar.

"Charlie, are you OK?" It's Esme's voice.

"No," I choke, starting to weep.

She opens the door and I start sobbing from the dream, and because I can't find any Kleenex and don't want tears and snot all over my satin sheets.

She hands me a tissue and gets in bed with me, putting her arms around me.

Ahh.

I feel her breath on the back of my neck. She smells like stroganoff. I stop crying and my breath becomes in sync with hers.

"I love you," I tell her, because I do. She's my best friend and confidant, the Betty White to my Rue McClanahan.

I hear her say, "I love you, too," before I fall asleep.

THE DRAMA

I wake up and it's nauseatingly bright—I'd forgotten to lower my room-darkening shades last night. And why does my mouth taste so bad?

I'm hit by the memory of last night's nightmare. Usually my dreams are filled with worlds where I'm successful, rich, handsome and highly sought after. But this dream was terrible. I tear up just thinking about it.

I hope Esme's home so I can tell her all about it since I can't afford a therapist.

I put on my kaftan—the flowing tie-dye rayon always makes me feel better. Instagram has been full of sexy men wearing kaftans around sparkling pools in Palm Springs. A lot of the time they are paid promotions which means they have a convenient link to where to buy them.

I liked to think that if I bought one I might look like these muscle bears, so I went immediately to the website, *Kafclan.com*. I chose a brown leopard print to coordinate with my bedroom and almost pressed "buy" until I saw it cost $185. For a schmata I'd wear, when? I couldn't afford Palm Springs. I didn't have a pool. So I'd wear it around the house... for who?

I left the site open in a browser tab for weeks, looking at it longingly until the rent came due and I had a brief moment of rationality and closed the tab.

But I didn't forget it! Esme and I share an Amazon Prime account and the next day the site started showing me kaftans. How'd it know? There was a plus-size model wearing a 1960's pink and yellow Pucci-esque print—for $18.96. $18.96. If it had been $19 I might have given it a second thought, but at that price, sold! It arrived two days later looking as chic as can be for $18.96. What's not to like?

>>>

Crap. I remembered the nightmare. Where's Esme?

She's in the kitchen, making waffles. Oh, lord, I love that girl. Oh, wait, she's not alone, there's another woman, I think it's a woman. She looks like actress Lea Delaria who calls herself "a big butch dyke." I saw Lea in an interactive theater piece in a sweaty Koreatown basement and she pulled me out of the crowd to sing a love song to me, so now I'm partial to big butch dykes.

"This is Buck," Esme says, glowing. I mean, she's actually glowing from the stove top flame as she flips the old-fashioned waffle maker over. "Buck, this is Charlie, I mean Chaz."

Buck strides up to me, thrusts out her/their hand and says, "Pleased to meet ya, pal!" She shakes like an auto mechanic I once had a crush on until he told me I needed a new somethingorother for my car and it cost $400 at which point he would basically be a rent-boy, not that there's anything wrong with that except I can't afford them.

"Hi, Buckaroo!" I say, oddly chipper, instantly wondering why I called her/them that and why my voice sounded like Pee Wee Herman.

"Buckaroo, I like that!" Buck says, pulling me into a hug that feels like a bear is crushing the life out of me, something I've imagined both in terror and sexually.

Esme looks at me funny and asks "What's wrong with your voice, Chaz?"

Buck releases me and I appreciate being able to breathe. "I dunno, it's the first time I talked today... and I had a nightmare."

"Yeah, what was it about?"

Esme puts a plate piled high with waffles in front of Buck who holds her/their knife in her/their fist, again like an actual bear might if it felt the need to use cutlery.

Wait, why do we call bears "it" when people have to be he/him/she/her/they/them? Wouldn't it be easier just to call everybody "it?"

>>>

"I dunno, yeah, I mean, you know, I don't want to talk about it... but I was in this hallway..."

Then I recalled my nightmare in minute detail, Buck was eating through the entire stack of waffles and taking the occasional bite of mine muttering, "You're so busy talking they're gonna get cold."

When I finish, Buck says, "Holy fuck, man, if you are a man, that was heavy shit." I didn't know if she/them was referring to my nightmare or the mass of waffles they'd just consumed.

"What do you think it means?" Esme asks. It was an annoying thing to say but I couldn't blame her because when we had these discussions she tried to talk like the psychiatrists she saw on TV and that's something they always asked.

"Sounds like you're suffocating!" Buck tosses out there, unasked.

"Um, yeah, that's pretty much what I was going to say," I sigh.

"Buck's a psychiatrist," Esme explains. "A real one, who can write prescriptions and everything."

"Xanax?" I ask, hopefully.

"Sure, but it sounds like you might need an antipsychotic. Come and see me, here's my card," she/them says, patting me hard on the back as if I have something lodged in my throat. "Gotta run, babe, thanks for last night and the waffles! Let's do this again, soon." Buck puts on a long duster as if she/them is going to hop on a horse, blows kisses at Esme, and slams the door with such ferocity I fear it'll fall off its hinges, and not for the first time.

"Well, they're fun," I say.

"You can't afford her," Esme explains. Ah, so Buck's a she! "Her office is in Beverly Hills and she charges $750 an hour, except for her pro bono work for the LGBTQ center..."

"...Then I'll go to the center..." I say, relieved.

"...for homeless teens and those in hospice," Esme finishes, disappointingly. I'm all for homeless teens and the dying getting help, but I, unfortunately or fortunately, don't fit into either category.

"Why do you feel like you're suffocating, Chip?" Esme's pet name for me is "Chip" as in "Chip and Dale," the animated chipmunks who are always causing havoc. I don't mind it from her, but from anyone else it makes me sound like a paint sample.

"How long can I continue to do... nothing?" I ask.

"You don't do nothing, You just spent the entire day at Debbie's, speaking of which, does she still have a boyfriend?"

"No, she dumped him when he asked her to send flowers to his wife."

"I've always felt I could turn her," Esme smiles. Esme's always had a thing for Debbie, I think it's the accent, but Debbie is into dick as much as I am.

Though, lately, I haven't thought about dick or even looked at pictures or videos of them. In fact, I'm starting to get worried because the last time I looked at a dick that wasn't mine it just looked weird. The whole thing, from tip to balls. There was a time when I found almost all dicks to be things of beauty, givers of life, an animal part I could put in my mouth without feeling guilty.

I still very much like my own dick as it brings me pleasure. Of course it could be longer—but nearly all men think that. That is except the ones with really long dicks who complain that they're "too big" to which I say, "fuck you and your big swinging dick."

But I *can* imagine it being a problem—that big thing stuffed in your underwear or hanging down your thigh, what do you do with it? And when it's hard, how many men (or even women) can deal with it? Yeah, OK, I'm sure it's a problem, but it's a problem 99.9% of men, me included, would be happy to have.

Until this moment I didn't even realize my fantasies lately haven't included cock? A lot of kissing, sure, again, it's like eating something delicious and completely calorie-free! Plus, the tongue is still alive, no, I haven't killed anything, and I can assume it's happy to be there in my mouth.

Kissing, holding, napping. Since when is napping a sexual fantasy? OMG, maybe I'm becoming sapiosexual (only attracted to brains) or demisexual (only attracted emotionally). I've always been objectusexual (sexually attracted to inanimate objects, but who hasn't found shag rugs erotic?), and autosexual (playing with myself!). But what if I'm becoming napisexual?

My head is swimming, so I lick the genuine maple syrup (one foodstuff where I've always preferred the real thing) off my plate, flicking my tongue as far around my beard as I can to get any stray drops.

>>>

"Earth to Chip, come in chip!" Esme says, pulling the pretty much already clean plate out of my hands. "Where'd you go?"

"I was thinking about dick."

"Of course you were."

"No, I was thinking about how I haven't been thinking about dick."

"That qualifies as still thinking about it."

"No, seriously, Ez, I'm going nowhere in my life and now I don't even care about sex. I need professional help and unfortunately I'm not a homeless teen."

"That's a terrible thing to say, even for you."

"I know, I'm sorry. Thank you for listening. Now, please tell me what to do with my life."

"Start washing the dishes."

I get up and my knees crack. Oh my fucking God, I've gotten completely old overnight. On the way to the kitchen I look in the hall mirror to see if my hair has turned completely silver, but no, I look pretty much the same, and the kaftan's cool.

I start washing dishes. Esme perches on the counter, drinking a big green smoothie made of God-know-what. Lately that's all she's eaten. "I want to get back to my girlish figure," she says.

"You're already built like a prepubescent boy," I tell her, knowing it will make her smile.

"That's sweet, but I gotta lose some baby fat," she says, patting her stomach.

I pat mine. "Me, too."

"Naw, Chip, you're cute and cuddly," she says, kissing my cheek.

"Speaking of cuddling, thank you for coming in last night. I'm sorry, I didn't know you had Duke in your bed."

"Her name's *Buck*. And you know I'm always happy to be there for you. It takes her forever to fall asleep, but once she finally does I could bake cookies on her stomach—bitch sleeps so hot. I was back in my bed in the morning so I could wake up with her."

"She really does seem nice," I say, meaning it. Esme had brought home a lot of losers (almost as many as I had). I'd like a Buck with a dick... except, did I really? It feels like something's very wrong with me, and unless I can masquerade as a teen I don't know who I can talk to for answers.

Esme starts to cry. I dry off my hands and hug her tight. "What? What's wrong, Ez?"

"I think I love her."

"So what're you so afraid of..." I start singing the old Partridge Family song.

"...I'm afraid that I'm not sure of a love there is no cure for..." she continues.

We sing a rousing duet while putting away the plates. *"I think I love you, isn't that what life is made of, though it worries me to say I never felt this way..."*

"Oh, shit, I'm so happy for you," I tell her sincerely.

"I know, but I don't know if she loves me—and if she does..."

Now it's me who starts to cry because I know what she's going to say. They'd move in together and I'd be alone and unable to pay the rent and have to get a roommate who might be an ax murderer, or worse, listen to Abba.

"I'm still happy for you," I manage to say—and now she's hugging me.

"Mess," she whispers in my ear and I laugh.

I've always been a mess. Really always, at least as long as I can remember. Maybe I wasn't a mess in the womb, but given that my mother's womb was clearly cramped and probably selfishly dry, I probably was then, too.

It was all *her* fault.

THE MOTHER

I don't like to think about her, but her well-coiffed head pops up in my head without warning. Mind you, I haven't seen her since I was three, so what I remember her looking like and what she looks like now are vastly different. I Googled and saw photos of her dressed up for charity events. Even I have to admit she has great taste, which must be where I get it.

To my three-year-old eyes, she'll always be a gorgeous gargoyle. To my Forty-(clear throat)-five-year-old eyes she's all glossy surface and no heart. The hardness is obvious even in photos—like her body is a fortress designed to keep you out. Keep *me* out.

Perhaps tired of hearing about Mother, Esme recommends I see her psychic, Andrew. Esme promised she didn't tell him anything about me and it would all be his reading.

At first I mistake Andrew for an accountant with his round clean-shaven face, blue button-down shirt tucked into Dockers above white socks and penny loafers. He gives me an odd hug—reaching out his arms like actress Norma Shearer at the end of *The Women*, a 1939 movie where there isn't a single man in the entire film. Everything about that movie is classic, right down to Joan Crawford's prototypical gold-digger bitch named *Crystal* and her art deco cut-glass bathtub.

Andrew reaches out his arms and I move in so my head is to his left and he guides me away—gently, but firmly. My mind immediately starts to wonder if there's something evil inside me (like my mother's genes), but he says, "We need to hug, heart-to-heart, so your head needs to be on my right."

Sounds like bunk, but I do it—and I can *feel* the connection. He doesn't hold me tightly, it's not a personal thing, but we stay in that hug for what feels like a long time, and the longer it goes on, the more I feel myself melt.

I breathe with him, and finally he takes one long, slow, deep breath, and steps back. If that's all he does it will have been enough.

"You have a wall around your heart," he says, seriously, gently, kindly. "It's to keep your mother out. But it's also keeping you from feeling love."

Cue the waterworks. So many tears I don't even bother to wipe them with the Kleenex he gives me.

"It's not your fault," he adds, making me cry harder. He puts his hand on mine and we sit this way until the tears stop. "It's not hers, either," he says, and I start feeling angry.

"But she..." I say.

"...She had to protect herself when she was young so she built a wall around her heart. Unfortunately, that's all she knew how to do and the wall got too high. Now nothing can get in or out," he explains.

I shake my head and shrug my shoulders. I understand... but it's not enough to make me less angry with her. "She's an adult, she had choices," I say. "I was a baby. A baby! I didn't have a choice!" The tears start again.

I look up and see him smiling sadly. "You're right. But she made the only choice she thought she could, and I'm feeling she did it *for* your own good."

"No, no, no, no, no, no, no, no, no, no. No! She's a selfish bitch, a terrible human being and I'm sorry that she's the one who gave birth to me because I want no part of her," I insist.

"I know *you* can't understand this now. *She* may never understand it. That's her terrible limitation and curse. It's very sad, really. But *you can* understand if you let go of the anger and hate. *You can*. And when you do, you can find love yourself."

Oh, shit. I already have—I am instantly and deeply in love with Andrew. I know this is projection or transference or some other technical term that one of the shrinks I saw told me after I professed my love to him. He was a schlubby nebbish, completely unappealing, but the fact that he was there, focused on me, wanting to help me, made me fall in love.

It didn't matter that I was paying him to do it!

Andrew put his hand on my heart and I tried not to recoil because the new love of my life was touching me so intimately. "You think you feel love, but what you feel is gratitude for being seen. I suspect you have a hard time actually feeling the love that's *given* to you. Is that right?"

I thought about it, and was pissed off to the point where I'd decided that Andrew and I were not going to have a future together.

I wanted to argue, to put him in his place and tell him he was a quack—but he was right. God dammit, he was right!

I loved my dad and he showed his love in his actions, but, looking back, I never quite felt it in my heart. As for my mother, "I'm so mad at her for building this wall in me that I can't imagine I'll ever forgive her!"

"You will—and when you do, you will be a radiant beacon of love."

What the fuck? A radiant beacon? Me? Now I knew that Andrew was a faker. I could not and would not believe any of this! It was probably the same bullshit that he tells everyone who wears a locket containing their mother's picture with a wooden stake through it. (I don't actually wear that locket, that would be insane, but I feel like it's tattooed on my chest, which is probably insane, too.)

When I get home I ask, "I'm a loving person, aren't I, Esme?"

"That's a leading question, Chip."

"That's not a *yes,* Esme."

"It's not a *no* either."

"So what is it?"

"You have a good heart, but you keep it locked away a lot of the time. I know you love me, and I love you. I'm happy you're my chosen brother. I'll be even happier when you can unlock all that love."

I sing to the tune of *Georgy Girl,* "'*Bring out all the love you hide and, oh, what a change there'd be, The world will see a new Charlie boy!*'"

Esme whistles the happy peppy song break, "*Da da da da, da da da da, da da da da, da da...*" and it makes me cry again.

"I don't know how to stop hating me... I mean *her.* I mean the *her* that's inside me, that's what I hate." I didn't hate all of me, I really didn't. I hated my body but that's different. Still, maybe that was her fault, too, even though she was as skinny as I wanted to be. Dad was a handsome man, but I didn't look like him. So *my* body *had* to be *her* fault.

"Do you hear yourself?" Esme asks, putting her arm around me. Esme is such a wonderful person and I really hope Buck loves her back. If not, I'd want to hurt Buck—though I know she'd be able to beat the shit out of me. I just want to believe I'd do anything to defend my beloved Esme. There, see, I can love. I do love.

"Yes, I heard myself and it's true, sometimes. But I love *you* always."

"Aw, you're a sweetheart," she kisses my cheek. She has lovely lips for a girl.

"A sweet heart surrounded by a tall wall," I reply. "I'm trying to take down the wall. Brick by brick." I am, but each time I feel fury towards my mother another brick is added.

"She abandoned you. It's natural to be angry. And I'm not taking her side here, but she's clearly got issues. I don't want you to end up like her," Esme wipes my tears with her soft fingers.

I want to protest and scream "How fucking dare you —I'll never be like her!" But I manage to avoid saying it out loud and as soon as the feeling passes, I know she's right, dammit!

I spend the rest of the day in bed, curled up with my chocolate bon bon pillows, trying to imagine what had made Mother so hard and unloving. I remember what Andrew said, that "she did it for my own good." She knew Dad was loving and she wasn't. If she'd stuck around I'd probably be even more fucked up than I am.

A brick falls away.

I find Esme on the sofa, reading my Vogue September issue. Not so much not reading as looking at the half-naked female models. I put my arms around her and hug her with all the love I have.

She smiles, happily, "You give good hug,"

"I learned it from Andrew."

"No, you always have." I stroke the back of her hair and she puts her head on my shoulder.

THE USUAL SUSPECTS

Normally when I wake up in the morning, I look around and am grateful to live in my chocolate box. Today I wake up and my nest feels empty. Something's missing. Is it a boyfriend? My stomach tightens, no, not a full-time thing, that feels suffocating. But to wake up *with* somebody, like Esme does with Buck. Why do I want that so much?

Probably because I'm a mammal. You don't see puppies or kittens sleeping on king-sized beds by themselves. No, they sleep in piles, on top of each other, because it's warm, cozy, and they know somebody else is there.

I know how to get a guy into bed, so I fire up *Boink* and go to my page of favorites. I have a couple of regulars I can call when I want a little *something something*.

Let's see, there's Tedd... what's he doing in this list? He's like a male model and only hooked up with me once because he'd broken up with his husband and was super drunk and was gone when he woke up from passing out. He's the type who usually only gets with guys who look just like him, which is totally narcissistic.

I fantasized about him for a while but it's time to remove him from this list because it's never gonna happen again. Deleted.

Lorenzo, OMG is he adorable. Like my own perfect younger version of Regé-Jean Page. Even has an English accent. But I got diarrhea the last two times we hooked up and I can only assume he has the world's strongest digestive system while mine is… normal for my age. It's sad I can't call him again, but I just can't. Delete.

Jerry… no, he just wants to be dominated. He likes to run around on all-fours and once asked me to *force him* to make dinner *and* wash the dishes. While that sounds like a dream come tru, he wasn't a good cook, left specs of food on the dishes after washing, and I felt guilty.

Tim—adorable and a total sweetheart, but mostly wants to bottom and that's way too much work.

Wiley. Wiley? I have no memory of this person. I read the messages where he thanked me for a hot night (he's nothing if not polite), but I don't remember him, or any hotness. Am I going senile? I'm only 45, I shouldn't be able to completely forget anything other than a colonoscopy. Was I drunk or on 'shrooms? I look at his face again. Doesn't ring a bell. His body. His cock. Nice, I should remember. I don't.

I decide to go shotgun—craft a clever message I'll paste into multiple profiles and see who replies.

"Hey? Wanna Cuddle? Seriously, just cuddle (and kiss, of course). Come 'n get it?" Hmm, the *come 'n get it,* part is a little too cute if not outright nauseating. Delete. I replace it with, "I'm here all day and can host, drop me a note 🎲." I'm shocked there's no emoji for *cuddle*, so I guess the kiss will do. Send. Send. Send. Send. Send. Send. Send. Send.

I lay in bed watching the screen as if they're all going to instantly reply, in which case, we can be like a litter of gay puppies, that'd be fun. But after five minutes of staring at the screen I realize how ludicrous it is to wait, so I put down the phone, do my morning ablutions—a word I only know from *Sweeny Todd* and I like to use it because "washing my face" sounds prosaic and I don't even like to *think* of my own toilet habits.

I do like to think of historical figures going to the bathroom, though. You never read about it—in all my history courses I learned about George Washington's wooden teeth, but never about his poop. It's hard to imagine a time without flushing toilets and two-ply extra-soft toilet paper. Nobody ever talks about how all those famous people, like Cleopatra must have had itchy asses. No wonder they were so dramatic and angry!

I've read Jane Austen and she never talks about what the characters wipe their behinds with! I went to England when I was 21 (not backpacking, what am I, a turtle?) and at one country pub there was an actual outhouse with newspaper for toilet paper. That's where my concern about historical hygiene started (along with my propensity for carrying a small pack of *WetOnes*, just in case—I mean, what if I got a papercut down there?)

Napoleon probably had someone to wipe his butt for him, using fine silk scarves. No, that would have been Louis XIV. Or they had sitz baths and bidets. Why don't most Americans have bidets? I bought a toilet seat attachment for $32 on Amazon that sprays water on my ass and it might be the single best thing I ever spent money on. So Fresh. So Clean...now I'm singing that Outkast song.

I go to the kitchen for some oatmeal, the instant packaged kind with brown sugar and cinnamon and raisin-like things. I love this stuff, but I can't forget Rober and his obsession with *real* food. I briefly consider buying those steel cut oats from Ireland (I do like the metal tin). I'd cook them for hours, season with cinnamon I've... where does cinnamon come from? I Google it. It's tree bark? Five minutes later after reading the entire Wikipedia page and wondering why I never knew any of this, I pour the packet in a bowl, cover it with water and microwave for a minute. Would ancient oats and scraping at tree bark with my fingernails really taste better? I can't imagine it could. Then I think of that damned butter. But that's butter, and this is just oats for fuck's sake.

I enjoy every last sticky sweet bite of it and even lick the bowl because nobody's around. Why isn't Esme here? She's allowed out without explaining it to me, but still. Probably at Costco buying food for *Tiny Dinners*, or maybe with Buck...

It's very quiet here now, other than the gas-powered leaf blower outside. Peaceful. Maybe I would like living alone. The leaf blower stops. Now it's *too* quiet and I want to talk to Esme. I don't like this alone business. I check my phone to see if there are replies on *Boink*. Yes —four of them!

I read the messages. Wiley: "Sorry, not into just cuddling, bro." Well, fuck you Wiley, except I won't because I don't even remember your stupid face. No, that's unkind, I must focus on kindness if I want these bricks to fall. "Thanks, Wiley, maybe another time, handsome," I message him. I actually don't think he's handsome but I say that anyway because it's nice and I like when other people say that to me even if they don't mean it.

Tedd: "New phone, who dis?" Oh, shit, I didn't mean to send him a message and, seriously, he's given me the lamest reply. Nobody's said that since 2009.

Mike: "If you punish me I'll do whatever you want." Holy mother of crap, no. I don't have the time or interest in punishing someone. Ick. I mean, whatever floats your boat, I am not judgemental, but I am also not interested. Why did I even message him? I must have been half-asleep.

Tim: "Hi, you know I love to cuddle after getting fucked." That's right, I remember, he's an amazing cuddler, so sensual. I don't remember much, because after all that effort I had to sleep, but for a few minutes while I was still conscious it was lovely. "Thanks, Tim, can't fuck right now, it's against doctors orders." I think about being more graphic, perhaps tossing in the word "oozing" but I'll just leave it at that. Send. Sigh. Silence.

Drip. Drip. Drip. I hear the kitchen sink dripping. I get up and turn it off completely, something Esme's always on me about.

I take a shower and sing "So Fresh, So Clean" and do my little shower dance that includes various Madonna poses and using the hand-held shower like a microphone.

I never dreamed of being a singer, or a star, or even famous. I dreamed of being a Disney princess and my dad even bought me a pink tutu which, I remember him saying, "Is only for wearing around the house, Charlie." I didn't know to appreciate how accepting that was of him, letting me be me while also protecting me from other kids who would not understand a boy in a tutu. I've grown out of tutus because I now find them unflattering, but not many dads would let their little boy pirouette around the house singing, "Some day my prince will come!"

In my club phase I went to a party at the Eagle called "Some day your prince will cum," but even then I didn't wear a tutu, I wore a pink hot pants and a crop top with a plastic jewel glued in my navel. It took two weeks for the glue to wear off so I could get that fucking jewel out. I have no memories of the rest of that night so either I was drinking or I unconsciously blocked out that I had to take an Uber home, alone, in that outfit. Maybe that's where I met Wiley. Sometimes it's best to not remember.

>>>

Lordy, all this reminiscing... I forgot I was in the shower and it's running out of hot water. I dry off with my colorful Turkish towel that doubles as a sarong, and look at my phone again. Nada. Nothing. Zilch.

My stomach makes a happy noise and I remember how delicious breakfast was, and how Rober would have frowned on it from his lofty Eames chair... Rober! He told me he only used licensed professional cuddlers. I could text ans ask him who he uses!

"Hey, Rober…" No, I can't say "hey." "Hello, Rober. This is Charlie. I ~~was~~ am so impressed with your approach to licensed cuddlers and was wondering if you'd share your ~~guy, man, person, rentboy,~~ cuddler because I ~~need a fix, feel empty, need to be held so I know I exist,~~ could use a cuddle myself. Thanks, and let's do dinner again, soon!" Send.

I do like dinner, even if it's another vicarious dinner. Sure, why not?

No reply. OK, I don't even like to admit this to myself, but sometimes I forget other people have lives. Intellectually I *know* they do, I know they exist outside of my world and they're not just extras in my movie. I *know* that.

But I also childishly wonder if they don't just kind of freeze and wait for me to come into the frame again… I can imagine Rober, frozen in his Eames chair until my message makes his phone ping, spurring him back to life.

Maybe I don't need a professional cuddler, maybe I need another therapist. But there's always something wrong with *them*. The guy with food in his teeth. The lady with a hairstyle from the 90s like she was preserved in amber. The young, handsome Israeli who had such a thick accent I couldn't understand him but didn't care for a while because he was pretty. The nebbish I fell in love with until, in a late-night google search, I discovered was married and had two kids. Ick. I'm forgetting someone. No, not a therapist but a psychic crystal healer named Henry I met on Instagram but after what he tried to do with those crystals it's probably yet another thing I'd prefer to forget.

Maybe I need a bartender with a good ear. I put on my most normcore jeans and t-shirt that says, "My eyes are down there," with an arrow pointing to my crotch. No, no, no, why do I even still have this shirt? Some guy left it here... or I liked it and hid it before he left. What possessed me to put it on now? Off it goes. Other T's: Mickey Mouse—fascist capitalist—Nope. Captain America? Why? We Bare Bears. Everybody loves them. I like to think of myself as *Ice Bear* but I'm probably more *Grizz*.

Wait, I'm worried about looking too gay? Why do I even think that? What, am I trying to pretend to be straight? Is that even possible? I'm the perfect test case for girls who claim to have gaydar. "What about him, Amy?" "Of, for sure, Susan, 100% sure." Well, duh.

Where are my keys? Esme put up a rack by the door where we were supposed to leave our coats, keys, wallets... I've got four fashionable coats that're too warm to ever wear in LA, so there's no room for anything else. My wallet and keys are always in my pants but they're not in these pants. I finally find them in the pants in the laundry hamper and am thankful I found them before they went into the wash—like last time.

Phone. Wallet. Mask. Hand sanitizer. Kleenex. Protein bar. Eyedrops (for that dewy look). Cough drops (TB isn't a sexy look). Tube of moisturizer (again with the dewy look). Quartz worry stone (dry panic). All the essentials. My pockets are bulging which makes it hard to walk. Lordy, I am a hothouse flower who hates the heat.

Wait—I forgot keys. Where are they? They could be any place in the entire apartment... I will never find them and be trapped here for eternity or until Esme comes home, whichever comes first. I unlock the front door and go down to the car in case they're still in the ignition, yes, that happens. No, they're not. Damn!

Ping! A message from Rober: "Hello, my lovely. Such joy to hear from you again. Yes, I'd love to watch you eat dinner, you name the place! My cuddler calls himself 'Terrence' and you can find him online at theboyfriendcuddleexperience.com - tell him I sent you! Kisses!"

Rober's so nice. If only he wasn't so weird. I seem to have felt that way about every man I've met. If only they were different they'd be perfect.

But I definitely will take him up on dinner. I'll Google Michelin star restaurants—if it's good enough for Bibendum, the Michelin man, it's good enough for his twin brother, me.

THE BOYFRIEND CUDDLE EXPERIENCE

I go to theboyfriendcuddleexperience.com - hmm. Clearly a stock photo: two pretty gay men having brunch. Well, that's the dream, isn't it. Brunch with the boyfriend, or at least a pretty man who chews with his mouth closed.

I only remember one pearl of wisdom from my mother, "Chew with your mouth closed!" and I have to admit it's served me well. I've been to dinner with some men who eat like pigs and it's gross. Thanks, Mother!

Oooh, another brick falls. I wonder how many more bricks I need to let go of before I'm a *radical bacon*... no, that's not what he called me. *Radiant beacon!* This shouldn't be hard, right?

Back to Terrence's website: "The Boyfriend Cuddle Experience is a rent-a-friend service designed to provide you with a warm human connection without the strings and arrows of a non-transactional relationship. Terrence DeSoto is a Certified Touch and Cuddle Therapist and offers a safe space for you to be touched and held in a completely non-sexual way. Terrence has been seen on Oprah and Yelp.com where his satisfied customers call him, 'Warm, tender, wholesome, giving, and the soul of good energy.' Cuddle experiences start at $750..."

WTF? I mean, W the actual F? $750? Oh, this guy can't just cuddle at that price. There must be some other transactional activity going on there! Unless he's a mind-boggling, skin-tingling-good-cuddler. Is it even possible to be that good?

And if Rober can pay seven and a half Benjamins for a cuddle, then he could be *paying me* to eat for him. I totally bet he would. How do I ask him without seeming... greedy. He could at least pay for an Uber and maybe new shoes and a wrist watch. Not to mention a selection of headgear, including, but not limited to, a crown, though last time I wore one it left marks on my forehead that took a whole day to go away. It was worth it.

My mind is still reeling from anyone having the balls to ask for $750 to *not* have sex. I used to be jealous of people like this—they must be rolling in it (or rolling *on* it while cuddling, which sounds like a baller thing to do). I imagine Terrence has a house in the hills, all glass with a gorgeous view of city lights. His clients arrive in Rolls' smelling of Tom Ford's *Fucking Fabulous* cologne and lie on his $40,000 leather sofa air-shipped from France by Roche Bobois, a company whose name I can't even pronounce.

He holds his clients for an hour, or maybe just 50 minutes like a shrink. They gratefully open a $6,000 Hermes leather weekender bag filled with $100 bills and leave so refreshed that they also leave the Hermes bag as a bonus.

But, in reality, I've seen guys who can put up a damned impressive website. You'd think they were as successful as they look on Instagram, sitting in a Ferrari, lounging by the pool at the Four Seasons... but it's all fake. The Ferrari was at the dealer where a friend of theirs washes cars and let them in after hours. They're at the Four Seasons to *clean* the pool. They share a one bedroom with another "glamorous" instagrammer and take turns shooting each other's photos—and sleeping on a sticky 1970s Naugahyde sofa.

Naugahyde was so cool when I was a kid. I really wanted a "Nauga" doll, kooky creatures made from vinyl that were supposedly the exclusive if not elusive source of the Nauga-hyde. I still wanted one well into my twenties when I did a search for one on eBay and suddenly the notion of turning a vegan leather product into something that came from an imaginary creature defeated the entire purpose! People were so weird in the 60's, probably from all the drinking and diet pills. It must have been wonderful.

Let me search for those Naugas again... what am I doing? No! I need to Google "Terrence DeSoto" and see what I find out. By not falling into eBay I just saved myself at least an hour and feel proudly productive for a moment!

Terrence's site mentioned Yelp. I always consult Yelp before going to a restaurant, then feel compelled to write reviews of every place I eat, even Arby's, and I quote, "Cheese goo is good for you as completely man-made foods build your immunity to the city. Sometimes, like after a colonoscopy, there's just nothing like a good Beef 'n Cheddar, where the processed cheese product creates a soothing and protective colon coating."

I love reading my own reviews and seeing how many people liked them. We can't all be official restaurant reviewers, even after sending our Yelp reviews to a number of national publications and hearing absolutely nothing back from them, the assholes.

I read Terrance's reviews: G. DeMarco of Encino wrote, "Terrence is the best, he makes life worth lifing." Nice spelling. Let's look at Mr. DeMarco's other reviews. Oh, wait, there are none. DeMarco... DeSoto? Could it be the same person? Next review: "Terrence is unlike anyone else I've ever met, so caring that he's worth every singly solitary penny. Run, do not walk to his websit and hire him!" That was from Lance DeMendez. Really? Another typo and another "De" name? Finally, "I depend on Terrence for all my cuddling needs, he's very clean and professional" From Robert Smith. Wait, what? Is Robert really Rober's name? And Smith? Really?

My head is spinning as I plop down on the couch...
Ouch! Oh, there are my car keys! That's gonna bruise. I
Google "Robert Smith" and I get the singer from *The
Cure* (I've always liked the song *Love Cats*), and about
6,580,000 other results. I try, "Robert Smith" and
"Encino" and now there are *only* 12,700 results!

Wait, I've forgotten what I was doing.

I go to the "about" page... what? The "About" text still
has *Lorem ipsum dolor sit amet, consectetur
adipiscing elit,* nonsense "Greeked" text graphic
designers use a placeholder until the real text comes
along. There is no real text.

Next are videos from YouTube. Here's one of him
cuddling—a long body pillow. The pillow looks happy
because he's drawn a smiley face on it. The other video
is an acting "reel:" A corpse on *CSI Cheboygan* where
the star of the show is personally reading his toe tag.
There he is as a waiter in a webisode where he has an
actual line, "More coffee, sir?" with a fake English
accent. There's a video of him on Oprah... clapping in
the audience.

Rober... or *Robert*, said his cuddler was *licensed*.
Terrence's site says "certified." Let's see your
credentials Mr. DeSoto... hmm, don't see any on your
site. Did Rober not do his due diligence? Maybe Rober
was remiss in checking his license to cuddle! Maybe it's
because Terrence is smoking hot. Armani underwear
model hot. The caption says he *was* a model for Armani
but left the business because it was too stressful. Poor
baby. No, I shouldn't negate his experience.

THE NEW THEORY OF RELATIVITY

When I read he was an underwear model my brain automatically thinks, "If he looks perfect then he must have a perfect life." Like so many things I know this is not true, but it's basically the crux of how all advertising works, "Buy our stuff and you'll look better so your life will be better." Or, the way I've always taken it, "If you don't buy our stuff you are doomed to be unattractive and unhappy—aka YOU!" I forgive myself for falling into this mental trap because advertisers spend billions every year to shove it in my face.

Yet I once overheard two perfectly muscle-bound guys leaving the gym (next door to an In-n-out, which is why I was there). The first guy sadly said, "It doesn't matter how hard I work out, I can only get a six pack, not an eight pack." The other guy nodded his head, "Totally, man. I had to get lipo because otherwise I didn't look cut enough." They nodded at each other with somber understanding. I surely didn't help by waving a double-double cheeseburger in their face, taking a bite and saying, "Oh, my God, this is the second best thing I've ever had in my mouth today," then sashaying away. Still, I understood that even for these perfect specimens, there was always someone better looking...

That's how I developed a theory I live by (except when I forget, which is most of the time). I call it *The New Theory of Relativity,* and it goes like this:

There's always someone better looking than you/not as good looking. Thinner/Fatter. Taller/Shorter. Younger/Older. Happier/Sadder. Smarter/Dumber. Richer/Poorer. Healthier/Sicker. More successful/less successful. More fulfilled/Less fulfilled. Kinder/Meaner. Healthier/sicker. More loved/less loved. Luckier/less lucky. Privileged/disadvantaged.

It literally doesn't matter who you are, there is always someone better off, or worse off than you. This even applies to the richest man in the world, Elon Musk where *most* of us are clearly saner and a lot less assholish.

A few years ago I got a job in PR (like spinning plates on roller skates while lying, difficult for me because I could never remember what story I'd spun). I was working for a very rich and successful software entrepreneur we all called "The Snake Charmer" because he could convince you of anything, even if you believed the opposite.

It happened to me more than once, I'd go to his office to explain why his marketing strategy of buying an $150,000 magazine spread and having both pages blank—not even a company name, was misguided if not wasteful (I avoided using the words "just plain stupid.")

He explained why it was genius and how it would generate buzz (it never did). Still, he was so convinced, and therefore convincing, that I left the meeting believing him... until a few hours later when I wondered how he'd brainwashed me.

The Charmer's company raised a hundred million dollars through his remarkable Steve Jobs-like "reality distortion field."

As the lowest person in the PR department, I was the one tasked with going to his house to deliver ad layouts —even those notorious blank pages. Why we couldn't just email them was a mystery, but I guess he just liked people going out of their way to deliver things to him.

His driveway was up a curvy road a full half a mile long. At the end of it, a Model X and an Audi R8 sports car were parked outside his house—a big cube made of glass—like an Apple store, only even colder.

Inside, it was so Zen there was no place to sit other than an occasional cushion on a cold, shiny marble floor. It must have been like living in an ice cube, but everywhere you looked there was an incredible view of Los Angeles, smoggy during the day, stunning at night.

One day he called me into his library, a cube within a cube. A glass desk was in front of yet another floor-to-ceiling window. The other three walls were lined with thick glass bookshelves covered in books arranged by color. I don't know how he ever found anything, in fact, while I was there he asked me to look for a book titled, *Go F*ck yourself: turning your self-loathing into success!*

I thought, "I need to read this book!" but then I noticed all the books in his library were self-help books on how to be either more successful, less sad, or both. Through the wall behind his glass desk I could see even bigger houses perched on the hills. Some looked like massive Tuscan villas, others like Greek temples, still others were glass cubes only slightly different from his —but twice as big!

He was visibly agitated as we both frantically looked for this book. Why didn't he just buy the ebook online? I was afraid to ask.

"I need this book—now!" he said, desperately.

At that moment it occurred to me that he was unhappy because he was *the poorest multi-millionaire on the block.*

All the other houses he could see were bigger and had more cars parked outside. His driveway was long, but it wasn't lined with dirty cars and trucks for a cadre of servants like in the other houses.

He had to answer his own front door—how demeaning was that? Why didn't he have a butler and a battalion of maids? Did he even have a personal chef? Is that why I was called over, just to have another human in his Fortress of Solitude?

For a split second I actually felt sorry for him. Maybe he was living beyond his means, like I was in my Jeannie-bottle studio apartment at the time.

It didn't matter how rich he was—or seemed. Someone else always had more, so it was never enough.

This was a valuable life lesson that sent me straight to HR for my very first "I need to spend my remaining weeks in Maui." I hoped The Charmer would send me a note and a nice big check, but that didn't happen. He was probably too concerned about his own future. The same week, the company stock which at one point reached $300, had plummeted to 5 cents and been delisted from NASDAQ. It was hard not to feel sorry for him, until he started another company that raised hundreds of millions more, then went bust overnight, without even warning his employees. Not so charming.

>>>

I pull out of this memory, surprised my right butt cheek is sore—oh, right, from sitting on my car keys!

I Google "Cuddling accreditation," and find everything from a 6-week in-person intensive in Seattle for $5,280, to a 2-hour video course which comes with a genuine parchment certificate for $169.

While I hear Seattle is lovely this time of year, there's no way I'm plunking down that kind of cash, even though their site calls it, "A sure-fire investment in your financial future." That wording alone makes me suspect that this is actually a "sure-fire investment in *their* future."

Besides, I'm not getting into this to make a fortune, I'm getting into this to help my fellow man!

What? No, I'm just looking for someone to cuddle with and my train-of-thought got derailed. But—maybe I can leverage my specific skill set of lying on the sofa and napping and turn it into an altruistic career that also makes me rich!

$750 an hour would be great—but given that I wasn't an underwear model, how much would be reasonable for 'Thanksgiving day parade balloon' me? To check out current prices I turn to rentboy.com where men sell themselves by the hour. It's a noble profession, some say the world's oldest. If they're consenting adults I see nothing wrong with it.

Let's see... the underwear model types are asking between $250 and $500 per hour. The... what would I call myself... I've aged into being a "daddy," which basically only means I'm over 35, but the "daddys" I'm seeing here all look like former underwear models, too... ah, wait, here's a normal guy with the headline, "Warm, accepting, non-threatening man won't make you feel self-conscious." Oooh, what an appealing way to market oneself. I'll remember that. He charges $99... ah, but with a 2-hour minimum—smart. I can learn from this guy, though I'm not going to hire him because I still cling to the belief that I can get someone to come over for free.

And, besides, I'm not looking for... what's that photo? Oooh, that's gotta hurt. The caption reads, "No extra-charge for kinks!" I didn't even know you could do that with avocados and wonder how long it'll take me to forget it.

$99 an hour. That sounds reasonable. $99 sounds so much more reasonable than $100, just the way *The 99 Cent Store* sounds a lot cheaper than *The Dollar Store*. Though the last time I went there to buy a frozen dinner it cost $1.25! My dad told me that *Motel 6* used to only cost $6! Can you even imagine. Sometimes I feel like I was born in the wrong era... then again, being gay was literally illegal in the past, so it's probably better now.

THE GRADUATE

I could do the $169 class—but I've never been big on school. Of course I graduated college, but now I can't remember anything I learned in those four years—except how to create my own degree, a *BA of Visual and Floral Arts*.

That BA that was BS. There was no such thing as a degree in *floral arts* but my friend Jimmie was sleeping with Dean Alkmar, so I simply suggested to the dean that his wife would surely approve of a degree in Floral

Arts... and voila. Was it mean? I didn't out him—and it wasn't as mean as Alkmar unceremoniously dumping sweet young Jimmie right after graduation and before a promised trip to Key West. Turns out Alkmar selected a new senior every year for special attention until they graduated but they never got to Key West. Ugh.

To make up for it, Jimmie and I went to Key West. I got eaten alive by mosquitoes and he got such a bad case of the clap he called it "Thunderous applause."

So instead of school, I will do what I do when I want to learn anything—go to YouTube! I search for "How to Cuddle," and oh, here are two very pretty gay men with 700,000 views. They show the basics but do it in a sexy way (though unfortunately with their clothes on—but then that's how professional cuddling is done).

While entertaining, I didn't learn anything I didn't already know. WikiHow has two animated blobs cuddling and a narrator explaining the basics of spooning, even though blobs can't spoon the way people can. Still nothing new.

Here's another cute gay guy—with blindingly white teeth. Honestly, I have to squint. Who thinks a fluorescent mouth is attractive? He says, "I've come up with a position I call spooning," like he invented it! He doesn't even demonstrate, he just keeps smiling and waving his hands. Next!

Ah, at last, a professional cuddler who explains: Set an intention; Breathe together; Here's where you can and cannot touch; Various positions. Also, the importance of a clear cuddling contract the client signs so they know the rules of conduct; And a suggestion to have a camera and a third party watching... that might even be an additional revenue source! That's a good start.

I watch another, and another, and another…

As I follow along I try the positions—on my back, stomach, side, feet, and one position I skipped because it looked like it required a yogi.

It's 8pm! I spent all day doing this and didn't even take a dinner break—but I feel great—as if I've actually cuddled someone, in this case, myself! I am so ready!

I Google "diplomas" and see what looks most official. The formats of Harvard and Yale are remarkably simple and easy to copy. I'm not using the name of either school, just the layout.

"Cuddle College" sounds too cutesy on its own, maybe a city name will add the dash of specificity required. *Coral Gables* comes to mind from the summer I spent there when Dad was working with Fairchild Tropical Gardens. Coral Gables sounds classy, and if anybody asks I can remember important things like my favorite place: the elegant Venetian Pool, or restaurant: Sunday brunch at the Biltmore (I only went once with Dad, but it was memorable, especially serving myself from giant silver bowls of chocolate mousse and bananas and cream). Now I'm hungry!

I finish the diploma: "*Coral Gables College of the Healing Arts* is proud to confer the title of *Certified Cuddler Summa Cum Laude* on *Mister Charles Jefferson Cooperman* and has admitted him to all its rights and privileges."

I admire the printed copy, though I do wonder whether "Cum Laude" could be misconstrued. I change it to "with Highest Honors." Yeah, that's safer. I'll buy some inkjet parchment paper to put it on my wall, and website.

But first, dinner. I make a grilled cheese sandwich, probably my single favorite food. Sourdough bread, French cultured butter (yes, I splurged), a light spread of honey mustard and grated extra-sharp Vermont Cheddar cheese. It's pure heaven on a plate.

Ever since dinner with Rober I've been trying something called "Conscious eating." I don't watch Netflix while I scarf down my food. Instead, I close my eyes and pay attention to every sensation—the crunch of the bread against my teeth, the warm butter on my tongue, the tang of mustard and the Cheddar umami. Oooh, mommy! Mommy. Mother. So skinny she probably never gets grilled cheese. I feel sorry for her—another brick falls.

And now, clearly as a cosmic reward for shedding yet another brick, a genius idea pops out, fully-formed, like Athena from Zeus's forehead. If the cuddling thing doesn't pan out—or even as a side hustle, I can be a *surrogate eater!* It'd be like reading books to the blind, but I'd eat food for those gay men on Kate Moss's trendy *An-Apple-A-Day—and-Nothing-Else* diet plan!

I can see it now—scores of rich, half-starving hunks, who aren't even drinking water because they need to look extra-cut for an Instagram "fitness" shoot, half-crazed with hunger and thirst! I breeze in singing, "No more hunger and thirst, but first be a person who needs people!" and I use all my strength to rip off a piece of bread like a wild animal tearing apart its prey! I slather it with fancy butter and stuff it in my mouth, washing it down with some fancy-ass white wine I didn't have to pay for.

The desperate fitness model nearly creams himself with excitement (but he can't really, because at this point he's too weak to do anything but scrunch his abs, or whatever they do, I wouldn't know), as I order anything I want from the a la carte menu and he pays the check *and* me.

He's dizzy with hunger so I go above and beyond and help him to the Uber we're sharing, at his expense because that's just how it works when you're professional, and when he passes out on the way to the apartment he shares with three other so-fitness models, the agreement he signed gives me "all rights and privileges" to feel his abs and glutes and whatever muscles he's got that I don't know the name of!

I'll call it the "Chubby Boyfriend Eating Experience," except that the word "chubby" would frighten them. "Hungry Boyfriend Eating Experience." Yes, that's better. Like Rober, they probably dream of someday actually being able to eat, but for now, they must content themselves reading the Kate Moss quote they've tattooed backwards on their butt crack so they can read it in a mirror, "Nothing tastes as good as skinny feels." I'll bet those skinny/angry Beverly Hills women would go for this, too.

I'm so excited about this new chapter of my life. When not busy cuddling, I'll be busy being paid to eat to keep up my cuddlish figure!

My future is secure—at fucking last!

Just then I hear the front door open and close with a bang worthy of Buck. Esme throws her bag on the floor and stomps into her bedroom, slamming that door. I give her time to cool off, then knock on her door and whisper, "Do you want to talk about it?"

"No!" she roars and I back away. I sit quietly on the sofa, making notes about the cuddling techniques I've learned today. After a while her door cracks open but she says nothing. I cautiously enter her room.

She's standing stiffly looking out the window, then spins around, "Get away from me!" she cries, her claws extended. I back away warily.

I try to soothe her, "Baby…"

"Don't call me *baby!*"

"Did I do something…"

"No! Stop attacking me!"

I want to explain that I'm not attacking her but she might take that as an attack so I don't. I do keep eye contact, something you're not supposed to do with a wild animal, but Esme's not all that feral.

"Can I help…" I ask?

"NO! Nobody can help!" Well, that makes my job easier, or impossible, depending on how I look at it. "Least of all you, what do you know about anything!" Her face is starting to look like Linda Blair in *The Exorcist* so I can suspect what's coming, "You're 45, you don't have a direction in your life or a relationship…"

I stop listening and wait for her head to spin around 360. It doesn't, which is both a disappointment and a relief.

I remember something from a video I watched today, it's *not about me* it's about *them*, so I remember she's *hurtmad* and wants to make me hurt and mad, too. I don't have to fall for that like I have in the past because then my trying to help turns into a screaming match which can only end with gallons of ice cream and the inevitable bloating. Nope, not this time. I'm here *for her.*

"Aren't you going to say anything? Defend yourself? Tell me you love me? You *butch* bitches are all the same!"

Ah… I get it—it's *not* about me. And… There's really nothing I can say. But there is something I can *do*. I move slowly towards her, keeping my face in what I hope is a loving gaze. I don't want to move too fast and scare her off. Her eyes are looking like she's waiting for me to get close enough to strike! But if she slapped me it'd feel campy and dramatic like in a Joan Crawford movie, so at least *something* in my life would be exciting.

As soon as I'm within arm's reach, I grab her—pulling her into a tight hug. I give her an Andrew-like heart-to-heart hug and hold her there, sending silent messages of love. That's it. No words. No explanations. No advice. Just love. It feels good for me. I hope she can feel it. She stops struggling, stops shaking, then lets out a sigh.

I do something very out of character and pick her up. I have very little upper body strength but I've had Halloween costumes that weighed more than Esme (I'm looking at you fake Lady Gaga meat dress made out of sequined bacon).

I put her gently on the bed and curl up next to her— the big spoon. Neither of us says anything as I practice my newly found cuddling skills. I pull her close, her head against my chest. I stroke her short hair, her shoulders, her arms and intertwine my fingers with hers. We lie like that, not making a sound, until I hear her cry and feel her tears soaking through my shirt. I pull her closer and match my breathing to hers, then consciously take longer, slower breaths so she will, too.

I can feel her body relax. She stops crying. I hand her a Kleenex and she blows her nose—long and snotty.

I want to ask her what happened. Is it her food cart? Buck? Life in general? Life in general is hard especially since we're all privates. I don't understand why the world is made so that every day can be a struggle? So that our moments of joy feel few and far between? I suppose we're supposed to be learning from all this suffering, but what?

"It's everything," she finally says.

"Everything is a pain in the ass," I reply, then think I should probably just keep my mouth shut and say, "Mmm."

I hate to see other people suffer. Even Republicans. I don't get joy from anyone's sorrow. No Schadenfreude. Though, to be honest, there are a few awful people in the world who have single-handedly caused so much pain that they deserve some pain of their own. If only their sociopathic hearts could break open and feel a little empathy. When I'm being kind, I think that these people are damaged—their hurt and fear coming out as anger. When I'm not kind, I know they're simply sociopaths. Still, I wonder if that was even their choice... like my mother. What if she's unable to love? How much sadder for her than for me.

Another brick falls.

Esme and I sleep cuddled up all night. I wake up and see her face, her mascara having run, making her look like a pretty Pagliacci.

It is nice to wake up and see a face I love. I have to stifle a laugh when a thought crosses my mind: I could put a mirror next to the bed! LOL. I'm not laughing at the conceit of it but the fact that for a moment I love myself. How funny that feels. A strange new sensation.

It's shocking. Embarrassing. Am I a narcissist like my mother? Are only narcissists allowed to love themselves? The thoughts fade as I imagine looking at my own face in the mirror next to the bed. Waking up, seeing my own kind face. Momentarily not even recognizing myself, like has happened in department stores where I don't know there's a mirror and just see a person walking towards me and they look good in that outfit and only then do I realize it's me and I wonder why I normally can't see myself that way—why I can't see myself as I am.

But right now I'm looking at Esme. I love being here for her. I love that I want to comfort other people. It makes me feel good. *Selfish altruism.*

Esme's eyes open, she sees me and smiles. "Good morning, sunshine."

I kiss her nose, "Good morning, my beautiful lass." I have no idea why I say something like "lass," it just feels right.

"Buck thinks we're moving too fast."

I smile—it's both amusing and annoying to see a woman like Buck being as stupid as a man. "Fear of commitment... and she's a shrink."

"Why do we love people who don't love us back?" she asks, as if she thinks I honestly have an answer.

"Ask my mother," I say, trying to remain serious but starting to giggle. My God, I've gone through my entire life asking this question and it's a relief to be reminded it's not just me.

"Let me bring my hat and my knife!" Esme says, starting to giggle too. I've always loved that this girl quotes Sondheim. When we were younger we had a cliche pact that we'd marry each other if we weren't otherwise engaged at 30. That came and went over a decade ago and we wisely decided to avoid the nuptials and remain friends instead. "That was some mighty fine cuddling, Mister," she says.

"I've been doing my homework." I reply.

"You're doin' swell, Dolly, I can tell, Dolly."

"It's Saturday. Let's go to the farmers market," I suggest, knowing how she loves her some farmers markets. I occasionally enjoy the cute farmers, or the stands for cheese or honey, but I've never really liked eating vegetables, much to my Dad's consternation. I find them beautiful, but, like eating animals, I feel bad killing them.

This is why I like processed food so much—I don't have to think about where the food comes from. Consider the humble Oreo—there's literally no recognizable nature in it! My Dad would be spinning in his grave if he hadn't been cremated and had me sprinkle him in his tulip garden before it was repossessed.

I don't mind cutting flowers—their life is so short anyway, I like to imagine they're happy to bring color and fragrance and joy into someone's life.

"You don't like farmers' markets," Esme says, knowing me so well.

"Maybe that cute asparagus farmer will be there," I add, hopefully. He has beautiful hands with dirt under his fingernails, like my dad. And no, it's not a daddy issue, I just see hands like that and think, "Love."

"Thanks, Chip." She kisses me on the cheek and gets in the shower. We share one bathroom and I have to pee but it doesn't matter, we can be in there at the same time. I feel very lucky.

THE GUINEA PiG

The farmers market is OK mostly because there's an adorable baker there who's as round as his loaves of bread. His hands, pink and clean and soft, hand me bread they made themselves. Crispy crust, light crumb. He smiles with crooked teeth, which, along with his wife and kids are deal breakers for me, but otherwise he's the almost-perfect man. I buy a loaf of bread, a brownie, and a sesame danish for Esme. Then I eat the danish and go back to buy another one. No, two.

It's sunny and hot, neither of which I like, but Esme looks as if she's forgotten about "everything" and is enjoying the sights, smells and tastes.

When we're done, Esme has a basket full of greens and I have a bag full of baked goods. On the way to the car I see a guy holding a sign that says, "Free Hugs." I hand my bag to Esme and go in for the hug. He feels tentative, scared and bony, not a good combination. I feel sorry for him and give him one of Debbie's rocking hugs while whispering, "It's OK, it's all OK."

I let him go and he looks stunned, pulls out his wallet and hands me a $20. I wave it away. "It was *my pleasure*," I tell him. As I walk away I see him hugging a woman using the rocking motion I just showed him—yes! Passing along positive energy!

We get home and Esme makes a cabbage salad. She knows how I feel about lettuce, "It tastes like lawn clippings," to which she always asks, "how do you know?" Honestly I've never eaten lawn clippings but they have a very distinctive smell that, to me at least, reminds me of lettuce. Also, there's so little to lettuce that I don't see the point.

But cabbage is substantial, the food of my ancestors! Still, it's best when layered with cheese, croutons, dressing and some kind of meat, though today Esme makes it with Chick'n patties which are surprisingly delicious fake meat and so far removed in taste and visual from their soy ancestors that I can eat them guilt-free.

After dinner we curl up on the sofa to watch "Sex Education" on Netflix. But before the episode starts Esme says, "You should cuddle with Buck."

"What? Why?"

"One, because I think she needs to learn to relax. Two, because she could give you feedback from a psychiatric point of view. Three, you might be able to tell me what's wrong with her."

"I'll do anything for you, Ez, but..."

"Good, I'll text her and tell her you need her help. She liked you. Said you didn't seem bad for a boy."

The next morning: I see a text from Esme. She sent it at 3am, but I don't see it until 10:30 because I put my phone on silent and airplane mode at night. I read something, somewhere, that said the cellular radiation waves can disturb your dreams and I believe it's true because before I did this I was constantly dreaming that my leg was buzzing like my phone was on vibrate. I could literally feel it in my dream and it would wake me up and I'd be disappointed because nobody was actually calling.

The straw that broke this camel's back was when I felt the dream-phone vibrate and it was Zach Ephron calling—just as I knew he someday would. Yes, I know he's straight and moved to Australia, but one of the tenets I live by is "Never let reality get in the way of a good fantasy," so I imagine taking him, the nice Jewish boy, home to meet my Mother…

WTF? Meet my mother? When did that enter into the fantasy? This obsession with having a mother is getting out of hand. Though, maybe, if I did have a really gorgeous, famous, rich, talented, and perhaps Jewish boyfriend, then my mother would love me…

Oh my God, oh, my God! I just had an epiphany—and yes, it was painful. I still want her love. Despite everything. Despite despising her. I have a micro-fantasy that perhaps she suffered a stroke which caused amnesia and she simply forgot she has a son. Maybe if I reminded her she would invite me to live at her Holmby Hills estate which, as I saw in Architectural Digest, has a pool house at least twice the size of my apartment. I could live there and skinny dip when she and her husband-creature are jetting off somewhere that I don't want to go, like India. Otherwise, I'd accompany her everywhere I can be bothered to go, like London or the Hermes store.

If I had a therapist I'd ask him or her or them what this obsession was with mother, and Hermes? Could Hermes actually be a symbol for that Greek God with wings on his ankles? I desperately wanted a pair of Jeremy Scott X Nike boots with wings on them but Nike shoes are always too narrow for my feet. I could barely walk around the store in them and decided they weren't worth the pain.

I try to remember my Greek mythology but now it's mixed up in those Marvel movies and I'm not sure what's real and what's Taika Waititi whose real name is David Cohen anyway.

Hermes was the messenger God, like the FTD Florist delivery man.

>>>

Oh—wait—maybe I *do* have a therapist, at least a temporary one, because Esme texted to say that Buck would be "delighted" to cuddle with me "for research."

"Delighted" seems both a bit dainty for Buck, who I keep thinking is named Duke. And "for research" sounds clinical and impersonal which feels offensive to me. Still, Esme has gone out of her way to set this up, partly for my benefit and partly on the off-chance I can wheedle something out of Buck as to why she won't commit to Esme who I know to be one of the nicest people on the planet even if, or perhaps because, she's flat chested.

Esme's next text: "3pm, her office in Beverly Hills. She has a big leather sofa which I know is big enough for two :)" She sends a Google Map link. Then adds, "She validates parking." How well she knows me.

I take a long shower, scrubbing with Esme's shower scrunchy thing. I eat plain yogurt with ginger jam. I brush my teeth and floss and gargle with mouthwash, twice. I avoid wearing my favorite shirt because I've already worn it once and it's on top of my dirty clothes hamper (not inside, because it might be possible to wear it again before washing).

But today I'm only wearing clothes I know to be freshly laundered and dried using *Nuzzle* Fabric Softener Sheets with the "Bimini Breeze" scent "that transports you to a tropical isle with notes of wild orchid, fresh coconut and a hint of musk." The musk part makes me think of monkeys who I find very cute. I like to imagine that cuteness exuding from my shorts, making me sexually irresistible. Obviously that won't work with Duke... shit, Buck... I don't want to call her the wrong name! Maybe, being butch, she'll find the musk calming the way I used to...

My brain flashes back to when I was very little and not feeling well. Mother would put her mink stole on the bed and let me cuddle on top of it. I loved the feel of the soft fur, and the particular smell it had, like a clean animal...

I'd forgotten that until now and it explains so much. 1) She didn't care about the mink stole because, while it was all dad could afford, it was too cheap for her,

otherwise why would she let a sick child lie on it? 2)
Now I understand why I'm attracted to hairy men. 3) I
can see how I, myself, can be a veritable mink stole for
someone else.

Off to Buck's office just off "Little Santa Monica
Boulevard" in one of those charming 1940s buildings
that I think of as, "Plantation Deco," single-story white-
washed brick buildings with columns, porticos and
shutters.

Back when I had my official clipboard that let me get
in almost anywhere, I snuck onto the old Selznick
Studios where *Gone with the Wind* was filmed. The
administration office was built to look like the *Tara*
plantation in the movie. Once on the lot I wandered
freely for hours. I discovered a series of WWII era
quonset huts—inside were racks and racks of film reels,
all baking in the uninsulated heat. I opened up a film
can marked "Gone with the Wind Reel One" and was hit
with the smell of vinegar, and the view of the film
literally melting. I felt sad that these important films
were treated so poorly that I almost felt the need to take
a bunch home and put them in my fridge but it was
already too full.

>>>

Parking $5 every fifteen minutes? Pshaw! I park at
Buck's without fear of insane charges and find my way
to her office, "Buck Winston: Queer Therapy
Associates." I always liked the word "Queer." I know it
wasn't meant nicely, but I've spent my life both trying
to fit in and having a fear of being normal, so it feels
just right.

The waiting room looks like an English hunting lodge except the animal heads on the wall are soft sculptures made of patterned pendleton blankets. The walls are paneled in oak with stacked stone wainscoting and it smells deliciously like there's a fireplace burning cedar logs.

I love my chocolate box room and all, but I could move right in. If Esme and Duke... fuck, *Buck*, I must remember, Buck, Buck, Buck, Buck, Buck! If they got together Buck could afford a home with a guest house for me to live in.

Geez, it's all about me, isn't it? No, today it's about my first client, *Buck* (rhymes with *fuck* so I can remember it now). It's about her need for deep relaxation and positive energy from one queer to another. I am here for her (and Esme). *It's not about me.*

I see a switch on the wall with a small brass sign reading, "Please flip switch so I know you're here and wait quietly as I'm in session." I flip the switch quietly and sit on the leather sofa that doesn't seem big enough for two, but I have to remember Esme is literally half my size.

The inner office door opens and Buck comes out, dressed like she's just come in from the stables, only clean. "Hey, Chazbo!" she smiles. I smile, too, because I like "Chazbo" and wish I'd had a friend like Buck in high school to give me a cool nickname so I didn't have to run around telling people to call me Chaz which they never remembered.

"Howdy, Buckaroo!" I say, saluting for no good reason I can think of, it just happens.

"Glad you're here. I've been reading psychiatric journals about cuddle therapy and am delighted that you're willing to give me a first-hand experience with it!"

Oooh, she actually did say *delighted* and in a friendly way. "I hope Esme told you I just graduated, so I'm not an expert, like you."

"It's an emerging field, nobody's an expert yet."

She ushers me into her office which evolves into an "English Country Lawyer" decor. Her desk is a massive leather-topped mahogany thing big enough to sleep under. The leather sofa here is twice as wide as the one in the lobby and definitely big enough for two, three if you're adventurous.

The wall behind her desk is covered with framed diplomas from Harvard, Stanford, the American Academy in Rome. "I forgot my diploma at home," I say, feeling insecure.

She laughs. I hadn't heard her laugh before, it's almost soprano, unlike her baritone speaking voice. "So, Chazbo, you take the lead. I've got an appointment in an hour but I assume your sessions are 50 minutes, like mine."

I suddenly feel shy, like I don't know what I'm doing, because I kind of don't. I do, intellectually, but I've never put it in practice before and I don't want Buck to text Esme later saying, "Your roomie is a quack."

I'm nervous. "OK, Buck. First, since this process is about honesty and openness, I'll say I'm a bit nervous because you're a professional and I'm new…"

She interrupts me, "The first rule of providing therapy is to relax and *act* confident, even if you're not. Otherwise you'll make your patient nervous."

"Is the second rule 'we don't talk about therapy club?"

Buck stares at me, "Actually, yes. So relax—breathe!" She commands and I do.

"OK, yes, sorry, rocky start. I'm fine now. I was going to say *breathe* but you already did." Please lie on the sofa in whatever way feels comfortable to you.

Buck's a big girl but she takes a leap and sinks into the cushions. She stares at me, daring me to get near her. Instinctively I want to take a step back, but I remember her advice, I *act confident* and sit on the edge of the leather cushions.

"Before we start, you should set an intention" I suggest.

"Oh, Lord. I'm not going to say it out loud."

"I can help you better if you do because then I know where to focus."

She nods, "That's a good move right there, doc."

I nod and wait for her to tell me her intention. She doesn't. "What is your intention?"

"What if I don't know?" she says obstinately.

"Tell me the first thing that comes into your head." I say, calmly.

"This is stupid," she smiles.

I'm annoyed and close my eyes for a second. I can either go into my head and get stuck on how I feel, or I can open my eyes and focus on how Buck feels. I open my eyes. "Then why did you ask me here if you already thought it was stupid?"

"I wanted to be sure?" she asks, not sounding sure.

"So you're going to make up your mind before actually investigating? Does that sound scientific to you?"

"Oh fuck you. Fine, my intention is to relinquish control."

"Thank you for sharing that. In that case, we're going to start simple, with the spoon."

"I'm always the big spoon," she tells me as if I didn't already know, given that she's clearly a serving spoon to Esme's demitasse.

"Today you're going to experience being a little spoon, so please roll over." She faces away from me. I explain what I'm doing and ask for consent. "I'm going to lie close to you and put my arms around you, is that OK?"

"You have my consent, *doctor cuddles*," she says, sarcastically.

"Is there anywhere on your body you don't want touched?"

"By a man? Yeah, the whole thing. By you—don't worry about it."

"Are you saying I'm not a man?" I laugh.

"Kinda, which is what I like about you." I choose to take it as a compliment.

I slowly move my body next to hers. Wow, she smells good, like saddle and smoke. I put one arm under her head and the other around her waist. I synchronize my breathing to hers.

As we lay like this I consciously try to send her calm, "It's fine to do nothing now" vibes. I am an expert in giving myself permission to do nothing, probably to excess, but here I feel it works.

It's interesting to feel her body—thick, strong, firm. The only woman I've ever cuddled is Esme and she feels like a teenage boy (which, for the record, doesn't turn me on). But Buck feels substantial and, dare I say it, sexy, and the last thing I want now is to get turned on.

I stroke her hair—a crew cut that's longer on top, fading to a buzz cut on the side. I love how a buzz cut feels, like mohair upholstery fabric. It tickles my fingers and just under my nails. Since it's on her lesbian head, I think of it as "homohair."

She sighs. Good—I'm getting somewhere.

"Should I talk about something?" Buck asks, a bit sleepily.

"You can if you want, but I suggest we just experiment with silence." We say nothing for a few minutes—I can see a clock on her wall, one of those iron ones that looks like it came from an old train station. I focus on breathing, feeling the warmth between us, stroking her hair and sending good vibes.

She starts to snore. Loud! That's good, she's relaxed, but maybe she just needed a nap in which case am I actually helping? But Esme said Buck had a hard time falling asleep, so this must be progress! Still, none of the YouTube videos covered this contingency! I clear my throat. Nothing. I lightly pull on her ear. Nothing. I tap her cheek. I pat her stomach, shake her and say, "Wake up, Buck!" Nothing.

Finally, in desperation, I lean in and whisper into her ear, "I love you, babe." She *jolts* awake.

"What? What did you say?" she says, squirming, trying to get away, but she's between the back cushions and a soft place, me, so she doesn't get anywhere.

"You were asleep. Did you dream I said something?" I'm not lying—I participated in 'therapeutic role play!' Her breathing gets faster and more shallow, I hear her sniffle. I explain, "We're going to move into the *half-spoon pose* now. I'll be on my back and you lie next to me with your leg over me and your head on my chest." She doesn't move. I feel her body stiffen. "Come on now, relinquish control and do what I ask."

Her body relaxes, she rolls over and puts her head in my chest. I tap her leg and she puts it over mine. I put my arms around her and feel her body relax more. I also hear more sniffling. "It's OK to feel whatever it is you're feeling, I'm here for you."

"I can hear your heartbeat," she says, now sounding like a little girl. Time passes. "I'm uncomfortable, I want to stop," Buck says, not moving.

"You can stop now if you want, but it might be better to work through the pain." This is something I heard a TV shrink say and it stuck with me, though not quite enough for me to practice it myself. Instead, I'll normally get a piece of chocolate or go to sleep. But if I suggested that to Buck I'd just be enabling her... like I enable myself. Oh, Lord, who's being therapized here?

She sits up suddenly and blurts out, "I don't have to do what you tell me, dad!" We both freeze. She sighs, "Oh fuck," and puts her head back on my chest.

I see the clock hand tick to *10 till*. I gently move back and forth. "That's our time," I say as nicely as I can, because it never seemed nice to me when my shrinks would say that. I always felt they were nickel and diming me out of 10 minutes, basically 20% of an hour! But now I finally understand—it's draining to give for

50 solid minutes. I've always thought I was a generous person but that took a lot out of me. If I had another client/patient, I'd need a few minutes to recover before doing it all again.

She sits up, wiping her eyes. "Well, that wasn't as stupid as I thought it was going to be."

"Um, thanks."

She gets up and straightens her vest. "Sorry, it wasn't stupid at all. It brought up a lot of stuff for me. That's good. Really good. But hard."

"You don't have to apologize. I hope it was helpful."

She won't look me in the eye. "I've got a patient in 10, thanks, man, you should be going."

I get up and pull at my clothes. I'm going to need to wear something stretchy in the future. "OK, uh," I don't know what to say to follow up, except, "Can you validate my parking?"

"Of course," she says, opening a drawer and pulling out an orange sticker. "You can go now."

I nod, wanting to thank her, or waiting for her to thank me. I turn to leave but can't find the door. I remember coming in to the left but I only see a bookcase. I move towards it and stupidly touch the wall looking for a knob.

"Pull *Pride and Prejudice*," she says, not looking up.

I see the book, ruby red with gold lettering, stuffed between other books so I can only reach the gilded edge at the top. I pull it and the door pops open. I slip out. There's a real knob on the other side, fancy brass. I pull it closed and lean against it.

"Intense, isn't she?" I hear a voice ask. I'm too off-balance to look up, so I only see thin legs in impressive emerald green alligator pumps. My eyes move up her legs and are stopped cold by her green alligator Birkin bag worth more than my rent for a year. "She's constantly making me remember things I'd rather not," the skinny woman says, her voice like familiar sandpaper, painful and comforting at the same time, giving me goosebumps.

"Yeah, totally," I say stupidly, finding it impossible to look away from her insanely expensive handbag. I nod and go outside. The sunlight surprises me. Buck's office was so dark I almost forgot I was in LA, and the whole experience has me shaken.

I clutch my parking validation and sit in the car trying to compose myself. Sometimes I wonder how much of my life is real and how much is imagined. Like that green Birkin bag, another Hermes symbol, can it be real? Am I having near-Rodeo-Drive hallucinations? And why did it give me goosebumps?

Why didn't I look at her face? Clearly something's wrong with me, and I berate myself for not using my time with Buck to ask her some questions about me! I know, it wasn't the time.

When I stop thinking about myself for a second (it's hard to do), I remember Buck was going through something and *I connected! I made a difference!* Have I ever done that before?

Suddenly everything's so quiet as I sit in my car in the underground garage. Quiet and dark and liminal, like a tulip bulb bursting to bloom!

The parking validation works, so what would have cost $30 is free! It's like I actually made $30 right there! Maybe I'll put it in the box under my bed where

I'm saving up for a trip to Morocco—$30 down, only $3,000 left. Wait, I don't actually have the $30 to put in that box. So pizza it is.

THE PARMESAN

The single best umami flavor in the world is Parmesan cheese. This is a scientific fact for which I am unwilling to accept any alternative opinions. So when I order Detroit-style deep-dish pizza from Appolonia's, I tell Justin behind the counter to fall down in the Parm.

If I was really rich I'd have a mattress made out of Parmesan. It sounds unsanitary but it's the kind of thing I imagine rich people can do. I wouldn't be a greedy rich person, though and once I'd showered and slept on the Parm I'd donate it to food banks.

I don't understand greed at someone else's expense. It literally doesn't make sense to me. Life isn't a zero-sum game. There's enough for everybody if a few greedy bastards weren't hoarding most of it!

I'm grateful just to have a place to live in a city where 50,000 people are sleeping on the street. I don't want to sleep on the street, though I tried it once because I was so afraid of it that Esme said, "Why don't you go sleep on the street and you'll see you don't have to worry about it. I asked her to come with me and she said, "Are you crazy?" but I still went.

OK—to be 100% clear about this, I didn't sleep overnight. I was doing extra work (the people in the background) on a very bad TV show with an enormous budget called *LAX 911*. Back then I liked extra work because it mostly involved waiting around and noshing at the "craft services" table which was always full of junk food. But then it got too competitive and boring and not worth the snacks.

This particular shoot was at an old warehouse near the airport, decorated with more mirror balls than I'd ever seen in one place outside of the bathroom in my first apartment. The set was supposed to look like a nightclub filled with 200 sweaty shirtless dancers and drag queens.

I don't do shirtless. I see no reason to subject the general public to such a graphic display. I will remove my shirt to swim unless I can get away with calling the shirt a "rash guard" which, in my case, is more of an "emotional rash."

Since the casting call had been for "shirtless partiers" they were a bit confused when I wouldn't remove my shirt. "Nobody wants to see this," I explained. They insisted. I removed my shirt. They said, "OK you can play a bouncer. Now put your shirt back on."

I always remember this as a confirmation that I'm hideous. I say not entirely in jest. Clearly there are men who are willing to allow me to be naked in their presence, and I've had no complaints either in person, or on YelpMen, a now defunct website where gay guys rated their dates, usually with their bitchiness set to kill. I used to search for "Chaz," the only name I used on the gay apps, and see if I got a 5 star review... or disparaging comments, like "Oh, the humanity!"

To *my* utter and complete horror, nobody ever said *anything* about me. Was I completely un-memorable? Was I like the Velveeta of sex? "If you're desperate, here's an orange square that tastes a bit like wax but can pass for food in a pinch."

Huh. Where was I? Even I lost track of my inner monologue. OK, I got it—I'm playing the bouncer on this terrible TV show, which means now I'm wearing a bad polyester suit and fedora they gave me that smelled like shrimp. And it's 100 degrees inside and everyone else is comfortably half-naked and I'm schvitzing.

The rest of them are happy to wait inside in the heat (and fake smoke, which, I was informed, is oil that you inhale until it gives you diarrhea). Movie making is so glamorous!

I chose to wait outside where it was only 80. I waited, and waited, and waited, because that's how it works. You arrive at 6am and your first shot isn't until noon, or in this case, 4pm... and extras don't get chairs. Nope, because extras are essentially sub-human props with legs. So, in lieu of a chair, I laid down on the sidewalk. Nobody noticed. I could have been dead. Nobody cared. And I discovered it wasn't so terrible sleeping on the sidewalk (during the day with a film crew around to protect you, or at least keep away strangers).

I slept so well, in fact, that I completely missed the shot I was supposed to be in—a pivotal moment: stage pyrotechnics cause a flaming drag queen to literally burst into flames sending the entire shirtless crowd running for the doors only to discover they're stuck which causes a stampede where any number of muscular people are trampled to death.

Tragic—and I missed it! This being show business and all, nobody was terribly trampled—Only a couple of extras were stepped on, but they escaped with their lives and another $25 in hazard pay so they were happy.

I woke up when the crowd burst through the doors, screaming like little girls. I got up, pretended to be part of the action and went back inside to do another take, but the assistant director shouted that they didn't need one because they had five expensive *Red* cameras shooting the whole thing. Then they made us sit around for another 6 hours for no reason before finally letting us go.

I later read in Variety that this single day of shooting cost upwards of $500,000. When I saw the episode on TV I expected it to be a masterpiece of mayhem. Instead, it looked like it was shot on a Sony Handycam circa 2000. It was fuzzy and dark and you could only see about 12 of the 200 extras. Even the literally flaming drag queen got less than a second of airtime, which was a shame, because I'd never seen such bad acting.

She was so memorably terrible that she got her own reality show called "Real Drag Housewives of The Castro," which ran for one season on a new gay cable network called *Boyzz* before it folded. How a gay network can go out of business is a mystery to me because gays can spend a lot of money on nonesense, since they rarely have kids to waste it on.

>>>

Oh, fuck, I was on autopilot and started to drive north on Coldwater Canyon towards home! Now I have to go south on LaBrea to get back to Wilshire to get my pizza. As Debbie said, I'm not good at keeping my brain in my body. Sometimes I can manage it while arranging flowers or decorating or having sex, but even then my mind can wander to more interesting things like Parmesan.

Luckily there's parking in front of Appolonia's so I can run in and get a few slices (with extra Parm). The slices are so big that one is a meal. I get three, one to eat in the car and two more to freeze in case of emergency.

THE ATTACK

"Where have you been?" Esme attacks me as I come through the door, almost knocking the precious pizza out of my hands.

"I just stopped to get pizza," I explain, innocently.

Esme grabs the pizza box. "I'm taking one," she says, grabbing one of the two slices and licking all around the edge to mark her territory. Little does she know that I don't care, I'll eat something she's licked because I know where she's been. She takes a huge preemptive bite in case I grab it back.

"I haven't heard from you, I haven't heard from Buck. What the fuck happened, Chip?"

After all the driving and Parm worship I'd kind of forgotten the whole Buck thing which was just a few hours ago. "Um..." I start, trying to remember, but mostly having psychedelic flashes of green pumps and Birkin bags.

"Did Buck say something about me?"

"Let me catch my breath for fuck's sake, will you? And don't eat that entire slice or your stomach will be distended."

She throws the pizza back in the box. "Tell me or I'm going to smother you in your sleep!"

Esme is not a violent person, so I take this threat with a grain of salt, but also seriously because I've always had a fear of being smothered by pillows held by everyone I'd ever met, like an Agatha Christie movie you can't possibly figure out because there aren't really clues, just a lot of English people yammering away in tweed.

"I'm sorry, Esme, I didn't mean to upset you. Honestly, I was overwhelmed, and there was this woman with a Birkin bag, and pizza..."

"You and your crazy Hermes obsession!"

"I know, I know, I don't know what it's about, I'm sorry."

"Go on!" She demands, a very loud voice coming out of her small body.

"Buck's office is beautifully decorated," I start.

"I know that!"

"She's very cuddly."

"I KNOW!"

"I told her I loved her." I whisper. There's a long, silent pause in which time I can hear my stomach rumbling for another piece of pizza, but I'm afraid to move.

"You WHAT?"

"I said..."

"I fucking heard you. You wait right here. Do not move, I'm getting my body pillow," she says, threateningly.

I am too scared to move and too scared not to move so I take the opportunity to take a bite of the piece of pizza because if I'm going to die at least I'll die happier. She comes back bearing the big pillow.

"Are you going to hit me or smother me? I just want to know so I can be prepared," I say, through a mouth full of pizza.

"Does she love you back?"

I'm speechless, which is pretty rare for me, but also my mouth is full and the cheese baked on this crust is scrumptious.

"Does she fucking love you back, you motherfucking, cock-sucking bastard!"

Now I know she's lost her mind, at least temporarily. Who would be both a motherfucker and a cocksucker? I know there are bisexual people so it's possible, but Esme knows me better than to think I go both ways.

I swallow. Geez, that was a big bite and I have to keep swallowing to get it down my gullet. I take her hand, tightly clinging to the pillow, and guide her to sit next to me.

"Honey, honey, honey, honey, honey," I say in my most soothing tone. "Breathe." I put my arm around her and breathe slowly and deeply until she starts to do it herself. "I don't love Buck. Don't get me wrong, I like her and she has great taste, but she's not my type."

"Why? What's wrong with her? Nevermind, go on," Esme sighs.

"She fell asleep..."

"It's hard for her to fall asleep, what did you do?"

"I... I... I don't remember... let me think... she was talking and I told her to try being silent..." I explained.

"You got her to stop talking?" Esme loosened her grip on the pillow.

"I asked nicely, that's all. Then she was snoring and I couldn't wake her up so I said what I thought *you'd* want to say 'I love you, babe,' and she jolted awake and kind of cried and wanted to quit and wouldn't look me in the eye."

"You really got to her, huh? That's interesting. I wonder what it means."

"Ask her," I suggest.

"That's too easy. I'd rather ruminate and lose sleep inventing scenarios of what's going on in her head and how it'll lead to my eventual heartbreak," Esme says, half-joking.

"I don't know what it means—only she does. So ask her."

"But then she'll know you told me and that's against the whole Code of the Hammerabi."

"Hippocratic Oath?" I wonder.

"Why are you always so caught up with minutiae? Why do you even remember shit like that when you can't remember normal everyday stuff taking out the trash?"

I sit, silent, because I don't know. Well, I do actually know about the trash. It's not that I forget, it's that I don't like carrying the big plastic bags downstairs. I'm always afraid I'll trip over it and break a leg, or worse, the bag will break open and I'll have to touch the trash. Ugh!

But I don't know why it's so much easier for me to remember trivia, than, say, the name of a friend I'd known for years. Like Gene, who liked to talk for hours after midnight, and I enjoyed his calls as they distracted me from real life. But we'd be talking and I'd literally forget his name. "Genius? Genie?" I'd wonder. I'd have to scroll through the G's in the contacts app on my phone to remember. I worry about early senility except I've always been like this probably because I bore easily so I don't pay attention.

>>>

"What are you off thinking about now, Chip? Honestly, my life is at stake here, at least my love life, so please, be here now."

"Look, I know there's clearly something wrong with my brain, OK? I'm doing the best I can within the sight of pizza. It's very distracting."

Esme shoves a slice at me. I take a bite and chew, slowly so as to appreciate all the flavors and not have to say anything.

I swallow and start to choke. Esme gets behind me and gives me the Heimlich maneuver, which I like to think of as the "Hamlish" maneuver where you sing, "Memories," from "The Way We Were," and it makes the patient gag...

I don't think I actually needed the maneuver, but it's a nice hug and makes me cough and sends the piece of pizza flying off into a mean-spirited Yucca plant even my neglect has been unable to kill. Maybe this will.

Just then Esme's phone makes the noise of some kind of animal I've never heard. She studies the text message, takes a deep breath, puts down her phone slowly and looks at me, accusingly.

"I can't stand the suspense, just tell me what I did wrong!" I tell her.

"It's from Buck."

"What did she say?"

She picks up the phone and holds it an inch from my nose, so close I can't possibly read it. I gently guide her hand further away until the words come into focus, "Thanks for sending Chazbo. I had an epiphany and want to talk about it. Come to my place."

"What does that mean?" Esme asks, like I know.

"I think it means she had an epiphany and wants to talk to you about it."

"I KNOW that!" she hisses. "Is she going to break up with me???"

Now I'm really sleepy and want to take a shower because despite how clean Buck appeared to be, she's a human who has, for lack of a better word, "cooties," and I want to wash off all traces of humanity and go to sleep. "I don't think so. I don't know. I'm tired."

"It's only 7pm. You can't be tired. How exhausted can you be from cuddling with my girlfriend for an hour..."

"50 minutes..."

"...even less exhausting."

"It was my first time, I was nervous, I thought she was going to judge me, and then she freaked out and I can't get those green pumps out of my head."

"Wait a second," Esme quizzes me, "Are you saying Buck was wearing heels? Buck doesn't wear heels. Are you sure you were in the right office?"

"Not Buck, his patient..."

"You and small leather goods, it's a sickness."

"I KNOW" I say, the way she did earlier. I once saw a tiny zippered Louis Vuitton leather pouch at the "Cat Lady Thrift Store" on Cahuenga. It had a price tag of $4 because they didn't know what it was worth. I almost fainted. I went to the register and bought it and every night I'd stick my nose in and fall asleep to the smell of money before bed.

Then a guy I'd never met before came over. He said his name was *Jazb* (that's not even a name!) and we had a moderately good time in bed but he was a little rough. At one point I had to yell, "Stop already!" and later that night I reached for my LV coin purse and it was *gone!* That fucker must have stolen it just because I yelled at him!

I wrote a scathing review of him on *YelpMen* to protect anyone else with valuable small leather goods he might abscond with. And—I flamed him on *Asstagram* the gay Instagram, and *FuckBook* the gay FaceBook but with fewer Russian trolls.

I was distraught and couldn't sleep and felt as if I'd lost something important in my life that I would never find again, unless I slept with the guy I met who worked at a Louis Vuitton store and could get 50% off, but even then this coin purse that could maybe hold four coins was still $300! I was finally able to sleep by remembering the smell, but it wasn't the same.

About three months later I found the missing coin purse in the back of my underwear drawer and remembered that I'd hidden it there in case anyone was tempted to steal it. I went to YelpMen to remove my review (I'm very conscientious that way), but by then the site had already gone out of business. I'm sure the guy's fine, besides, Jazb couldn't possibly be his real name.

>>>

I come back to the moment by feeling Esme's nails digging into my arm. "Oh my God, Ez, just wait an hour for traffic to calm down because you're not getting through the Cahuenga pass now with a concert at the Bowl. Once the performance starts, the traffic's clear to her house. You go. You talk. As much as I wish I was,

I'm not a fucking mind reader, I don't know what Buck wants to tell you."

She loosens her grip and I notice the nail marks in my skin and think, "That would make an interesting tattoo if I didn't have such a low threshold of pain that it's unmitigated agony just to get a popcorn kernel stuck in my teeth."

"I still may kill you," Esme said, not unkindly, kissing me on the cheek.

"That's always an option, babe," I reassure her.

THE CLIENT

I finish the second piece of pizza and am stuffed in a good way when I hear mysterious windchimes, which I often think are outside but really mean I've got a text from an unknown number. The message says, "You were recommended. Need appointment."

I stare at it for a long time until the words don't make sense, like when you say a word too much until it loses all meaning. Appointment. Appointment. App *ointment.* How is that even a thing?

I feel like the room lights up and a shower of firework sparkles are landing on me. The song, "This Could be the Start of Something Big!" starts playing in my head, sung by that lady singer with the hair from the 50s... she was married to that very handsome singer and they'd sing together but I always wondered what he saw in her...Steve and Eydie—I mean, who spells their name that way? Eydie Gormé, so sophisticated for a nice Jewish girl from the Bronx.

I see a call coming from an unknown number. I never answer these calls because if they're important they'll leave a message and otherwise they're just trying to sell me an extended warranty for my car.

I press the volume key which silences the call, but lights up my screen, reminding me of the text message. I should probably do something about this.

App ointment. Hmm. I will check my calendar and see when I'm free. Let's see... always. But just like an empty restaurant, if it's not hard to get in I don't want to go, so I decide to make myself sound busy.

"Hello! Thank you for your text! I'm so glad I was recommended to you..." by who? Who else? It's gotta be Buck. OMG, what if it's the green leather lady? She was very bony. The only time I've ever cuddled with a skinny person, other than Esme, was that guy who was visiting from Vietnam. He was very nice but his ribs kept jabbing into me so I claimed to be hungry and he took me to a Vietnamese restaurant and ordered stuff which gave me diarrhea.

Oh, text message... I won't say 'Buck' just in case it wasn't her but who else could it be? 'I'm so glad you were recommended!' I'm using a lot of exclamation marks but I want to sound... I can't even think of the word... enthusiastic? Happy? 'This week my only availability is Tuesday at 2pm." Send. I chose Tuesday because nothing has ever happened on a Tuesday and 2pm means I don't have to wake up early. Oh, damn, I should have asked where they live. What if this person is a long drive away in the wrong direction for traffic... This gives me an idea—I'll charge for travel time!

A minute passes, then I get another text, "I rescheduled my botox/boxing session so Tuesday at 2 works. You need to come to me, 'cause I have a tantric sex lesson at 4."

I immediately decide to double my hourly rate. "Where are you located?" I reply.

"Beverly Hills. The flats. On Alpine. OK?"

They hope that's OK? Why would that *not* be OK? Are they ashamed to live in the flats and not the actual hills? I silently double my hourly rate again. "That's fine, please text me your address."

"Thanks! Let me know what to wear."

What should she/he wear? Clearly a Chanel suit! I shouldn't mock, it's a good question, and one that I'll answer on the "How to prepare for your cuddling session," sheet I need to put together for future clients after this... Man... Woman... *person* recommends me to all their friends and I'm so busy I have to hire minions to do my bidding.

"Something comfortable and chic," I reply and accidentally hit "send" before I can backspace over "chic" because that was just my little joke.

"I have just the thing, a *Chihuahua West* cashmere tracksuit," the reply appears. *Chihuahua West*? That's the expensive brand run by this gorgeous guy with perfect eyebrows who's always posing semi-naked on Instagram which I'd do if I looked like him, too. Could this be him? I'm freaking out. He's got a perfectly flat stomach which is annoying but he's always showing closeups of his treasure trail and I'm sure there's a pot-o-gold at the end of that rainbow! He can't keep his tongue in his mouth, either, so he must love to French... No, it cannot possibly be him as he's Lady GaGa's best friend so there must be a line of thirsty male models around his block willing to service him for a scarf...

Back to reality. I text, "Sounds fab!" I use "fab" so it's clear I'm gay in case the therapist hasn't told this person and if they're a man wearing a cashmere tracksuit they might as well be gay and if they're a woman then they'll know they have nothing to fear from me, like groping or wearing Axe body spray.

I set the phone down because that text message exchange feels weighty and I'm weak with excitement.

The address appears in my text and I immediately Google Map it, then use Street View to see what the house looks like. It's big. White. Ultra Modern. Looks like a cross between a Four Seasons Hotel and a high-security prison.

Maybe I should get a spray tan this weekend. Or go on a grapefruit diet and lose 5 pounds. Or maybe what I really need is a cashmere tracksuit. I go to the *Chihuahua West* site and they're $2,600... and don't even come in my size!

Fuck Mr. Perfect Eyebrows. I can find something almost identical on Amazon. There it is—*Cashmerish* brand—with pictures of hip young people laughing, skateboarding, and drinking cocktails in their faux cashmere sweats. Do I want *Sahara Taupe, Santa Barbra* [sic] *Sand,* or *Soho Greige?* No, no, no, I clearly need *Sonoran Silver* which is really gray so it'll bring out the sparkle in my beard. The description says, "Sheek 100% pure and breathable cashmere-like-acrylic fibers. *Machine washable.* $26. Because it's Asian sizing where an XL is equivalent to a US size XS, I'll need an 9X, but that's OK. Free shipping and returns. *Buy it now*. Get it tomorrow. Bingo!

I lay back in bed, my head nestled between two chocolate bon bon pillows. My eyes grow heavy.

Shit, wait, I forgot to take a shower! I drag myself to the bathroom which I have to myself because Esme seems to have left for Buck's. If Buck was going to break up with her she'd have just sent her an "I'm sorry" text message like everyone else.

I turn the hot water up because I love that I don't have to pay for the hot water, and I'm more tense than usual because of today's challenge and Esme's death threat and now this mysterious client who could make my future if I don't fuck it up.

I use the lavender soap Debbie gave me for Hanukkah but which I've been saving for a special occasion and this seems special enough, except as soon as I get it wet I think I could have saved it for the mystery client but there's no putting this genie back in the bottle. After what I'll charge them I can buy a whole *case* of lavender soaps—the hard-milled kind (whatever that means) from France!

I dry off and lay naked on my bed, feeling the heat rising from my soon-to-be-rich-and-successful body.

THE GOOD NEWS

Before I can fall asleep, my phone blows up playing Cher's *Dark Lady* song, which is Esme's ringtone *and* text-sound because of the whole Esmerelda fortune teller joke. She's texting *and* calling at the same time, making Cher sing on top of herself, sounding even worse than she did before being famously autotuned by the *Pet Shop Boys*. I love the story of how when Cher heard the auto-tuned version where she sounds a bit like a robot, she asked them, "How'd you think of that?" and they answered, "Because you sounded bad and we had to do something."

I look at the text first in case Esme's coming to kill me, in which case why answer her call? The text reads, "ANSWER YOUR FUCKING PHONE!"

I answer the fucking phone. I say nothing and listen to hear if Esme is crying from sadness, or panting from running upstairs with a machete.

I hear a laugh and she says, "Oh, stop it, Buck, I'm on the phone!"

That sounds good, except it could be hysterical laughing and maybe she and Buck and both coming over with machetes. I continue to strain against every fiber of my being to remain silent.

"Are you there, Chippy Whippy Doo Dah?" she giggles. That's not good. Sounds like she's snapped ala the Joker in Batman and is coming to wreak or reek havoc on me, or both. Batman is boring. The movies always feel like I'm watching the kink of the director.

Kinks are fun if they're yours (like my kink of making out in boutique changing rooms), but it's pretty boring to watch anyone else's because, unlike mine, they rarely make any sense.

I've thought about this a lot. Where in our DNA are the little switches that make us attracted to a man in uniform (which I understand) vs a man in an animal costume (no judgment, but I don't get this at all, the suits must get sweaty and be expensive to dry-clean, and it's an awful lot of bother to unwrap and get to the creamy center).

Why does the human genetic language make young guys like older guys (I'm all for that one), or instruct other guys to like being tied up, spanked, and crawl on all fours wearing a leather puppy mask and leash (don't get me started).

Kinks aren't random things, people all over the world like the same strange stuff. Why are some people the S or M in S&M? Personally, I am repulsed by anything involving pain or inconvenience, so the whole S&M thing doesn't work for me. Also, it seems to require a lot of equipment, and while I'm all for shopping for cute outfits, I don't want to have to carry a bag of heavy torture tools and toys with me just so I can get off—that's too much schlepping.

>>>

"Chazbot, have you wandered back into the dark recesses of your head again?" Esme asks. Why does her voice sound odd?

"Um... no... sorry Ez... I was..." I want to lie and say I was making toast and didn't want it to burn. So often my first impulse is to make up a story to make myself sound better. Nobody can blame a guy for making toast, that universally beloved delicacy. My ex, Vevan (his real name, though he refused to explain why), came back from Japan and gave me a loaf of bread he bought there. I was hoping for a kimono, cloisonne jewelry or a tea set, so a loaf of bread felt like a warning that things were rocky.

The slices were so thick they wouldn't fit into the toaster because they were meant to be toasted in the toaster oven—with a little water in a tiny, heat-resistant glass cup so it creates steam. I tried this and it was, without a doubt, the most incredible toast I'd ever had —crisp on the outside, tender, dare I say *pillowy*, on the inside. I didn't know about Rober's magic French butter at the time or I might have O.D.'d on toast, but it was still heavenly with crap butter and cinnamon sugar sprinkled on it.

The only problem was if I wanted another loaf I'd have to catch a flight to Kyoto. I blamed Vevan for this impossible situation, and when he refused to fly back to buy more bread, I naturally had to break up with him.

>>>

Jesus, I've forgotten Esme was on the phone.

She titters, "What's up, pickle pop?"

Oh—Esme is just high! That's the only time she calls me bizarre food-related pet names, like Pepe Le Pew's "my petit kumquat."

"I was just going to sleep. Everything OK with you?"

"Hunky dory, Mr. Mori!" Buck says, sending Esme gasping with giggles.

I assume by this hilarity on both their parts that things are just fine. Buck clearly didn't break up with Esme, they both got high and probably had sex.

I've never understood how lesbians have sex. While I won't Google it because I don't really want to know, my casual guess is that it involves a combination of tongue, fingers and frottage. I have no idea as I find the female body a complete mystery. Esme tried to show me her lady parts once when we were both very drunk but all I remember is us laughing so hard she peed herself.

Men are easy. Our man parts are right there, hanging out for the world to see. I've wondered if this makes much practical sense—I imagine ancient men running in the wilderness, their dangling private parts getting snagged on thorns while women could just breeze through, unharmed.

But the advantage of men is that we're so obvious. Nothing's hidden (except the prostate but nobody wants to *see* that). Also, as a man, I have the same parts (if sometimes not as big), as my partner. I understand how they work and what I like, so I can make an educated guess as to what another man likes.

But how does *anyone* have sex with a woman? I know it happens all the time, but I suspect too many men have no idea so their wives and girlfriends have to fake it. At least this is what I've heard from my female friends. The straight male ego is too fragile so women are afraid of saying, "No, you clumsy dolt, it's that part there, lick it!"

Ironically, while straight men consider gay men *less of a man,* we tend to think we're *more manly* because we have to deal with other "big strong men." I'm sure that's offensively sexist in some way, but I don't mean it to be. Most of my best friends are women because overall they're smarter, more sensitive and smell better.

During sex, gay men generally aren't shy about hissing, "Don't do that, do this!" because it's just easier than expecting our partners to be mind readers. Personally, I'd still find mind-reading a useful trait in a sexual partner, though not in a romantic one. I don't want them always knowing what I'm thinking, lest they hear something like, "Oh, no! His bottom teeth are a little crooked." That's what I thought when I realized I had absolutely fallen *out* of love with Vevan. When I'm in love I never see their flaws.

I hear Vevan has since had them straightened which kind of makes me want him back, but his pinkie toe jutted out at a strange angle and I don't think there's any way to fix that other than losing the toe, like I did.

>>>

Oh, God. Esme hung up. She was probably talking and I didn't answer. I don't move a muscle, standing stock still so I can listen more closely in case Esme and Buck are sneaking up the stairs. Why am I still worried about that when they were clearly happy...

My phone screams *Dark Lady* again. It's a text from Esme. "Get your ass over here, Honey Woney Ding Dong." Oh, Lord. The names are getting worse. I once tried to get Esme to eat a Hostess Ding Dong, clearly one of the most impressive results of corporate food invention. Only science could create a cake that's always moist and filled with creme but requires no refrigeration. It stays fresh for eternity while managing to taste like a high-end French pastry as reimagined by a mad scientist with a penchant for hydrogenated fats.

When Hostess went bankrupt I cried and rushed to the supermarket to buy a few cases of Ding Dongs and Twinkies. My nefarious plan was to store them under my bed for a few years, sell them for a fortune on eBay, then retire to the part of the South of France where they speak English. But after a few years I looked under the bed and they were all gone! Was this another theft by a visiting paramour with a sweet tooth? Turns out *I* ate them. All. A Twinkie here, a Ding Dong there, and after two years there was nothing left!

In the end it didn't matter as Hostess's cake business assets were scooped up by two investment firms who understood that nobody goes broke underestimating the palate of the American consumer, like me.

You can still buy them at the market and my stash wouldn't have been worth any more than I paid for it, so it was just as well that I ate my own investment.

>>>

I reply to Esme's text, "Where are you, Sweetie Peetie Pie?" That's not a very good name but she's high so it doesn't matter.

I wait for a reply. There is none. I wait and wait and wait and wait and wait and fall asleep.

It's sunny outside when I wake to *Dark Lady* and check my phone. There are 36 messages from Esme, from 2am until just now. That means my phone was blaring this song all night and I slept right through it. Even though this might hurt Cher's feelings, I'm very proud.

Mostly the text messages are either random emoji, or like that game where you have to figure out what a phrase is from the various symbols and how they sound. I've never been good at those games so I don't play them. What are those things called? I Google it. "Rebus." I don't even like that word.

Buried amidst all the emojis are the occasional words like, "OK" and "Happy" and "I owe you," which I take a screenshot of in case she's too high to remember it later. *Somewhere in my youth or childhood, I must have done something good...* that song from *The Sound of Music* plays in my head, then stops when I remember I've never thought, "youth *or* childhood" were very good lyrics—they're basically the same thing. I couldn't understand it, as lyricist Oscar Hammerstein's work was usually flawless. Then I read Richard Rogers wrote this song himself, lyrics and all, to try to win an Oscar® award for the movie version after Oscar H. died... that explains it!

I scroll down to Esme's most recent message of a minute ago, "OK, you misfit toy who didn't come over or answer my last 37 messages, all I can say is that you missed one hell of a time in Vegas!"

Vegas? She went to Vegas without me just because I say to anyone who will listen how much I loathe Vegas? Sure, they have enticing all-you-can-eat buffets, but after getting food poisoning from them not once, or even twice, but three times, they have landed firmly on my "no eat" list.

Vegas? Did they get married? OMFG. I immediately call her. Her phone answers but all I can hear is clanging either from slot machines or one of her fortune-teller dangly earrings hitting the phone.

"Esme? Are congratulations in order?"

"You don't congratulate the bride," Buck's voice says over the din. Must be slot machines as I can't imagine Buck in dangly earrings.

"Which one of you is the bride?" I ask rudely. I once did flowers for a gay wedding and stayed to watch and torture myself with their happiness. Also because they had King Crab legs at the reception, if you can believe it, which I couldn't.

After the ceremony, an older woman went up to the happy couple, both wearing matching Dolce and Gabbana suits (which explained why they could afford crab legs) and asked, "Which one of you is the bride?" Luckily both the grooms were drunk and laughed but I was deeply offended and had to eat three crab legs and drink half-a-bottle of Veuve Clicquot champagne before I could regain my composure.

But in this case, both Esme and Buck *are* brides, right? Right. Oh, but being only half-awake I'd forgotten the *Emily Post Etiquette* rule of "You don't congratulate the bride as that makes it sound as if she *landed* the groom. Instead, you offer your *best wishes*," which is sexist because you *do* congratulate the groom!

I feel strongly that anytime someone convinces someone else to get married, either congratulations or condolences are in order.

It strikes me now that Esme and Buck will move in together and I'll be left alone. If this had happened just a few days ago I would have been thrown into a Pop-Tart-eating panic about how I'd be evicted from my apartment and onto the street where it would be impossible to keep ice cream frozen.

But now I am actually happy for them both. What an interesting sensation—to be genuinely happy for people who aren't me. But I am. I want Esme to be happy, and Buck launched my career among the hoi polloi... no, that's the wrong word, it always sounds fancy but it means "common people." No, Buck launched my career with the elite, crème de la crème, upper-crust or at least the rich who won't mind paying $400 an hour (which now doesn't sound like quite enough) for cuddling.

I've already fantasized about moving to Malibu and opening an ocean-view "cuddling studio," so I can be happy for them without being terrified for myself.

Everybody is happy!

Then I get a text from a different number with no name, "Where are you?"

WTF?

I check my phone. 2pm. I slept late even for me. But I've got nothing to do today except perhaps watch a few more YouTube videos to polish up my cuddling act.

Wait, what? I thought it was Monday. Phone says *Tuesday*—Phone must be broken. I check Laptop as I do when phone is clearly confused. Laptop says, "Tuesday, June 8."

They're *both* wrong? Then I remember I have something on Tuesday... at 2... Oh, fuck! My first cuddling session with the unknown Beverly Hills rich person!!!

THE BAD NEWS

My entire future crumbles before my eyes!

Tears land on the text message, magnifying it, yet making the screen unresponsive to my touch.

My hysterical chant of "What do I do? What do I do? What do I do?" is interrupted by the song "What's new, Pussycat?" playing briefly in my head until I slap myself on the forehead.

I briefly consider the "I'm dying and had to go to Hawaii" line. I reconsider because in this case it would get in the way of future bookings.

Loathe as I am to lie, I can't think of any honest way to address this. "My best friend went to Vegas and got married and I had to be the best man so I'm in Vegas and am so sorry, I will make it up for a free session." The fuck I'll do a free session! Rich people don't value anything they can get for free, not even a Rolex in an Oscar gift bag, which is how I almost got a drunk Ben Affleck to give one to me before his bitch of a publicist snatched it away for herself.

But—If my lie was true, then why didn't I message the client last night to apologize? I'll have to call Buck and tell her that I was with them last night even if she can't remember it just in case one of her patients asks... too complicated.

Plus, none of that sounds remotely professional. Needs to be something more urgent like, "I had to go to the ER. My phone battery died but thankfully I didn't. Was only able to recharge when I was released a few minutes ago. Sorry, I'm not contagious and can meet Tomorrow at 2." Not bad!

I stare at the message before hitting *send,* which I still don't do because I want to make sure there isn't something better I can say. Maybe, "I had a cuddle-related injury and..." oh, please, even I don't believe that one.

But I've always been a fan of the sympathy play, so I hit *send* on the ER tale and hold my breath.

Finally I can't hold it anymore and gasp for air, but keep staring at my phone. Ping! A reply! "Glad you're not dead, mate. Tomorrow at 2 I have a zoom with my psychic stock advisor, Claus, in Liechtenstein. He's a night owl, or, as I've oft suspected, a vampire. I don't discriminate. I'll re-sked with him and hope he doesn't burst into flames. G'day."

My future starts to reassemble itself, piece by piece. I imagine that this person (I really should ask who he or she is) will be transformed, then their friends, and who knows, my fame could spread to Liechtenstein. Is it even possible to cuddle a vampire? No, it's probably best to franchise in countries like Transylvania.

The sheer relief has made me ravenously hungry. But before I do anything else I set the alarm of my phone for Thursday at 11am so I'll have plenty of time to clean up, choose my ensemble and get to Beverly Hills.

My phone moans like a moose. It's Buck. "My patient let me know that you're fine after your night in the ER. You should have told us! But it was kind of you not to put a damper on our joyful night, so thanks, bub."

OMG, I killed two birds with one lie!

I decide to celebrate and order a breakfast burrito because it's always 9am somewhere! I drive through and eat in my car, remembering the first time I had a breakfast burrito. I was an extra on *Friday the 13th, part 13, He's Back Yet Again!* It was shot in South Pasadena and while I hate horror movies, I thought it would be fun because the casting notice said, "Must have good aim for throwing bricks through windows." How could anyone resist that?

Naturally the call time was an absurd 5am, the only good part being there was no traffic. Driving LA freeways at 5am is absolutely magical—you fly down the road the way I imagine the freeway designers expected the system to work. It only took 15 minutes to get to Pasadena whereas the last time I drove there during normal human hours it took an hour-and-a-half.

While there were once again no chairs for extras, they were feeding us! At least, after the cast and crew, and rent-a-cops, street sweepers and set-crashers who wandered in off the street carrying clipboards (that's where I learned that trick).

I'd never even heard of something called a Breakfast burrito, but, apparently, it had long been a staple of the "roach coach," the nickname for film set food trucks. I was handed a large, foil wrapped torpedo which, when unwrapped and bitten into, revealed a soft tortilla, scrambled eggs, hash browns and bacon in one warm, handheld package.

The magic was short-lived as it started to rain and there was no dry place for the extras. Being fed, and fed up, I snuck into one of the prop cop cars. This emboldened six other extras who piled in with me. I made sure to roll down a window a little, lest we suffocate which would be bad publicity for the film: "Horror Film Set Cursed! Nameless Extras Suffocate! Nobody Cares!" We all fell asleep until noon, at which time a production assistant knocked on the window and yelled "Lunch!"

I don't remember lunch, but I do remember our first shot wasn't 'till sunset. We stood in the drizzle in front of the famous Halloween House and got to throw bricks through the window. I've never been able to throw anything much further than the length of my arm so I didn't get the joy of breaking a window, though I almost broke my toe.

They released us before they had to feed us another meal, but being hungry, I hung around anyway to avoid traffic on the 110 and 134 and ate some impressive fried chicken and biscuits.

>>>

After finishing the burrito I make a quick stop at Ralph's to get groceries. I head back home to study cuddling, determined that since God or my lie has given me a second chance I am going to make good!

There's an Amazon package in front of my door. It's my *Cashmerish* tracksuit! I rip open the box, tear the plastic bag and gasp—it's so soft! The color coordinates perfectly with my ever-increasing silver hairs. I put it on and feel like I'm wrapped in the downy undercoat of a Kashmir goat. And it's got a cargo pocket for my phone! I might have to order a dozen more as these will clearly by my work uniforms—which means I can write them off.

Thus swaddled, I lay on the sofa watching people cuddling on YouTube and feeling very professional.

THE RESTING SMILE FACE

Esme didn't come home last night. I smell a trend. One that's fine as long as my cuddling career takes off. Otherwise I might have to move home with my parents (like my friends), only in my case this would be complicated by the fact that both are dead. Or at least I tend to think of my mother as dead. Can you imagine the look on her stretched and filled face if I showed up at her door with my suitcases?

I have, in fact, driven by her manse, though I couldn't actually get to the front door because there were big iron gates on the driveway and I was afraid of pressing the intercom button because I might blurt out, "Mommy?" and no good could come from that!

If I could manage to get through her gates, I wonder if she could find a corner for me in the potting shed next to the gardener's riding mower... no, I am not going there. I must think kindly of her. If I *really* needed her, I can imagine she might be able to find a place in her small hard heart to help me. She might even lend me a liver if she still has one left. Do I hear a brick falling? Yeah, no. Though maybe I've loosened a bit of grout.

Esme sent a cute photo of herself, Buck and Buck's dog, *Wino*, so named because as a puppy she lapped up an entire bottle of chablis she knocked off a coffee table. From then on she would seek out alcohol of any kind. Buck had to remind party guests not to leave their glasses on any surface the dog could reach. Turns out, the dog, a short-legged Jack Russell, could reach most any through a combination of jumping and/or sad puppy eyes.

In the pic, the three of them are cuddled up on what appears to be a camel-colored suede divan. Suede, with an alcoholic dog? That's brave, even for Buck.

I'm nervous. Today is my big day—my first *professional* cuddling gig. I once again do the whole ablutions thing, taking as long as I want because I don't have to worry about their being hot water for Esme. I desperately want to put product in my hair, but the site of that suede divan makes me wary—what if this client has some kind of delicate upholstery and my hair product stains it?

Antimacassar comes to mind. When I grew up people would put a doily on the top of their sofa cushion. I never understood why until a very swishy friend who had been a sailor, or a *seaman* as he loved to call it, explained that sailors, sorry, *seamen*, used to oil their hair with macassar oil. It made their hair shine (and killed head lice), but the oil also stained everything, including their uniforms, which is why they ended up with those big cute sailor collars to keep the oil off the rest of their uniform. Ladies—of the evening, one supposes—tired of seamen staining their sofas, started crocheted lace doilies between customers so they could keep the men from despoiling their furniture before or after they despoiled them.

Anyway—I think of this because if I put product in my hair and it gets on the clients upholstery without my first having despoiled them to the point where they no longer care, then that's not going to be good for business.

I must moisturize, of course, but with a product scientifically designed to sink into the skin. I prefer scientific beauty products after spending untold thousands on those that merely had beautiful packaging —like those pretty ones from the Province that smell great and do absolutely nothing other than make macassar-like stains on my late-great metallic turquoise 1984 Honda Civic Hatchback's headrest. I never could get those stains out, so luckily my car was totaled by a Range Rover backing up in the library parking lot. It only made a 4" dent in my fender but my car was worth so little the insurance company totalled it.

AAA insurance sent me a check for $2,125.42. I could never figure out how they came up with that exact figure. To celebrate and also make it a more even number, I spent $5.42 on an imitation crab cake lunch at a short-lived drive through chain called *You Call This Seafood?* and wondered what I could get with the rest of that pittance.

Luckily, my drag queen friend, *Dame Zizi Caliente,* who had the distinction of being the first one kicked out of RuPaul's Drag Race season 23, had still gained notoriety because almost every word she said on the show had to be bleeped. She changed her drag name to *Bleepy Be-atch* and got a string of demeaning but lucrative jobs hurling insults at strangers for sex shop openings and the occasional gay boy Bar Mitzvah.

Thus moving up in the world, she was trying to unload her 2002 Lexus GS with genuine imitation rosewood dash trim installed by Bleepy's boyfriend at the time, a tattoo artist named *Sloth.* True to his name he installed the woodish trim slightly askew, but I didn't care, the car ran just fine (being a gussied up Toyota and all), only had 130,000 miles on it, and had a cream leather interior which made me feel like a king, or at least a jester joyriding in the king's old car. Most importantly, it had air conditioning that made me feel like I was driving a Sub-Zero fridge.

I bought it for two grand but *had* to spend $125 on detailing to remove the smell of fish which Bleepy could never believably explain. Since it had a salvage title it's possible that the car spent some time underwater, but who hasn't?

>>>

I'm looking at myself in the mirror, moisturizer slathered over my face, trying to remember why I bothered to wake up early and pretty myself up... Ah, right, first client. I'd lose my mind if it wasn't screwed up.

I almost apply the hair product when I remember the whole michegas with the macassar. I'm pleased my hair still looks pretty good at my advanced age. I call the growing number of silver hairs "free highlights." In the right light they do sparkle plenty.

I rub the moisturizer in, leaning towards the mirror and inspecting my skin. I'm surprised to see *me* staring back at me. I normally avoid looking in mirrors lest I notice I have wrinkles. Wrinkles! Nature's way of reminding you that you're going to die. Mine aren't too bad because I'm not skinny, but they're still there, including the two vertical lines between my eyebrows that a cosmetologist/astrologist once told me meant I was a perfectionist. I laughed at this, and cried at the haircut she gave me: an asymmetrical wavy bob that made me look like a jazzercise instructor with a lazy eye.

By 45, my father was a successful landscape architect. What am I, besides stylish and multi-talented when I can bother? It's sad, because I know I can do things. If only someone would pay me what I think I'm worth, I'm sure I could wow them. Hell, I do that with flowers without being paid what I'm worth.

But mostly I feel invisible, which is why I sometimes resort to wearing a kilt and construction boots to the supermarket—so that *somebody* might notice me. Sometimes I'm even surprised to see myself looking back at me in the mirror—I don't know what I expect to see—I guess *nothing*.

But here I am. A person. A man. I let out a dramatic sigh and arrange my curly hair in a manbun, before thinking better of it. No, I'm going to let it all hang out like a lion's mane, only dark brown, with silver highlights.

I am not a bad-looking human being. I feel lucky I don't have what I call an *unfortunate face*, those people you look at and think, "How do they get through life with that face?" It's not their fault, like me, it's their parents' fault. But at least I'm symmetrical at first glance, and I have a "RSF," Resting Smile Face.

I was at the airport coming back from Kansas where nobody should be forced to go and this older lady, wrinkled but with a good, honest, sweet *gramma* face, out of the blue said to me, "What're you so happy about, asshole?"

She might have seen me eyeing her clear plastic purse full of hard boiled eggs, but I really was just looking forward to getting back to Los Angeles where people didn't think *Ranunculus* was a dirty word, or, if they did, were into it.

Clearly she had unresolved attitude problems, but I found it fascinating when she took out her teeth to eat the eggs, whole. And it was a rare instance where I took someone else's uninvited words in a positive way.

I wasn't actually happy, I just *looked* happy. How wonderful is that? That's like the epitome of advertising! It doesn't matter how you really feel, as long as other people feel you're happier than they are!

On the flight home I felt the corners of my mouth as they turned up, then regretted it because I'd touched the armrest and now assumed the international germs of thousands were crawling their way inexorably into my mouth. But I still smiled, because no matter what bacteria or virus I might contract, nobody else could see it. They could only see my *resting smile face* and imagine I was happier than they were.

I bravely look into the mirror again. I appear to be smiling.

THE PREMIERE LEAGUE

Normally, I have to fret over what I'm going to wear. What will be the most appropriate? What will be the most stylish, or at least cutest? What won't require Spanx. I have a pair but they make it difficult to breathe. That works for some people as it gives them a sexy breathless look. It mostly makes me appear asphyxiated. I used to wear them when going out to dinner precisely because it kept me from eating more than a requisite gay bite or two. Any more and I felt I was going to puke. Too bad Rober didn't know about this trick.

But now I have my *Cashmerish* tracksuit! Oh, happy day! What with my resting smile face and my ersatz-cashmere clothing, I am going to slay! Bad choice of words, since I don't want to get the reputation of killing my clients.

Oh, fuck, I never thought of that before. What if, while we're cuddling, whoever this is has a stroke from the sheer joy of it? That would not be good for business. Maybe I could salvage it by focusing on those people who actively want to die, but is that the audience I want? No, no, no, no, no, no, no. No return customers!

I stop and breathe, the Cashmerish already feeling a bit warm. I check the weather today, it's going to be 88, but with a breeze so it only feels like 86. I'm sure that the client's house in Beverly Hills will be chilled to a comfortable 68 degrees so as to better preserve the occupants. I'll be fine.

The sweat I'm feeling isn't from heat, but anxiety. Breathe. Breathe. Breathe. Look at me, pulling my own schtick on myself, and it's working.

My stomach rumbles, I'm hungry. I'd better take off the tracksuit because I can't have yogurt landing on my crotch. That happened once before I went to Debbie's and she said customers would get the wrong idea. She forced me to change into a pair of overalls. She insisted they were the latest thing, but I felt like a farmer.

It's nice and cool wearing nothing but my boxers. It would probably be nice to cuddle this way but now I'm confusing personal cuddling with business and I must not do that.

I eat yogurt with apricot jam. It's a bold choice but today calls for bold action. Then I brush my teeth especially hard, like Donnie Osmond, who, I read, brushed his teeth six times a day until they all fell out. This didn't sound right, so I went to Snopes which said this wasn't true and their perfect teeth were genetic but that Donny does suffer from social anxiety disorder. At least he *looks* happy!

Back in the tracksuit, I feel like I'm already cuddling with a bunny. I'm pleased no animal was harmed in the making of this *Cashmerish*, except maybe the ones who've had their habitat lost to factories or died from polluted water. OMG, why must I always find some way to feel guilty for everything?

No, I tell myself this is responsibly sourced acrylic... maybe recycled from those terrible acrylic paintings on velvet of children with big eyes. I am ridding the world of bad scary art and blessing it with my soft, fuzzy presence! I repeat that to myself until it almost makes sense.

I get in my Lexus. It may be old and have crooked wood on the dash, but if it was 20 years ago this car would be hot shit. The GPS guides me over Coldwater Canyon. I know the route, but I never go anywhere without the GPS sparing me from unnecessary traffic. Sometimes it gives me routes so convoluted that I wonder why I've had to take 27 turns down side streets, but I rest easy knowing it's getting me around other people.

Today it's a pretty straight shot, not even much traffic as I breeze along, the breeze of the AC pummeling me.

OMG, why do I have to pee? I'm assuming it's nerves and not the sudden-onset of a rare bladder disorder, but either way it's distracting. One used to be able to pull over on Coldwater Canyon and pee into anyone's landscaping, but now with security cameras everywhere that's not wise.

I'll just ask to use the client's bathroom when I get there. Do I use the word "bathroom," which makes it sound like I'm going to bathe, or "toilet" which sounds too graphic, or perhaps the more genteel "powder room," or the twee "commode?" I can't just come out and say, "Excuse me, I need to pee," though at least then they know I'm not going to stink up their room.

They surely have some fancy potpourri or high-tech fragrance spray like they had when I worked in men's shoes at Neiman's for two weeks. One of my responsibilities was checking the fluid level of the "ambiance adjustment device," so that it would never stop misting a smell I could only describe as "new money—like the intoxicating scent of $100 bills fresh from the bank.

Other departments had other scents, so sometimes if you stood in just the wrong place you could find yourself in an olfactory vortex of old-money, peonies and pheromones. Sometimes when I was on break I'd head to that sweet spot and let myself get dizzy—it helped me make it through the day. Before I quit, I told my friend Arthur there'd be an opening—the job was much more his kind of thing as he had a foot fetish.

Personally, I find hands very sexy, so when forced to look at toes they just seem like stumpy fingers. Not hot.

The GPS has me turn right on Sunset, and left on Alpine where there's a traffic light. I'm always super careful of traffic lights in Beverly Hills because each one has a hidden camera that can send you an expensive ticket if you do anything wrong. I read that the back tires of your car have to be all the way through the intersection before it turns red, or it can cost you $480 plus a trip to traffic school. I was forced to go to "comedy traffic school" once and the instructor must have been a comedy club dropout because his act didn't so much kill as make me wish I was dead.

The houses on this verdant block look like sets from
Zorro or *Downton Abbey* or *Gone with the Gale* (an
unlicensed 1982 remake of *Gone With the Wind*
starring the-next-big-thing *Gale Warning*. She's since
gone on to become a respected realtor in Tarzana who
advertises by putting her face on shopping carts).

I immediately recognize the foreboding white box of
a house I saw on Google Maps. I can see the Bauhaus
effect they were going for but failed. Now the only way
to save it, other than a complete teardown, would be
some jaunty striped awnings and a shit ton of ivy. I
might mention it and, who knows, launch a decorating
career, too! Possibilities!

I pull up at the gate and press the intercom. A posh
English accented voice crackles through the speaker,
"Explain yourself."

That throws me. "I... I have an appointment... for
cuddling... with..." I stop there since I don't know the
name of the client.

"With *whom?*" the voice asks. I have no answer. Am I
really going to be stuck outside and miss my
appointment and end up living in the gutter because
this person failed to give me their name... and I failed to
ask? I'm already a failure.

"He's here for me," I hear another voice, deeper, with
an odd accent. I think "thank you, man."

The gate slowly slides back, and I inch up the
driveway made up of concrete squares surrounded by
perfectly trimmed grass. I take three deep breaths and
clear my mind. Today is going to be fine. My future is
going to be fine.

I open my car door and am knocked back by a wall of hot air. This can't be 88 degrees. Yes, I was nearly shivering in my car (just the way I like it) but this feels like Vegas. I've never understood how anything could live in Vegas. I've been there a couple of times with friends who liked to gamble because the hotels are fancy and, if you go during the worst months, cheap. If you're willing to sit through a 2-hour high-pressure time-share presentation you can even get a free lunch.

I hate gambling, to me you might as well just flush the cash down the commode. I'd rather throw it away on clothes, accessories, or virtually anything else. The *only* reason to go to Vegas is to see magicians and tigers, not necessarily in that order.

Every time I left a hotel or casino in Vegas I felt like I was walking into an air fryer—hot swirling winds that would clearly turn me into a human French Fry if I didn't get into another air-conditioned car or building fast.

>>>

I don't have time for such reflections as 1) I can't be late, and 2) if I stand out in this desiccating wind I run the risk of melting inside my Cashmerish.

I lock the car out of habit, even though I'm in a gated driveway in Beverly Hills.

I nearly fall into a narrow moat between the driveway and the front step. I look down at this little strip of water full of tiny bright blue fish I assume are pygmy piranha. One wrong step and I could lose a foot like the old movie *Amazoniacs* I saw streaming on Amazon where a group of attractive young people are lured to the jungle by... no, this is not the time!

I make it up the stairs intact and stand in front of the glossy red doors with giant brass knobs shaped like soccer balls, the white parts made of white opals.

Do I knock? Find a doorbell? Wait for the trap door under my feet to drop me into a pit of snakes? The doors open slowly, revealing a 6'3", if he's an inch, brawny butler in full regalia, his buttons and tie-pin all made out of opals. His head reminds me of the ones at Easter Island.

"Who goes there?" he says, in an accent I now recognize as either Australian or New Zealand, I've always had a hard time telling them apart. I never guess as I've heard New Zealanders are offended if you think they're from Australia while Australians generally don't care about much of anything other than beer and telling stories about how they lost a limb to sharks.

I follow this hulking man into a playing-field of an entrance, two stories high. It's carpeted in astroturf and seems big enough to play football in—not that I'd know as I tend to think of sports as "theater for straight people."

The butler leads me to a white wooden bench and gestures for me to sit. He nods at my feet, and I see, for the first time, that he's wearing white sports shoes with cleats. I stare dumbly for a bit, wondering if he's unable to speak or if he just enjoys toying with me. I decide it's the latter, and that he hates me but I try not to care because I'm sure he's not the client.

He points to my feet and I remove my Fendi-esque loafers with orange monster eyes. I bought them from a cheap Chinese website. They took three months to arrive but looked so perfect that I wore them into the

Fendi store on Rodeo Drive where the fashionably emaciated salesman took one look and exclaimed, "Orange eyes! I'm obsessed! You could only buy that colorway in Milan!" I nodded, after which he was flirting with me until he saw me leaving without buying anything.

I am so glad I remembered to wear brand new socks since you cannot cuddle wearing shoes. You can try, but it's something YouTube videos specifically warned against.

The butler clears his throat and points to a rack of painfully white sports shoes that match the ones on his feet. Would it really be so hard for him to tell me what he wanted me to do? I make a guess: Each shoe is labeled with a size. I chose 12, because I'm really an 11.5 but if they're narrow I'll need a 12 or I won't even be able to get my feet into them.

The butler produces a long, white marble shoe horn which is handy because even in size 12 the shoes are narrow, tight—and ugly. I can understand wearing these if you actually play a sport where it's required by law, but otherwise, why?

I lace them which necessitates bending over, something I'd rather not do as I find it hard to breathe, hence all my shoes being loafers, clogs or sandals.

I stand up and wobble until I find my balance on the unnecessarily narrow soles studded with cleats that make me feel like I'm standing on tiny stilts.

The butler motions for me to follow him again. I feel unsteady like the first time I tried to wear heels. I know they make your calves look better, but, honestly, they were uncomfortable verging on dangerous. I wore a pair to a dance party once and by the end of the night was in so much pain I literally had to crawl home. Never again.

I almost get used to the cleats on the astroturf, then we go through a set of massive sliding glass panels to the backyard onto a teak deck. My cleats slide into the cracks between the slats and I have to fight to keep from falling into another moat filled with tiny deadly fish.

I am so busy trying to avoid them I almost run into a wide platform with a thick black leather pad on top. The butler once again gestures, this time for me to get on the platform which has to be a mistake because it's in direct sun with no AC, an environment that feels potentially fatal.

I climb onto the platform and sweat when I feel a meaty hand on my shoulder. "Ahoy, Mate!" The hand spins me around. My eyes are at the level of his impressively tanned, muscular, bare chest. I always wondered what a chiseled chest would feel like and here it is, glistening with either sweat or oil, like it matters which. His body looks like that of a 35 year old athlete. His face... is at least 65, maybe 80, it's hard to tell given its smooth, shiny, mask-like appearance.

He pulls his hand from my shoulder and thrusts it towards me, "Teddy Timbers, as if you didn't know," he rumbles, like an Australian earthquake.

His hand is so big mine doesn't quite fit around it and he shakes so vigorously I'm afraid I might lose a limb.

"You're gonna croak in that getup," he says, reaching under the platform and pulling out a pair of thin white running shorts.

"Yeah, sorry, you said you were wearing... and I thought we'd be inside..."

"Too beautiful of a day to be trapped inside," he says, smiling with stalactite teeth.

I look down and notice he's wearing the same white shorts with nothing under them because I can clearly see the outline of his impressive dick. I cannot afford to get an erection now so I think about sanddabs which I always find repellant.

"Take your kit off," he commands like I'm going to strip down in front of him and his butler in direct sun.

It's time to take control. "Thanks for the shorts, but in professional cuddling both parties should be fully clothed..."

"...Don't be a pussy," he laughs, "What'cha think I'm gonna take advantage of ya?" The butler laughs, too. I hate the butler. "Just cuz I was the first gay player in the Australian Football League doesn't mean you're my type!" More laughing from both of them.

I am torn between feeling deeply rejected, appreciating the guts it must have taken him to come out in professional sports, and wondering if I'm being Punk'd. Maybe all the traffic cameras in Beverly Hills are really just part of an elaborate city-wide Candid-Camera like comedy show and I'm this week's unsuspecting guest. It may be mortifying, but it could also be great publicity so I play along just in case.

I slide off the platform, trying to find my footing despite the stupid cleats. "Hahaha!" I fake-laugh as I figure out what to say. "Before our session it's always a good idea to make sure you're well-hydrated and have used the... loo," I say, momentarily proud I thought of a British-sounding word for toilet which I hoped they also used in Oz.

"Good I.D. mate," he says, slapping my ass so hard it tingles in way too good of a way. "My butler, Bastard, will show you to the dunny." I only understand half of that sentence, but figure it out when the butler eyes me, disgustedly, and leads me down a hall lined in lockers to a bathroom the size of my apartment.

I tear off my damp *Chasmerish* tracksuit and sigh as I hang it on a hook where it's not going to dry by the time I have to put it back on. I slide the little white shorts on over my boxers.

Oh, God. I look like the Pillsbury Dough Boy rolled in poppy seeds. I've always been almost translucently white. I don't tan, only burn then peel then go right back to white again. That, combined with the mostly dark curly hair on my chest (now flecked with "silver"), and I feel like a kosher dough boy.

If the rest of my life didn't depend on this cuddling session, I would have jumped back in my wet clothes and run to my car. Maybe not run, as I don't believe in running unless I'm being chased by a lion and even then it makes more sense to lie down and play dead. But I'd get to the car somehow, drive away and never look back.

That simply isn't an option now. I think about stuffing a sock in my underwear so I look more endowed, but because I'm wearing boxers, the socks could fall out at any time which would be highly embarrassing. I look back at the stupid cleat shoes and have to draw the line somewhere.

I step out of the bathroom, barefoot. The bastard Butler's face betrays subtle signs of snickering. He looks down at my feet and silently snorts, then walks back down the long hall towards the backyard into blinding sunlight—searing my quivering white flesh. I was clearly made for cloudy, northern climes and if I don't get a third-degree burn it's going to be a miracle.

Teddy's reclining, Burt-Reynolds-centerfold-pose, grinning like a gator. He pats the leather pad and says, "Come on boy, time to get this game in play."

I want to jump up in a single elegant move, but the platform's too high. Instead, I awkwardly hoist up one leg and claw at the slippery leather until Teddy's huge paw yanks me off the ground.

"OK, mate, work your magic!" Teddy demands.

I'm sweating from nerves and the sun. I take a deep breath. "Lie on your side—you're the *little* spoon."

"I've never been the little spoon in my entire life! I was bigger than my ma when I was three!" Teddy roars.

Now I'm *sure* someone is punking me, or this is a really bad dream. I hadn't considered that until now, but it seems like a definite possibility. That's a relief, because if it's a dream it doesn't matter, I can say whatever I want!

"You've paid me to be here so clearly you need something you don't already have. Lay on your side. Now." I'm forceful in a quiet way that even surprises me. He does what I've told him to do.

I get behind him. He feels twice as wide as even I am, and I reach my arms around him—but they're not long enough to wrap around. Luckily we're both slippery so I can slide my right arm up under his neck and onto that chest, lightly, first to hold him, but also to feel what a muscled chest feels like. I'm surprised, because it's not hard as a rock, it's kind of spongy.

I reach my left arm around as far as I can around his stomach, which does feel hard. I gently hug tighter, since that's a good place to start—but my arms just slide across his glistening skin. He grabs my left hand and pulls it tight, pushing the wind out of me.

"Mmm," he says, which I take to be a good sign. Normally I'd want my mouth near his ear so I can breathe lightly into it and hum. In the videos the cuddlee is compelled to start humming, too, which stimulates their vagus nerve because it's connected to the vocal cords.

But he's so big I'm looking at the back of his neck. Oh, what the heck, I breathe warmly onto him, and start to hum. Then he starts to hum, which, coming from him, sounds a bit like a lawnmower.

I gently rock back and forth, so focused on him that I've forgotten my own embarrassment, and the fact that the sun is beating down on me probably giving me skin cancer. Nope, just remembered that for a second. Focus on him.

Suddenly I'm hit with a wall of bliss. I tingle all over. It's like a bolt of joy-lighting has hit me and is running from my toes up to my spine, making my brain do backflips. I feel fulfilled and happy, I'm using my dubious talents to get paid good money for something that, like flower arranging, I'd do for free.

I feel myself gasp, and I'm cool all over—like the relief of taking a shower after a hot day. I feel his hard body soften and momentarily hope he's not dead, but even if he is, he's surely gone happy. No, he's still breathing.

I return to reality, finding the sun's warmth giving me energy I can share with him. My mind starts to spin about what kind of person I might become after this experience.

Then an odd thing happens—my brain simply stops. I have a vision of lounge chairs for tanning, future cuddling always half-naked in the sun... then it all goes away and I am here, now. I feel his breathing—we're sharing the same air.

Everything is *sensation*. I *feel* everything, this warm creature in front of me, the sun on my back, the slickness of our skin, the smell of bodies and sweat and lawn and trees is almost overwhelming. Through my closed eyes I see bright orange light on which organic shapes swim. The bird song pierces me like sweet sonic arrows. Finally, a sixth sense of this other human's energy, pulsing and roiling through me like electrified air.

It's a transcendent connection...

...Interrupted by an annoying smartphone beep that takes me out of the moment, into the hot sun, my arms around a massive slippery man. I open my eyes to see Bastard filming us on his iPhone and if I had a free arm I'd knock it out of his hands, but I can't move.

"Time to stop for your next appointment, sir," The bastard says.

I feel Teddy stirring. He sits up, freeing my arms. My hands have lost all feeling.

Teddy exclaims, "That was crackers, mate! Haven't relaxed like that since the 90s when Jeff Goldblum and I fucked like jackrabbits high on coke," I can't tell if he's serious or still mocking me, but he does *look* different. His hard, shiny mask of a face has softened into something akin to a real person.

Teddy pats my cheek, which almost knocks me off the table, then he slides off the table and takes the phone out of Bastard's hands, walking away.

"Did you shoot the whole thing, Bastard?" I say, worried that I wasn't supposed to call him that.

"Uh huh. Now I can do it for him without having to call you," he sniggers. Oh—so he *is* able to speak! The few muscles I know I have tighten and if he wasn't so big I'd want to punch him, not that I've ever punched anything in my entire life, except for a throw pillow embroidered with a poppy and it wasn't the pillow's fault.

"Excuse me," I say, sitting up, once again realizing I'm a marshmallow in the company of fiery Greek Gods, I briefly consider reaching into the moat and tossing the baby piranhas at him, but instead say, "my sessions are proprietary and if you want to perform this service you will need to get certified by me."

"Sounds fun, sign me up," he laughs—the bastard!

"I would also appreciate it if you and your boss would recommend me to your friends," I say, stupidly.

"I'll tell the master you asked," Bastard replies, leading me back to the bathroom.. "You need to sign the NDA on the bench before you shower," he says, standing there as if I'm supposed to sign while he watches. I quickly read the agreement because I've been burned before by signing things I never read. That's why, for several years, a photo of my belly button was the "before" in a web banner ad for a fat burning pill that was eventually banned because it was mostly sawdust.

I read that I'm not allowed to tell anyone I was here, or mention Teddy's name. Doesn't say anything about not tossing Bastard's name about! I speed read the three pages and cross out the part that says they can sue me for $1 million dollars and the use of my photo in a "before" picture, because my momma didn't raise no fool.

Momma. She lives not far from here. I could stop by for tea and little sandwiches and some gossip, wouldn't that be fun. Oh, God, I'm insane.

I snap back quicker than usual, finish scanning the pages and sign the bottom with a scribble that's not at all like my real signature. If anything, it looks a bit like "Stay-Puft marshmallow man." Fuck the both of them.

But I could pretty much live in this bathroom which looks like a locker room made of glowing back-lit white marble. The shower has a rain head above and I count 14 heads on the sides pummeling me with warm, vanilla-scented water from all angles. I'm surprised when doors in the walls open and spinning chamois brushes emerge like a human car wash, slapping me gently. I stand there for I don't know how long, nearing nirvana again when I hear a knock on the glass shower door and see Bastard's face leering over the top of it.

"Time to go, sir."

"OK, asshole," I say.

"Bastard," he reminds me.

"Fuck you," I say, waiting for him to move his big head away.

"Promise?" he smiles, showing no teeth that might reveal himself to be something other than human.

I hear the bathroom door close, get out and look for a towel. There are none. I hear a whooshing noise coming from the shower and go back in—all 15 shower heads are now blowing warm air at me until I'm perfectly dry. I think it's all over when there's one last mist of what smells like *Tom Ford's Ombre Leather* cologne. A nice touch.

I get ready to put on what I think will be my damp *Cashmerish* but I notice it's hanging on a wide wooden hanger and smells like it's been dry cleaned by a family of tangerines. It feels better than new as it slides over my surprisingly soft skin.

I'm torn between being angry with Teddy and the Bastard for not making this a weekly, if not biweekly appointment, and being grateful I had a short visit to the lovely land of the very, very rich. I like it here. I don't want to leave. I want to take another shower so I sit in marble splendor and wonder if they'll notice I didn't go.

The door swings open like the FBI is raiding, so I assume Bastard noticed. "I will show you the way out," he booms. I liked it better when he didn't talk.

I follow him to the astroturf lobby and remember I haven't been paid. "That will be $400, and travel time" I say as forcefully as I can.

Bastard thrusts his right hand down the front of his pants to his crotch and pulls out a stack of $100 bills, counting them condescendingly, "One, two, three, four, five," finishing with a chuckle.

I lose it. I'm not getting any more money or showers from these two so for once I say exactly what I'm thinking, "What exactly do you find so amusing, you bastard?"

He looks me in the eye, "You." Well, I asked. He reaches his arms around me and picks me up like a child. "You're so darn cute!" He shakes me, then plants a very hard kiss on my mouth, his tongue trying to force its way into my mouth—but I'm so stunned I seem to have lockjaw. He drops me, and hands me a card. "Call me," he says, guiding me out the front door with his hand on my ass before closing the door firmly behind me.

Intrigued and angry, I consider dropping his card into the piranha moat, but slip it in my pocket instead.

My inner-voice is still speechless as I drive away.

I feel Bastard's card in my pocket. I pull over in a shady spot in front of a mansion that looks like *Wuthering Heights*, and take the card out. It's engraved with only the word, "Bastard" set in a simple sans serif, and his phone number. I can't call now, I have to make him wait. And why do I want to call him anyway other than he was tall and well-built and has access to a shower that buffed me like a Ferrari?

Nope. Back in my pocket it goes and I drive home, my mind staying resolutely in my body. It's a new experience for me. I notice architecture and trees and signs and none of them send me off into a miasma of memories.

I consider turning on the radio to drown out this silence, but it's so interesting to notice the sounds of the tires spinning against the pavement. I'm feeling everything, the cold breeze against my cheeks, the leather of the steering wheel, the *Chasmerish* against my skin, my stomach rumbling.

I stop at In-n-out which usually has a line around the block but now only has six cars ahead of me. I briefly wonder if there's been a tragic outbreak of salmonella and most people are avoiding the place, then let that thought slide as I order a double-double, animal style. I find a parking spot under a tree and unwrap the burger. I've eaten countless burgers here, only now, I am engulfed by the way the bun feels against my teeth, the smell of the meat, the sweet grilled onions and that final tang of genuine American cheese.

Normally I wolf these down, but now I chew one bite until it insists on being swallowed, savoring every bite, taking 15 minutes to finish the burger. It's like I've never eaten one before.

When I actually pay attention, this $4 burger has as many flavor sensations as Rober's $12 pat of butter. I'd forgotten to cover myself with my normal 16 napkins to catch the drips so I look down expecting to find a Jackson Pollock tracksuit, but no, it's pristine.

I get home, shed my clothes and lie naked on my chocolate box bed. I smell of Tom Ford's idea of leather. I reach down and pull the five crisp $100 bills out of my pocket. I hadn't noticed because of where they came from, but they've clearly been ironed and starched.

My bliss turns to self-pity when I realize I've been living in the wrong world my entire life. My mother could have brought me into the rich world as a child. But no. Maybe it's for the best, maybe I wouldn't appreciate it the way I do now. A shard of my wall falls.

Part of living in LA is always seeing into the windows of the rich—shop windows, car windows. Separated by glass, security systems, and mostly by the people who've made it who don't want to lose their position to you.

Hmm, maybe I can marry Bastard and live at Teddy's! This far-fetched fantasy is interrupted when I hear a Moose—Buck's message tone. "How was it with Teddy?"

Oh, shit, I should have thanked her. "~~Eh. OK. Good.~~ Great! Thanks, Buck."

Buck texts: "Esme says 'Hi' and that there's leftover frozen stroganoff if you want it. Toodles!"

Toodles? I'm learning that some people who seem tough are only big. Good lesson I'm bound to forget.

But I don't want to forget how that bliss felt earlier, and how the silence sounds now. I breathe and remember the feeling, over and over and over, hoping it'll stick.

THE ROO

I fall asleep and dream I'm a kangaroo, hopping through the outback. I feel the warm wind as I bound effortlessly across the red, red earth.

Everything is so vivid—the vibration of the colors, the pungent smells of wildflowers, the simmering sun beating down on my fur.

It's all about intense feeling—and everything feels right. There are no thoughts to distract or mute my physical sensations.

I lay down in the shade of a green, green bush and feel something move in my pouch. I look down and a baby roo looks up at me. It feels natural to have a place within me to hold him. Having him there makes me feel —complete—as the sky and land merge in a crimson sunset.

THE NEXT DAY...

I wake rubbing my tummy and feel a paunch but no pouch. I smell coffee, throw on my kaftan and shuffle into the kitchen. It's Esme!

"Good morning, beautiful," I say, holding her in a hug. Her energy is different, less spikey, smoother.

She puts her hands on my cheeks, "What happened to you? Are you OK?"

I put my hands on hers, "Yeah."

"Why were you in the hospital?" I don't know what she's talking about. "Oh, you poor baby, you should sit down."

Oh, right, I lied. "I'm OK... now."

"You don't look so good." She looks in my eyes like she's trying to find something, "And you're too quiet."

I take in her words without trying to generate a response first, like I used to do. "Yup."

"You didn't have a stroke, did you?"

"Maybe—a stroke of luck."

"Tell me about it," she says, opening a cabinet door and pulling out a frying pan only big enough for one egg. "Buck's got a big, empty kitchen, so I thought I'd take a few things over."

I wonder if I should make up a story about why I was in the hospital but now it's all gotten very complicated. Instead, I tell her about the house, the Teddy, the Bastard. About how my mind shut off and I could feel everything. About how calm it made me feel. When I say, "Now I know I have something to give," I start to cry.

"You've always been a giving person, to people who were open to accepting it," she says, sweetly patting my back.

"I didn't know. I couldn't feel it. Now I can."

"What did the doctors say you should eat?"

She won't let this go and I don't want to lie to her of all people. "I didn't really have to go to the hospital."

"But Buck said..."

"Look, I fucked up. I was going to miss my first cuddling appointment so I made up for a story for the client and didn't know they'd text Buck."

"I was worried, you little shit!" She holds up the mini frying pan in a way that might be menacing if it wasn't so small. "It's not like you to lie."

"I know, I'm sorry!"

"So you just couldn't be bothered to come to my first and hopefully only wedding?"

"You were high, you never said you were getting married—and you didn't tell me where you were!"

"So?" she says, throwing the pan in a box with a crash.

I put my arms around her and send her my very best cuddling energy. "I love you, girl, I'm happy for you and

I will buy anything within reason on your wedding registry except that $2500 steam oven that simultaneously roasts a turkey and gives you a facial. You know I would do anything for you, except that oven thing, and even though I hate Vegas I would have flown there. But I couldn't exactly wander the streets yelling 'ESME!' like Brando in *Streetcar Named Desire* to find you."

"Sure you could, and it would have been hilarious," she softens. "It's OK, I don't even remember where we got hitched except it smelled like it used to be an iHop. You want pancakes?"

THE NETWORK

I help Esme take boxes of kitchen stuff to her car. "You gonna be OK without me here?" she asks.

"I think so." I reply, hugging her. "You don't have to worry about me."

"I will anyway."

"Thank you. I really do love you," I start to tear up again.

"I'll just be a few miles away," she pulls me closer.

I think—but *don't* say, "That's what my mother said."

"You can always come over," I hear her sniffle.

I think—but *don't* say, "My mother never said that." I *do say,* "You don't think you can keep me away, do you?"

"I hope not."

"You run along back to Buck. I'm going to see if I can drum up more clients!"

"You're what? This isn't like you at all," Esme looks at me, quizzically.

"I know—wonderful, isn't it?"

I've never consciously networked before, but now it doesn't feel like me pushing myself on other people, but like I have a gift to give and want to find people who need it. I have a mission.

I drive over to Debbie's flower shop.

"What'cha doin here on a Friday, doll?" She says through a stand of daffodils.

"Can I talk to you for a minute? I can make an arrangement at the same time."

"'Course! I've got the perfect one for you. A rainbow of roses for a boy named Rick's coming out gift to his mother."

"Oh, sweet! And I finally get to use some of the blue and purple roses you love to dye and I've always thought were dreadful... oh, sorry."

"They *are* dreadful, but..."

We recite together, "A lady's always prepared for any contingency."

I make a rainbow arc of roses, floating on a sea of, what else, baby's breath, and tell her about my professional cuddling.

"So people pay you to hug them... like a hooker?"

"No, our clothes are on."

"But you're still getting paid..."

"Yes," I explain, "Like you get paid to arrange flowers."

"So you're saying I'm a flower whore?" She laughs.

"Yup. And I'm a... hug whore!" I laugh.

"Won't that look pretty on your business card!"

"Speaking of which," I start, "I could use some referrals. I have an expensive Beverly Hills shrink recommending me to her customers, but with all the people you know..."

"...You want *me* to be your pimp?" she asks, incredulously?

"No, but how very Tennessee Williams of you, Deb. You're simply offering your customers an exclusive entree to the newest new way to enhance their lives!" I tastefully sprinkle a few star anise across the rainbow of roses and say, "Voila!"

"Nice touch. OK, Charlie. What do you want me to do, sprinkle flyers in with the flowers?"

"I thought I could borrow your email list and tell them about..." I have a rare moment struggling for words, "how they can find a feeling of inner peace through a session of..." now "cuddling" sounds too cutesy and... I have no trouble coming up with clever names for Esme's food cart, but I realize I've never thought up a pithy name for my own business.

Contact... embrace... embracing tranquility... *embracing equanimity,* I like that but does anybody know what equanimity means? Equanimous is a lovely sounding word that even I wouldn't know how to pronounce if I hadn't seen a website of "words you probably mispronounce" and I did, calling it "equan·an·amous" when it's really "e·quan·i·mous" like "The dawning of the age of equanimous."

>>>

"Yoo hoo! Charlie? Is anybody home?" I hear Debbie say as she waves at me.

"Sorry, I was thinking. I'm trying to stop that."

"Like a frog trying to change his croak."

"I love your old southern expressions!"

"Southern my ass," she drawls, "I just heard it on the cartoon channel. I had no idea where Madagascar was."

"So?"

She winces. "No."

"But..."

"You gotta be kidding? This is my business, Charlie, I can't have you spam my celebs with your little hobby."

OK, now I'm insulted. "It's not a hobby, it's a calling."

"I love you, doll, but it's a hard no. Now I gotta pee," she kisses my cheek, then she rushes away, her legs together.

Her laptop is right there. Unlocked. All I'd have to do is forward her email list to myself...

I can only *imagine* what I could do with them...

THE LETTERS

If this was a movie everything would get wavy as I fall into a fantasy...

Diane Keaton? OMG, I love her! I want her to be my BFF, go hat shopping together, complain about men together. She's definitely getting a personalized email. Wait—everybody needs to get a personalized email—not just a Dear (your name here) email, either, one where I say something meaningful about how their work has impacted me and how my work can impact them! That's going to take a long time.

I look at my phone. No endless string of desperate texts asking me to come as soon as possible! Not a single text, actually. I've got time.

Dear Diane:

Debbie LaPlant from *Southern Fried Flowers* recommended I drop you a note, ~~though if you ask she'll say she was hacked~~.

~~Ever since I was a small child I've loved you and wanted to be your best friend... Have I got a hat for you!~~ I've followed your career and I follow you on Instagram and your energy is so wonderful that I'd like to give something back to you. ~~Wait, that sounds like I stole something, which I didn't, actually, you stole my heart.~~

My name is ~~Charlie Chaz~~ Charles Jefferson Cooperman, and I'm a professional cuddler. I tried to come up with a fancier name for what I do, like *embracing equanimity* but even I didn't know what it meant. The truth is, what I do is simple—but profound.

It comes down to the mammalian need to be held. And while your friends and family might hug you, there's always a layer of baggage with them. They stole your favorite scarf. They ate your last bite of scalloped potatoes. They slept with your boyfriend. Little things that gnaw at your mind and keep you from being able to let go—completely.

But as someone you don't know (but can trust because of my credentials and references), I can hold space to hold you—like the universe does.

~~It would be my honor to hold you and help you relax, because you always seem a bit hyper, not a criticism, it's fun, just an observation.~~

~~Normally, this universe charges $400, but in your case, because I love up to but not the point of being a stalker, I want to give you a session for free.~~

Please contact me (phone number below) and I will ~~schedule an appointment at your convenience~~ look forward to creating a space for you.

Equanimously yours,

CJC

I can't believe I've just written a letter to Diane Keaton! I also can't believe how bad it is. The trouble is, I don't know what else to say because this is what I *want* to say. I consider emailing my brilliant friend Erin who writes screenplays for herself and her handsome Italian husband, Carlo. They're one of those nauseating couples who are gorgeous, talented and *nice*, too. She could write something artistic *and* official and made me sound like Oprah's next coming.

That's what I would have done in the past, but now, *I Gotta Me Me! I gotta be me! Who else can I be than who I am!* That rousing song flares up in my brain, even if those are pretty banal lyrics. I have this gut feeling, not unlike the kind you get when you've eaten just enough cheese, that the *only* way to present myself here is honestly—because what they see is what they're going to get.

I'm not going to be like one of those movie trailers I hate where they make the movie into something it isn't. Then the people who would have loved the movie miss it, but people who really aren't the right audience see it and hate it. That never made any sense to me... even if I did once tried to present myself as one of those tough-ass cigar chomping sports coach "daddy" types in hopes of luring an athlete to my bed. I only tried it once because when he arrived, all 6'6" of solid muscle, I literally didn't know what to do with him. It was embarrassing and I had to pretend I pulled my groin, the only sexy sounding yet athletic injury I could think of. If it happened today, I could spoon him into submission, but I didn't know that back then.

I reread the letter to Diane. It's not like I have anything to lose...

WHAT? WAIT! For a nanosecond it's as if reality peels back—showing a new world behind the curtain where *I have nothing to lose!*

All this time I've been afraid: What if I lost what little I had—what little money, what little promise, what little space I've managed to scrape out for myself in this big, scary world. What would happen to me? I'd drown in my own fear!

That made everything so important it was hard to do anything! So I did nothing.

But if I have nothing to lose then I can do anything!

I can send this email to Diane Keaton who probably won't ever reply anyway, so what does it matter? At least I'll know that I put myself out to her. Maybe she won't be able to receive me for whatever reason—most likely not even related to me but more about her dog or kids or busy schedule or fear that she might fall in love with me and want to marry me even though she said she'd never get married. The last one is the least likely but I just wanted to throw it in there even if there's only a .00001% chance of it being possible, because then it's *not outside the realm of possibility!*) But maybe, she'll reply. Maybe! That's exciting!

I spell check it because I don't want to look like a moron or stalker—and press *send*!

I wait to feel the bile rise like I want to throw up, but it doesn't happen. I'm just happy, picturing Diane in her beautiful Nancy Meyers-like modern farmhouse sitting on her Eames chair, reading *my* email... and laughing! Laughing would be a good response.

OMG, Oscar Issac is on Debbie's list. Hmm, the address is listed as the Hotel Bel Air, but the delivery was only last week so he might be there. I Google him. He's making a movie at Sony called *Love Bites*, a comedy about gay vampires with overbites. He's *so* getting an email.

Dear Oscar... ~~A gay vampire walks into a blood bank...~~

>>>

THE REALITY

I snap out of it. I can't take the list. I mean, I could, I know how, but I would never do that to Debbie... even though I still have time because she always takes forever in the bathroom. I've always wondered what she's really doing in there—watching porn and masturbating? What else could possibly take this long?

I close her laptop. There's got to be another way to contact these celebs. Maybe a subscription to IMDB pro where I could get her agent's contact info? Right like an agent would bother to forward an email when there's no possibility of them getting 10%. Maybe I could just get a list of agents and cuddle them, but my actor friends say agents aren't human. Do reptiles cuddle?

Debbie finally emerges from the bathroom. She's glowing. Who am I to judge?

THE FREEZER

Back home I keep staring at my phone as if somebody's going to beg me to cuddle them. Nothing.

My stomach growls. I've forgotten to eat. That's a first. Either this is a very good sign or I am losing my mind. Probably a very fine line between the two.

I dig into the permafrost of the freezer, excavating all the way to the back where I'm pretty sure there's a piece of birthday cake from my 40th. I couldn't choke it down then, it's time to swallow it now.

After much ice chipping I find it—a rainbow layer cake. I unwrap the plastic and take a sniff, but it's as frozen as a wooly mammoth in the Siberian tundra so it has no smell. I set the microwave to "stun" and give it 15 seconds. Now it smells sweet with a hint of raspberry. That's good. I pry off a piece of still frozen frosting, throw caution to the wind and put it in my mouth. It's sweet, with a hint of almond. Almonds are good, but wait, doesn't cyanide taste like almonds? I spit the frosting out into my hand until I realize cyanide can't just develop by itself in a freezer and if nobody died 5 years ago when they first ate this cake, it wasn't going to be poisoned now. I stick the frosting back in my mouth.

So this is what 40 tasted like. How young I was! How carefree! Yet I thought I was old! Now I'm 45 and I think I'm old but in five years I'll think I was young! So why don't I just think I'm young now? And why do I have to be young to be happy? So many questions, so little frosting.

I bite off a piece from the purple layer on the bottom. It's a little dry. I guess it was meant to taste like blackberry but now it tastes a little like sawdust and sugar. Not terrible.

While waiting for the rest of the cake to defrost I take the time to hack all the ice out of the freezer. Esme never did this because she never froze anything. "You can't freeze kale," she'd say, dismissively, like I was ever in danger of eating kale for any reason. I refuse to eat a vegetable I have to massage first. Besides, I don't believe Kale is a food, I suspect it's a massive trick by farmers who had a lot of weeds on their land and figured out a way to sell them to an unsuspecting health-food-deluded public.

Most of the stuff in the freezer is expected—vintage leftovers, antique pizza, a half loaf of challah I made once and thought was so incredible I wanted to save it and now it's been reduced to a brick.

What's this in foil? Oh, my God, my little toe! My dad saved it and I've carefully moved it with me all these years. I thought it might be like Walt Disney's frozen head, and someday the medical technology would be advanced enough to reattach it. I suspect it's got freezer burn but I'm not about to open it and look.

And here's my old GI Joseph! That's what I called him because "Joe" seemed too prosaic. He's always been an arctic explorer, as well as extraordinarily buff and *almost* anatomically correct. He doesn't appear to have suffered from hypothermia, though a chunk of his beard just snapped off. We had many happy times together.

My hands are numb, so I run them under warm water which hurts. I hear a ping from my computer and see I have an email! Is it from Diane?

I dry my hands and run back to the computer only to see it's my cash-back report for my PayPal debit card. I've earned 63 cents! That and ten bucks will buy a coffee.

It dawns on me that I only *fantasized* about sending that email to Diane, I never actually sent it. Now I'm starting to confuse dreams with reality. Probably not good.

I go back to the disaster zone otherwise known as the freezer. Back goes my pinkie toe. Do I really need to save this? Wouldn't it be too small now anyway? Somehow I can't throw it out. I take another bite of 5-year-old birthday cake. It reminds me of my fifth birthday. Other kids were having their parties at Chuck-E-Cheese, but dad arranged for mine at the beautiful UCLA Japanese garden, complete with giant koi. None of the other kids knew what to make of the place and a docent had to keep them from feeding M&Ms to the koi, but I was enchanted by the whole place. I wanted to live there. I think that's where I got the GI Joe, from a little girl named Sam who I had a crush on because she looked like a little boy. I tried to kiss her behind the bamboo and she screamed, which should have given everyone a clue about me and girls.

How long ago that was—40 years! My memory itself is middle-aged! The UCLA Japanese garden was sold to some random rich person and closed to the public. So sad—and now that I think about it, it was just a few blocks away from my mother's mansion—so near yet so far.

GI Joseph goes back in to protect the toe. None of this makes any sense and it doesn't really matter. They're frozen tidbits of my life. Should there be a prolonged power failure I can see letting go of them before they get really nasty, but for now, I shove them back in, along with some not-too-old pizza, a Lean Cuisine Chicken Enchilada Suiza (staves off starvation in just six minutes), a package of Boca burgers (meat-like-luxury made of soy. I don't mind eating soy because it acts superior and calls itself *Edamame*).

I put a bath towel on the floor to mop up the melting ice caps and symbolically finish the cake: the past is past—it can either become fuel or shit—sometimes, if we're lucky, both.

THE CLIENT WITH BENEFITS

I'm exhausted and a little nauseous from the cake and decide it's time to go to sleep.

I wake up the next morning expecting to see referrals from Buck. There are none.

I feel like I have something up my nose and pull out a piece of orange frosting.

Even though it's already hot in the room I feel a chill —like I'm in the freezer instead of GI Joseph. I'm all ready for action and everything's frozen.

That's OK, that's OK, I can be patient... I can be patient... I *can't* be patient!

I have a sharp pain in my sinus. I can't tell if it's more frosting or a literal brainstorm. Wait—I know, for certain, one person who wants professional cuddling! Rober! Yes, he might still be working with that hack, but there's no reason I can't message him a copy of my diploma and say I'm available for an evening of certified professional cuddling *and* vicarious eating!

Sent. I go to the bathroom to spray saline solution up my nose in case there's any more frosting there.

My phone pings. Aha! It's Rober, texting! "That sounds wonderful, are you free tonight?"

I am most certainly free tonight. I just need to decide what *I* want to eat while he watches! I have a hankering for Pasta Carbonara or Fettuccine Alfredo. Italian again. Since we've already been to Spago, I want to find an even more expensive place to order one, or both.

Hmm. I wonder if the cuddling should come before dinner? Otherwise, I might burp while cuddling and that's not classy. I feel overwhelmed with choice so I cede all control to the universe and message Rober, "I want the best Carbonara or Alfredo. Where do you recommend?" Send.

Not 15 seconds later I get a reply, "Roman." Is he serious? Are we going to Rome? Do I have anything to wear? I will have to charge him a daily rate, but still, why not?

"I'm up for Italy!" I reply.

"I mean my personal chef, Roman. He cooks and freezes a week's worth of food for me in one small Tupperware container, but I can have him come over and make a full meal for you."

Thank you, Universe! This solves so many problems at once. I'll get to see his house. Maybe I'll go skinny dipping. We can cuddle while Roman makes pasta. Then I can eat while Rober watches.

I'm excited, until I feel like it's a step backwards. The old me wanted a free dinner. The new me wants to be paid for my services then I can buy my own damn dinner, thank you, like a fully-grown independent man-child.

But it's not like I have other offers, the cuddling will still be professional, and Rober can be a "client with benefits." That sounds professional-ish.

"Sounds fab," I message Rober. "What time and where?"

"7pm. Here's the google maps link…" he replies. Encino hills. Perfect—I can take Mulholland west into the sunset and avoid the 101.

Being a professional, I shall fast all day so I can do my best eating for Rober. Except I'm hungry now. In order to assure my taste buds are refined, I make myself a piece of Japanese-style toaster oven toast (I eventually found a Japantown market that sold the magic bread) and slather it with Rober's fancy butter. That should hold me for the rest of the day, or until I'm hungry again in an hour.

There's definitely a downside to my new whatever it is, not success yet, drive? Dare I say, "Ambition?" Now I feel like I should *always* be doing *something* to pave my future!

I text Buck, "Thanks again for referring Teddy. Let me know if you have other patients who could use my help. Kiss Esme for me!" *Send.*

I only have 8 hours until I meet Rober... What other professional and productive things can I cram into the day? I'm already hungry again. I decide to forgo meals and only snack. I finish a box of Triscuits and only then notice the box says, "Family Size." If I contain multitudes, do I count as a family?

I go back to bed with the clear conviction that conserving my energy is the most professional thing I can do for my client tonight.

I fall asleep and I'm in a busy highrise office, the glass walls overlooking the Beverly Hills Country Club. The words, *"Embraceable You"* shine in 6 foot high chrome letters along a black marble wall.

A row of cuddlers is lined up for inspection. They stand at attention in their *Cashmerish* tracksuits, arranged by color. I give them the once-over as I walk by, nodding approvingly to all but the last one who has frosting on his upper lip. "That will never do," I say in a fatherly way. He tears up and I give him a hug. "There, there, you're doing fine!" I say, encouragingly.

Phones are ringing and a wall of monitors is showing a tally of "patients booked today" followed by the number 1021, followed by a statement, "5-star ratings today" and the number 1020. I whisper to my assistant who scurries off to get to the bottom of that one missing 5-star rating!

It's a veritable beehive of activity, people on the phones booking sessions, rooms filled with newly hired cuddlers in training, and Esme's food carts rolling up and down the aisles offering free food and drink to the scores of happy *Cuddle Concierges.*

My assistant reminds me I have an appointment to cuddle President Buttigieg who's in town for a fundraiser. My pilot is firing up the *cuddle copter* so I don't have to deal with traffic.

It's all very exciting and tiring. I sit at my enormous desk made of a thick sheet of glass cantilevered out from a boulder and I look at a small framed picture next to my computer. It's me, in my first Cashmerish, smiling. How simple it was then.

I wake up, sweating. It wasn't the dream, it's just hot. I turn on the AC and bask in the glory of cold air blowing over my body.

Is that what my future holds? A career sounds good and all, until it becomes—oh, my God, *work!* Somehow I've gotten this far without thinking of this as a job. It felt like a *calling*, which was great and spiritual, but if it's work I don't want to do it!

No, it was just a dream. Just a possible scenario of my success. If I don't want to run a big company I can sell it to Disney. Imagine the possibilities, "Cuddles by Mickey!" "Goofy's Magic Touch!" "Pooh and You!"

I think back on the dream and remember the name, "Embraceable You." I like it! "*You* are embraceable!" Starting there feels right because it instantly makes a person feel better! I'll work out the details of selling my billion-dollar business later.

I sit down and design a business card for "Embraceable You!" I like the exclamation point! I set it in a breezy script font. Looks like a feminine hygiene product. Needs to be OK for men, too. Sans serif? Too hard. It's got to feel cozy yet official. Round and soft, yet firm. Too round and it looks like a child's birthday party. Too sharp and it looks painful.

I try the Beverly Hills Hotel script lettering. It's 'aight. Oozes cachet. Maybe too girlish. The London Underground font? Official. Not too hard. Better all caps.

Ah, that leads me to Gill Sans (often confused for the Underground font), and their new Nova Inline, which means unlike normal fonts it's made up of double lines with white space between them. I like that—it shows two things coming together.

That's good for now because the words are starting to look wrong. *Embraceable* is very long. Embra ceable.

I type my phone number and that's it. No website. No email address. Not even my own name. Elegant.

It looks fine. It looks terrible. I can't look at this anymore. I print a sheet of 12, cut them only slightly crooked and put all but one in my wallet. I look at that one. There's more I could add, like "Let us help you Discover Your Embraceable You!" Or "Transformational Touch." Maybe later, for now I remember the old adage "KISS: keep it simple, stupid."

I'm hungry again. What time is it? Only 2pm. I can't possibly fast until 7, I could get low blood sugar and faint—I'm driving Mulholland, I have to be alert. I'll only allow myself a snack, so I polish off what's left in the "family size" box of Cheez-Its. They're very salty and I need a big glass of water. Now I'm too full.

I slosh back into my room to choose an outfit for tonight. I could, of course, wear my *Cashmerish,* but it's warm and if we cuddle out by the pool it'll be too much, even at night. I fire up my Amazon app to look for more summer-appropriate cuddling attire, not that I can get it by tonight.

Oh, I already have just the thing, a Japanese Jinbei I found when I was looking for the toasting bread. It's an airy light-cotton summer outfit, almost like pajamas but more stylish in striped indigo. I can totally wear that with some sandals after I give myself a pedicure so my toenails don't look quite so prehensile.

I wonder if I should exercise to work off the excess snacks. Naw, I'm going to lie down until the feeling passes.

THE ViCΛRIꙨUS

It's a beautiful sunset drive going west on Mulholland. I love the windy road and the lack of traffic, both so un-LA yet without actually having to leave LA which takes too much effort. While some Angelinos joke that the valley is a no-man's land, from high above it glows into the horizon like a stunning alien planet.

I turn down a steep street of mid-century houses, some recently remodeled by gays into a versions more elegant than they were when new. Others—still clinging onto their original elderly owners who haven't remodeled since 1963—show just how tacky mid century design could actually look.

Rober's house is at the end of a cul de sac and stands out with its dramatically lit display of cacti. I park on the street and follow flickering flame lights up the path to the front door—a single massive frosted glass panel. I knock but it doesn't make much noise. I find the illuminated door bell and press it, and old-fashioned sounding bells begin to chime.

Rober opens the door which pivots on a center hinge. He's wearing a black and gold silk Versace dressing gown and strappy sandals with wings... like the Roman God Mercury... or the Greek God Hermes! It's a fucking sign! A sign of what I don't know, but it's surely a sign. I could totally rock those sandals. He's going to have to take them off for the cuddle and then all bets are off!

"Lovely to see you, my dear. Come, come inside, Roman has made you an amuse bouche to start!"

Inside, the house is agleam from hidden lighting: aiming up from a rock garden wall; aiming down from the beamed ceiling; backlit bookshelves; even illumination under the long, low white nubby sofa that appears to float. The entire back wall is glass with a view of the valley, like a tapestry made of fireflies.

Rober proffers a plate of appetizers, "Grilled fig stuffed with blue cheese and walnut?"

"I'll have one if you have one," I tease.

"I think I can manage one, but that's all, the rest is for you!" He puts the fig in my mouth then waits expectantly, so I put one in his. The sweetness of the fig, the tartness of the cheese, the earthiness of the walnut. It's so good it makes me feel lightheaded.

It's times like this I wish I could only eat a tiny bit, like this. The taste is so sublime it's almost enough by itself and for a moment I understand Rober a little better. But I'm also looking forward to a plate full of pasta!

"Let's cuddle before dinner," I start, "it's always best on an empty stomach."

Rober's eyes light up, "At last, someone who understands that everything is better on an empty stomach!"

I don't really understand that, but I'm happy he's happy. I remember reading something Hemingway wrote about his mind being clearer on an empty stomach, but I think he was having hunger hallucinations.

I think *I'm* hallucinating when I see patterns of blue light flicker across the ceiling, then I realize it's the pool and say, "Let's cuddle under the stars."

I follow him out through sliding glass doors to an electric blue infinity pool that reflects and melts into the city lights—quintessential LA. I sigh. This glittering man-made body of water is just about the most glamorous thing I've ever seen.

I don't ask, I just take his hand and lead him to the water. He slips off his sandals, I kick off mine. He drops his robe, revealing matching Versace silk boxers. I shed my jinbei down to my Hanes 4-way stretch knit boxers and step into the beach-like, gradually sloping pool. The water is almost as warm as the night air as I lay down in the shallows. He lays next to me, the little spoon, and I wrap my arms around him.

I can hear the faint sound of pots and pans clanging inside, but outside there's the gentle water lapping, the leaves rustling in the trees and an occasional Rolls Royce gliding along Mulholland. This is how LA was meant to be experienced—right here, in this very moment. Warm breeze, warm water, sparkling view, a hint of night-blooming jasmine and garlic.

I channel this feeling into the energy I give to Rober, his skin slick with water. We lay there, taking it all in through our bodies, our senses. Wet, warm, quiet, chlorine, with a lingering taste of blue cheese.

Sublime calm... until I hear a rumble spreading out from the valley up into the hills. The water starts to splash, like surf. Everything shakes. Earthquake.

Normally I'd get tense and worry about being crushed by a bookcase, but here out in the open is the safest place to be.

I let the vibrations ripple through us. Unlike previous quakes which have felt angry, this one feels like the earth is trembling with joy.

The rumbling quiets. The waves subside. The vibration calms to a most remarkable serenity. Another fucking sign this is not a job, it's my *calling*.

I hear an owl hooting, followed by a patio door sliding open.

"Dinner is served," a man with a heavy Italian accent announces.

Rober and I stir (having already been shaken). We've barely spoken and all I did was hold him, but now he feels to me like a different person—like someone I know.

I stand up, take his hand and slowly walk out of the water. The warm air feels so good I don't need to dry off. "Can we eat out here?" I ask.

"*You* can eat anywhere you'd like." He pads in and talks to Roman, who comes out with a tray of meats and cheeses arranged the way I'd arrange flowers. I take a bite of a prosciutto-wrapped piece of cheese and chew it slowly. "Tell me how it tastes!" Rober whispers conspiratorially.

"Salt. Pepper. Pork." I inhale and let the flavors swirl around my head. My phone chimes. I try to ignore it but the chiming is insistent. "I'm sorry, but this may be my best friend and I have to..." he nods and waves my concern away.

I leave the table and out of the corner of my eye see him nibble a piece of salami. I look down at the phone and there's a message from an unknown number. It reads, "I absolutely must see you."

Who is this? Does it even matter—I'm *wanted*. Wanted. That brings up an image of an old west poster with a drawing of me in the center, "#1 most wanted," it says under my name. I can almost hear the whistled theme of *The Good, the Bad and the Ugly* floating up from the valley.

I'm not just wanted by one person whose neuroses happen to mesh with mine, no. This is more like *fame*, having complete strangers want me. I know, I know, people who are already famous say it's empty, meaningless, only good for getting the reservations at popular restaurants and or the occasional groupie.

But I've always wanted to be loved by everyone. I couldn't stand it if someone didn't like, much less love me, because I worked so hard to be loved. If I wasn't loved then I must be doing something wrong, right?

I hear a tiny tapping sound on my right temple, like an important thought is trying to get in but I brush it away. I don't want thoughts now, I just want to swim in this feeling of being wanted. By everybody. I know it'll pass. I know I'll go back to being an ordinary person who's lucky enough to have a best friend even if she's now got a wife she loves more, but in a totally different way.

I don't want to feel invisible again. I've done that all my life. I'd spent so much time trying to distract myself from this feeling: Going shopping, going to a movie, going to dinner, going on imaginary flights of fancy—anything but having to be where I am.

I hear the tapping inside my head now. I know what it wants to say—that "everybody" includes the woman who gave birth to me then gave me away.

Aren't I too old for all this childhood bullshit? I know it's there, I get it, I can't get rid of it. But do I have to care about it? I silently scold myself—so what if I feel like I was *emotionally* dropped on my head as a child? So what—my brain still works—move on!

I'm angry with myself now for having already lost that glorious feeling of calm... and my new freedom of being wanted.... and for possibly letting my pasta get cold.

Now I need to focus on *now!* I reply to the text, "Autoreply: I'm in session now and will get back to you tomorrow."

I turn my phone to silent and balance it face down on the spines of a saguaro cactus. Tonight I am here. Tomorrow I am wanted. That's all I need to know.

"Sorry about that, Rober," I say as he surreptitiously swallows. I reach out and take his hand. "I want to thank you, Rober, meeting you has changed my life."

Rober gulps and pulls his hand away. "I... you..." he stammers.

"Not personally. Well, yes, personally, but not in a personal relationship kind of way... I'm going to shut up now."

Rober reaches back over and pats my hand. "It's just me, I have a hard time with connection."

"You introduced me to professional cuddling and that's changed me, that's what I wanted to thank you for. And I know what you mean about connection—but *this* kind of connection—personal yet universal—this works for me."

"Yes, yes! Meaningful but not messy!" he says, his eyes misty.

We sit, nodding gently at each other in understanding. I eat a piece of salami-wrapped provolone and it breaks any tension there might have been.

Roman arrives with a large steaming platter of pasta, Alfredo on the right, Carbonara on the left. He places it in front of me, rolls his eyes then turns on his heels and leaves.

"Roman doesn't believe these two should be served together, but I explained that you're eccentric and I'd pay him double."

"*I'm* eccentric. Well, I guess I am! Or indecisive—I couldn't decide between the two because they're both sublime!" I turn my fork in the Alfredo first, watching the noodles and buttery parmesan sauce swirl sensuously. I raise it to my mouth and feel a drop of sauce land on my chin, then drip down onto my bare chest. I slide the forkful into my mouth and let it sit there, the butter coating my mouth, the parmesan tickling my taste buds and the garlic wafting into my nose.

The pasta is so fresh it starts to dissolve in my mouth even without chewing. If this is the last bite of food I ever eat it will be enough.

Rober sighs, reaches over and picks up a single slippery noodle between his fingers. He opens his mouth, sticks out his tongue and slowly lowers the pasta onto it. He shivers, gasps, and a single tear rolls down his cheek.

He may be weird, but he also knows how to appreciate every single bite. I love the first and last bites—the first because I know the first will quell my hunger and the last is beautiful because there's no more —so I'm reminded to enjoy it. But in between, I just eat, or I did. I think I've changed. I hope I have.

I dip my fork into the carbonara, spinning the pasta and rich sauce of eggs, parmesan, pancetta and pepper. Is seeing it enough? Smelling it? I almost don't even need to eat it as I'm already satisfied, but I put it in my mouth anyway and let the flavors assault me from within.

It feels like the world is trying to invade me through a brilliant trick of temptation. The ingredients are becoming part of me, cows and pigs and peppercorns. These tiny bits of the world will replace tiny bits of me with new cells. I'm flooded with images of farms and craftspeople and a colorfully psychedelic montage of their cells replacing mine.

I open my eyes, I don't know how long they've been closed.

Rober smiles. "Thank you for... understanding. Most people don't. They look at me and think I'm boring, or strange when I'm more than that—I'm both."

"I wouldn't say boring."

"Really? How wonderful. I've always felt boring. Most of my life has been spent running errands for other people. I managed a large bank in Beverly Hills. Very rich clients. They had everything and appreciated nothing. I was invisible to them, just someone to do the necessary paperwork before that paper was shredded. Pointless, really. It all would have happened without me. I felt like I'd never really lived, so I embezzled millions from people who wouldn't miss it—and built this new life."

I swallow hard but try to hide it. He daintily picks up another strand of pasta and slurps it into his mouth.

I'm not judging him. I'm not even all that shocked. Everything in LA is some kind of racket. Movie studio bookkeeping is inherently criminal. I actually like that he appreciates the money and has the taste to know what to do with it.

"Thank you for sharing that with me. I admire what you did."

He smiles broadly, then dabs his lips with a napkin which he keeps over his mouth. "Do you really?"

I nod before forking a combination of both Alfredo and carbonara into a single, forbidden bite. God, I hope this feeling lasts.

A duck lands in the pool with a splash, sending pool light rippling across us.

Rober reaches over and touches my cheek. "Just the fact that you think what I told you might be true makes me very happy. Maybe I'm not that boring anymore."

"I hope it's true," I tell him.

He bursts out laughing. "It is! I've never told anyone! I so wanted someone else to know. I assume we have cuddler-client privilege so I told you. You're not going to turn me in?"

"Why? Did anyone miss the money?"

"Nobody. For them it's a rounding error."

"Then good for you, Rober. Your courage gives me courage. You're an inspiration."

He raises the napkin over his face and bawls into it. I stop eating and try to take this all in, but it's too much, and I start crying, too, feeling my nose get stuffy so I won't be able to fully appreciate the pasta anyway.

I don't quite know what just happened. It's like someone strung an electric wire between us and we sparked off each other—not romantic love, but it is a connection so vital, so powerful.

It feels like the time I met an older man who I thought actually loved me. I was too young to understand or appreciate it so I was just frightened— like he was looking around inside my head, able to see all my shit, dirty secrets and broken dreams.

I almost immediately slept with his ex to push him away and ensure he couldn't get too deep inside my head. Turned out my head wasn't what he wanted to get deep inside anyway, and that feeling of love was all in *my* head.

But I felt it, and I ran from it, and I've been running ever since. Just now I felt it again and it felt completely different. It felt like I was no longer alone.

Rober stops crying. I blow my nose. I turn my head and see Roman standing behind me. "Why aren't you eating?" he asks like a Jewish/Italian mother/chef.

"It's so sublime, Roman, that it made us very emotional," I tell him.

He smiles. "Sì," he smiles.

Rober lowers the napkin and now he's giggling—the kind where you can't stop and it starts me laughing, too. I've only taken a few bites but I feel so full—and happy. I can't eat another bite.

Anything exquisite in small doses can become excruciating when you have too much.

THE iNTERROBANG?

Not another car on the road. My headlights sweep across the curves with the valley lights on one side, the city on the other. It feels like flying.

Before I left, Rober said, "Aren't you forgetting something?" He handed me a pile of aluminum catering trays with all the food Roman made, including the almond pear cake that smelled so good but I didn't have room for. On top was a red envelope with the words "thank you" scrawled calligraphically in gold.

He kissed me on the cheek and said, "See you next Friday," and I stumbled back to my car in a daze. I sat quietly in the driver's seat, feeling a bit shaky. I noticed the envelope and opened it—there were ten, 100-dollar bills inside. It was nice to see his ill gotten gains going to a good cause.

But I'd honestly forgotten about the money when I was leaving. It wasn't important. It's never been important to me. Sure, I need it, especially now that I'm paying the rent by myself. I'll need new tires soon, too, I think, as I take the Mullholland turns fast enough to make them squeal.

So why am I doing this? I don't know. Yes, I actually do, I just won't admit it to myself because I know once I think it clearly I can't go back. I am doing it for the *connection*. To feel like part of the world, part of humanity.

I don't have to be everything all unto myself. That's what I thought in the past. I just want to be a *part* of it, rather than standing outside looking at other people's lives. I can have my own life. I'm allowed.

Maybe it isn't the life I thought I'd have as a kid—so few young men grow up to be genies—but it isn't boring. It isn't paperwork. It feels meaningful!

But it's for rich people. Does that matter? I can start doing pro-bono work for underprivileged people. I can train them to become cuddlers and change their lives, too.

I see a glowing set of eyes in the middle of the road and slam on the brakes. A mountain lion stands proudly, then hops onto the hood of my car, drops a rat on my windshield and sprints away.

I can't take any more of these fucking signs.

I wake up in bed trying to remember what from last night was real and what was a dream. There's a text from Rober, just emojis "🌍 🍜🥡 🍸" so that part was true. I'm hoping that mountain lion part was a dream, otherwise the guys at the car wash are certain to ask questions.

Over on my dresser sits the little Louis Vuitton coin purse, stuffed with $1,500. My rent is covered. I want to talk to Esme, but I don't want it to interrupt her time with Buck or have it be all about me.

I pick up the phone to send her a short, happy text when I see the mysterious message from last night, "I absolutely must see you as soon as possible." What time is it? Only 9am? Normally I'd go back to sleep, but I am in momentum building mode, so I'm going to reply ASAP.

"I have time this afternoon at 2pm," I text, then immediately wish I knew who this was. I have to create some kind of system, like an online form, where people give me their real names and referrals. Otherwise, how can I keep track of which marketing is working? Is this person from Buck or recommended by Teddy or the Bastard?

The Bastard. Hmm. I never did call him. I don't know if I have time for that now, focused as I am on my calling of creating connections. Besides, he was... odd. I'm coming to think that everybody's odd, albeit in their own ways, but some are odder than others. It's hard to imagine a soft center to Bastard's rock hard exterior, but maybe inside he's just a wounded child. Which I don't want.

I never wanted children. Why subject someone else to childhood when I had to suffer through one. It seems selfish to keep bringing kids into the world—another way to distract oneself from an otherwise empty life. Fill it with kids, then you have no choice but to take care of them... oh, wait, some people did make another choice... like my Mother... What if that was the *right* one?

Ping. A text from the client who must see me. "2pm. San Vicente Bungalows. Tell Rolf you're here for Madame X."

I'd read about San Vicente Bungalows—a super exclusive club known for privacy—no smartphones or photos or you're kicked out. The only way to become a member is to be recommended by another member, so this must be somebody really famous—and rich. But who?

It's ironic that the rich and famous want to be invisible, while the invisible everyday people want to be seen.

I'm definitely wearing the *Cashmerish,* but if anyone asks, it's *Chihuahua West.* Unless Madame X is the *Chihuahua West* guy, in which case he'll know immediately and I'll say, "It's from my new line," which isn't a lie because I probably should resell these outfits to clients. I could get them embroidered with my logo—which I've just had a vision of:

It's an Interrobang. ‽ A rarely used typographic symbol that's a combination of an exclamation point and a question mark. The question mark part can be embracing the exclamation point—that's the point!

I'm excited. I'm scared. What if Madame X turns out to be someone I'm a fan of? Can I contain myself? Worse, what if it's someone I loathe, like virtually any Republican. Can I really imbue them with positive energy? Actually, yes, yes, I can—because that would be doing the world good. Filling haters with good juju and seeing how that changes their otherwise selfish attitudes!

Or, if it's a certain president, I could take the opportunity to send him to the great beyond by squeezing what little life he has out of him with his own brand of cheap, Chinese-made, neckties. The world would thank me—but I'm not going to dwell on that because it could get me locked up. Besides, he doesn't need me, he has porn stars and Russian hookers.

Damn, I've fallen back into a mental bear trap. I don't have time for this. I have to be physically—and emotionally put together. I have to float into that exclusive club, while at the same time being fully grounded.

Breakfast: Carbonara because it has egg in the sauce and the pancetta is like Italian bacon, both of which are breakfast food. I hungrily take the first bite—then remember it's not just about staving off physical hunger, it's about ingesting *life!*

I take a full half hour to eat a small plate, my eyes closed the whole time. I will bring the energy of the world to Madame X whoever she or he may be. I will do it in a wholly connected way while still maintaining distance to keep it from being personal.

I'm going to rock their world! OK, I went too far there. *I am going to make them feel at one with the universe!* Nice intention but perhaps a bit lofty. I need to shoot for something achievable, like, *I'm going to offer healing energy.* Yes, yes, I can do that! I like the whole *offer* thing because how they *receive* it is up to them. It's not about my controlling their experience, it's about my *offering*.

I take a shower with the lavender soap. Then I wonder if this person is one of those fragrance-sensitive people who'll start sneezing uncontrollably and call the West Hollywood Perfume Police. I do an extra scrub and rinse with hot water, then turn it off to smell myself.

Oooh, no, I'm exuding garlic from the pasta! It's coming out of my pores! I fill the tub with hot water and epsom salts to draw it out and soak until I can't smell any more garlic. Though maybe I've just gotten used to it and can't smell it. If Esme was here she would smell me, but she's not.

I throw on my bathrobe, go out and knock on my next door neighbor's door. Old Mrs. Grossman answers.

"I need to see Becky," I say plainly.

"Becky!" she yells, "That pervert from next door wants to see you!" She never takes her squinty eyes off me.

Becky is 12, has bright red hair, and has a nose like a bloodhound. Esme hired her to shop at farmers markets because she could sniff out the best produce. Becky arrives at the door, her face buried in her phone. "What?"

"How do I smell?"

She takes a long sniff without looking up. "Fine."

I hand her a $5 bill and she closes the door. From inside I hear Mrs. Grossman, "What are you doing smelling a pervert?" then Becky's half-attention reply, "If he was a pervert how come you called me?" and Mrs. Grossman, "Everybody's a pervert these days," and

Becky, "He's not a pervert, he's just gay," and finally Mrs. Grossman, "Exactly!"

I should have given Becky a $10. I look at my phone—how is it already noon? I don't understand time. Maybe I'm confused by daylight saving time which never makes any sense, it's like getting jet lag without going anywhere.

I go back inside and stand in front of my AC and breathe in the clean cold air. I visualize it's coming from clean electricity—miles of wind turbines, generating power, sending it over wires to this box in my window. More connections.

I check Google Maps and it says it'll take 35 minutes to get there. I'll leave at 1pm so I can arrive very early. If the mysterious X isn't ready to see me then maybe I can wait in the bar and casually drop some business cards.

I want to steel myself for any possibility—but steel is too inflexible. I will be bamboo—bending without breaking. I bamboozle by way down to the car, crank up the AC, start the GPS and drive into the future.

THE X-FACTOR

I pull up at the address and see no building—just a two storey high wall of shrubbery with a lone valet parking attendant standing outside. I roll up and roll down my window. "Is this the San Vicente bungalows?"

The valet says nothing.

"I was told to ask for Rolf—I'm here to see madam X," I say, and suddenly he snaps to attention.

"We've been expecting you," he says, flatly, gesturing to pull over to the curb. He sprints over, opening my door. "I'll take it from here."

I don't like handing my car over to valets. Even if it's 20 years old, I never know what they're going to do—take it for a joy ride? Not a big possibility. Sell it for parts? Possibly. But I'm sure this is the cheapest car they've ever seen here so I'm not going to worry about it.

I step onto the sidewalk and a concierge-like person appears. He's wearing a shorts suit in a green and white fern print, his tanned legs culminating in dark green patent leather ankle boots. "Right this way, sir," he says, guiding me into an almost invisible slice in the shrubbery.

We emerge into a small clearing still surrounded by foliage. He says, "Your phone, please." I hand him my phone which he drops into a metallic silver bag and slips into his pocket. "I'll hold this until your return." Return from where?

He proffers what looks like a balaclava but with only a hole for the mouth. No opening for the eyes. "I will need to put this on you for privacy protection."

I hold my hand out—I don't want this over my head. "Do you require all guests to wear this medieval contraption?" I demand.

"Not guests, sir. Service providers." Ah, yes, I'd forgotten that's what I am. I'm here only in service. "You may refuse, of course, in which case you will need to leave and pay for parking. It's your choice."

Not much of a choice. In a blinding flash of optimism, I think, "Okay! This will be another new experience for me—since I won't be able to see it will all come down to touch."

I relent and he slides the thing over my head. I'm alarmed to feel something tighten around my neck with a click. I am even more surprised when I feel him put a pair of headphones over my ears. I'm engulfed in trance music like something from a French hasheesh bar. Now two of my five senses are gone.

He puts an arm around my waist and guides my steps. I use the sense of touch and my feet to try to figure out what I am walking on. Feels like brick.

The trance music is interrupted with a transmission from this man, "We are crossing the threshold," he says portentously, as if I have left the plain of everyday existence and entered into a world so rarefied I'm not allowed to actually experience it.

Perhaps this is for my own good, because once experienced, maybe the rest of the world becomes so pale in comparison that mere mortals cannot survive the inevitable disappointment.

I go with it because in the past I paid for an experience like this. I went to dinner at a restaurant called *Pitch Black* run by blind chefs and servers. The restaurant literally had no light which was disorienting to me, but not the people who worked here. In the dark, I had to experience the food with only my sense of smell, taste, and occasionally touch (messy). Mostly I remember there was sand in the salad and when I asked the server about it she explained this was a "textural choice by the chef." Sure it was.

We keep walking. I hear a knock at a door. I catch a whiff of something... what is it? Carnations? Lily of the valley? Daffodil? Suddenly I feel anxious—claustrophobic. I force myself to take slow, deep breaths through my mouth. I'm not being smothered by a pillow, that old fear of mine. I'm not being buried alive. This is simply in an exclusive club where the members are clearly freakish. I can deal as long as it doesn't involve pain, specifically mine.

I hear some mumbled voices through the music. I feel a new set of hands around my waist—skinny—no, bony—like I imagine the hands of death must feel.

I'm not going there—I'm not going to imagine I'm in some sort of twisted ritual where rich people prolong their lives through human sacrifice because I've always heard that kind of thing works better with a virgin.

A robotic voice comes through the headphones, "I. Apologize. For. The. Precautions." Wait, this sounds like Stephen Hawkings. But he's dead, right? "Thank you. For. Understanding the. Sensitive. Nature of. This. Encounter. And respecting. My need. To remain. Anonymous."

I shrug, my muscles relaxing—not having a choice is a huge relief. I've often thought about how little we can actually control. We like to think we are captains of our own ship, masters of our own fate, but in reality there's so little we have control over. Some people say you are only in control of your own emotions, but even that's not true.

I let go of the illusion of control and the bony hands lead me to what I can reach out and feel is a bed—with a suede bedspread. I take a deep breath—I don't believe in touching much less lying on hotel bedspreads, but maybe at a place like this everything is sanitized to protect the rich.

I crawl onto the bed and await further instructions but this is getting suspiciously close to somebody else's kink and we all know how boring those are.

I feel the bony body lie down in front of me. I put my arms around it... I think it's a she, but it's impossible to tell without being inappropriate. I decide to think of it as a *her* because it's necessary to humanize whatever this is. I feel embarrassingly old-fashioned to be obsessed with binaries—but still think they're a *she* from the floral perfume.

She feels cold and slightly leathery, like a lizard that's missing the sun.

I can't do this. I can't. I can't have this awful trance music playing in my ear and still concentrate on sending positive energy to this desiccated creature. Despite my deepest instincts not to touch the bedspread, I rub my head against it until the headphones slip off. The silence is a relief, then I hear her give out a small cough, like the infant of a mother who smoked.

"Disappointed," she wheezes.

I stop breathing. I have the sudden urge to push her off the bed but don't because I'm afraid she'll break and they'll never remove this thing from my head, they'll just send me right off to Guantanamo, or wherever rich people send anyone who does them wrong, Anaheim, maybe.

"Disappointed." I whisper back, not in agreement, but mirroring, something I saw on YouTube that shows the cuddlee they're seen, heard, felt. I'm sorry if she's disappointed in me but I can hardly be faulted for not being at my best in this situation.

"You understand," she coughs.

I don't understand.

"Everything in my life disappoints me," she sighs.

I have goosebumps—worse, my skin is crawling and I want to let go but it's like touching a live electric outlet, my muscles won't release.

"Breathe," I say, as much to calm myself as her. I finally feel her starting to relax. She coughs again. I pull her a little closer.

I wish I could leave but I wouldn't be able to find my way out—and I want to do something good for this person, whoever or whatever she is.

It's as if I can literally feel her sadness through her skin. Her perfume is giving me a headache, or maybe it's a lack of oxygen or lingering fear, but it feels like the blood in my brain is starting to boil.

I gasp—tears coming to my eyes. I can't stop myself— this isn't supposed to be about me. I chastise myself silently.

I start to hum—not a song, but what feels like a lullaby from long ago that comes into my head.

"Oh baby," she coughs before crying... which begets weeping... which becomes sobbing... ugly and loud like a sick animal.

I feel her shaking so I hold her tight, not so tight as to possibly break a bone, but to hold her in place.

I'm painfully uncomfortable like I'm eavesdropping on a conversation I was never meant to hear.

A song wells up in my head—one I found soothing as a child when I'd pretend that Doris Day was my mother. I whisper, *"Que será, será. Whatever will be will be..."*

She stiffens. *"The future's not ours to see, que será, será... When I was just a little boy..."*

"No!" she cries, extricating herself from my hug and getting off the bed. "Get out!" she cries. I slide off the bed but don't know which way the door is. "Get him out!" she yells. A door opens. A beefy hand grabs me and pulls me away. I hear ice clinking in a glass, then a cough, then a door closing.

I'm dragged away, sliding on my heels. I smell cigar smoke and hear voices laughing. Someone says, "That's what I love about this place!"

I find myself back in the clearing, and the original butler unlocks the collar around my neck and says, "Return to the light," before pulling off the balaclava.

I should have closed my eyes but I didn't, and the light is blinding. I squint, tears in my eyes. What the fuck just happened? He hands me my phone which is blowing up with text messages I can't read yet because my eyes are too watery.

"Your car is waiting." He puts his hand on my lower back and presses me out through the tall hedge.

There's my car. Washed. Well, that's something. I fall into the driver's seat as the valet slams the door. I drive around the corner and park under a tree, trying to catch my breath.

I look at the notifications—$500 in my Venmo account. It feels dirty, but I earned it.

The rest of the messages are all from Buck. "OMG, I told her she wasn't ready! What happened?" "Text me." "Call me." And eight other messages I don't bother to read.

I call Buck. "What the fuck was that, Buck?"

"She's a patient—I can't tell you."

"And I'm your wife's best-friend, you owe me an explanation."

"Are you OK?"

"Of course not and you know it."

"I'm sorry, I told her not to."

"I can't do this over the phone. I'm coming to your office." I hang up and head down little Santa Monica to Beverly hills. I park under Buck's building because she's going to validate this if it's the last thing she does.

I storm into her office. She's waiting. "I'm sorry, Chazbo," she says.

I was all set to yell at her but her sincerity disarms me. All I can say is, "What?"

"You tell me."

"I don't know. They put a mask over my head like I was being kidnapped..." I recounted the story to her to the point where I sang *Que Sera Sera* and she freaked out.

Buck puts her hand on my shoulder and pulls me into a hug. "She said she wanted to see you and I *explicitly* told her *not* to. She went behind my back anyway." Buck holds me tighter, slowly swaying me to the right and left, "She's very... resourceful.... and she's dying."

"Oh, my God, did I kill her?" I wonder aloud.

"No, she's got... I can't tell you but she wanted to do this before she died." Buck is a good hugger. I start to relax. I'm glad Esme is in good hands. "I can tell you after she dies."

I want her dead *now*... I don't mean that. Yes, I do! I feel myself cracking open, a fissure in my wall starting at my head and splitting down my core, pulling apart, revealing flames. I can't hold it in—I let out the wail of a wounded animal. I feel my bricks shatter—a furnace, long buried but now exposed to air—exploding.

Buck holds me tighter. I hear the door open and feel another set of arms around me—Esme. Fuck. I literally can't hold myself together. A lifetime of sadness and rage fuel the flames and I don't want to burn alone—I want to set fire to everything! Remake the world in my own image. I get it now! All those people who hate! I get it and hate them right back, harder! I want them all dead. All of them, but first I want them to suffer! Fuck them! Fuck everybody who's not me! Fuck them all!!!

Then I hear Esme repeating, "I love you, Chip, I love you." Fuck her, she's harshing my hate! "I love you, Chip," damn... it's like a warm wave washes over me— turning the flames to steam—my cries to wheezes, my sobs to heavy breathing. I start to relax and catch my breath—the oxygen now feeding me instead of the flames.

Esme and Buck hold me and I melt into their embrace. I feel like a newborn, shocked and terrified by the world outside the womb. No longer floating, protected inside my mother but exposed to the elements where I can't swim—but must slog through, fighting, fighting, fighting the gravity.

"This is good, Chazbo, it feels bad, but it's good," Buck says. I love Buck. I want a Buck of my own but am happy Esme has this one.

My breathing slows, their tight embrace starting to feel constrictive. "I'm... OK, I guess..." I push them away but they hold fast. "I need... I need some space." I feel them loosen their grip. Esme has tears in her eyes. "Do you know who that woman was, Esme?"

She shakes her head. "Buck can't tell me, but said you'd need me so I rushed over."

"What are you feeling?" Buck asks, like a therapist.

I want to tell her but the words are stuck in my throat —too much to swallow. I sit down on her leather sofa. She sits to my left and Esme to my right, both with their hands on my shoulders.

"Disappointed." is the only word that'll come out.

"Sounds like more than that, buddy," Buck says.

It starts spilling out, "That's what this woman said. 'Disappointed.' In me. I've been doing so good, you guys. Feeling like this is my calling—my superpower. *Giving* without expecting anything in return yet getting so much in return—because I've felt *received*. That's what I've needed."

Esme puts her head on my shoulder. I feel Buck put her arm around both of us.

"But I couldn't get through to this woman. She refused to receive me and it felt like the worst rejection —like she was negating who I am—and who I want to be. I was just starting to feel I had a future and she made it feel impossible—like I'd have to go back to... what? What did I have? Odd jobs and thrift store shopping? Sinking in a world where I knew it was possible to float? I felt confident in myself for the first time and now..."

"You're bruised, it's natural," Buck says, quietly. "The confidence you found is still there, under the rubble. Sweep it away—you'll feel the confidence again and have an even better view of yourself."

Esme starts to hum, "On a Clear Day You Can See Forever."

I feel a smile on my face but then tears roll down my face again. "I love you, Esme." I turn to Buck, "Since you know more than I do about this—what do I do?"

"You're doing it. You're feeling the feelings."

"I don't like these feelings," I admit.

"Then you're doing it right."

That made me feel better. If I'm going to feel like shit, at least I know I'm doing it right!

"OK, but now I have doubts about my ability to keep helping people."

"Congratulations. Here's a quote for you, from art critic Robert Hughes, 'The greater the artist, the greater the doubt. Perfect confidence is granted to the less talented as a consolation prize.'"

"I'm not great," I sigh.

Buck leans in, "You have it in you—I felt it—that's why I recommend you to clients. But not her."

"Why not her?" I ask.

"Because..." Buck starts, "I can't tell you. I'll just say she wasn't ready, and, sadly, might never be. What happened wasn't about your ability, but her inability. Can that be enough for you?"

I take a deep breath.

I hear a chime. "My next patient is here, Chazbo, I gotta go," she says, leaning over and kissing me on my cheek. I'm surprised by how soft her lips are. Esme kisses my other cheek and I feel like the filling in a love sandwich.

"Call me if you need me," Buck says, and the simplicity but depth of her words makes me smile.

Esme takes my hand and we're almost out of the office before I ask, "Can you validate my parking?"

"For you—*always*," Buck says, handing me a validation sticker. Validated parking never fails to make me feel better.

Outside everything looks so colorful—the green of the trees like spearmint, the blue of the sky like lapis lazuli. Esme is still holding my hand. She leads me down the street, around the corner and into a cheese shop.

THE CHEESE

I don't need to talk. I sniff. I taste. *I see*. I am back in the world.

THE "STUF"

Back at home it's way too quiet. Why isn't Buck referring more of her patients? Did Madame X blow it for me? A thought flies through my mind like a comet, "I wish she was dead!" I feel like I'm a bad person for thinking it, but, no, I'm a good person who had a bad thought. It happens.

I decide a shower will help but even the water feels hard. It's too cold, too hot, soap too smelly, tub too slippery, towel too rough—everything's infuriating.

I'm thirsty and get a glass from the cabinet. What's that? In the back, behind the old jam jars I once thought were hip to use as tumblers? Is that a shiny blue bag? Oreos! I forgot I'd hidden them there for emergencies. This definitely qualifies.

Even better—they're not just Ores, but "Oreo Thins." Fewer calories, so you can eat more. Chocolate cream filling—so much better than the white "stuf" filling which has no recognizable flavor other than sweet.

Of course, the *only* correct way to eat an Oreo is to separate the two halves, eat one, scrape the filling off with your teeth, then eat the other. Anyone who thinks different is a heathen. That said, sometimes the aforementioned process can feel painfully slow, in which case I shove an entire cookie into my mouth at once and suck on it until it dissolves so I don't even have to put in the effort to chew.

I know Oreos aren't good for me physically—but emotionally? You simply cannot argue against their power—like chocolate Xanax!

Having finished half the package, I lie in bed and I distract myself with Instagram. I have a crush on a Spanish guy who bakes bread but he's in Madrid and I don't speak Spanish, so what chance do I have? This makes me truly sad because if he loves squeezing dough he'd love squeezing me.

After an hour of doomscrolling cute animals, cute boys, and cute desserts made to look like cute animals or boys, my battery is almost dead, and so is my arm.

I simply cannot risk an Instagram injury when I need my arms for cuddling. Cuddling who? It's not like anybody's begging me. Yes, there's Rober. I could live off his $1K a week, but then I'd feel like a gigolo. Or as Debbie would put it, a high-class HugWhore.

But maybe that's all I really am. All these lofty ideas of helping people and I'm really just helping myself like a cheap trick who charges a lot. Eech. That leaves a bad taste in my mouth (it can't possibly be the Oreos). I chew some Tums and fall asleep.

I wake up at 1pm the next day. I check my phone. No messages. No texts.

I wait for something to happen. I take a three hour nap. No messages. No texts.

I have a Little Caesars deep dish pizza delivered and I eat it while watching episodes of *I Love Lucy* making chocolate and stomping grapes. Before I know it, half the pizza is gone and I don't remember eating it yet I'm too bloated to move.

No messages. No texts. All disappointment.

How many times have I stopped myself from going after something I truly want just to spare myself the inevitable disappointment of not getting it? Why didn't I do that this time? Now I'm actually going to be disappointed and it hurts too much.

My only escape is sleep.

I wake up at noon and check my phone. No messages. No texts. Oh, well... So that's that.

I truly believed I could do something useful with my life—ha! I thought I had a gift—I bought my own bullshit.

God, I hate myself. I tolerated myself in the past because I held out a tiny shred of hope that someday I'd figure out life. Now I *thought* I'd figured it out—but no! I just deluding myself that I had something to give.

I eat the other half of the pizza while binging six straight episodes of *The Gilmore Girls*. Such a comforting fantasy—Lorelei and her daughter Rory talking nonstop while eating huge meals and never gaining weight. Real life isn't like that. Good thing my *Cashmerish* has a stretch waistband. Not that I'll ever need to wear it again...

I should take a shower but that sounds so wet. Instead, I lay in bed, my eyes refusing to close. I'll probably never sleep again. My life will become one torturous Mobius strip of regret—breathlessly running over and over its endless surface.

The pizza isn't digesting. I chew a Tums. Then another, then I toss a handful in my mouth—as if I can O.D. on them. Can you O.D. on them? I Google it. No. I'm disappointed and relieved, not to mention nauseous.

I watch headlights play across the ceiling. I hear Mrs. Grossman's TV loudly playing *Now Voyager*. Bette Davis says, "Oh, Jerry, don't let's ask for the moon. We have the stars." You can't see stars in LA, at least not in the sky.

I give up. I've done it so many times before it feels natural.

Like when I gave up on my glamorous dream to be the personal assistant to a star. In my fantasy I'd be Jake Gyllenhaal's right hand man. Jake would treat me like a paid bestie and we'd fly first class and Netflix and chill and I'd help him learn his lines and scrub his back in the bath.

But that dream was shattered a few months ago when I slept with a guy because he was Ellen De-Generes's personal assistant—and had really good eyebrows.

He spent most of the night complaining. Not about my performance, thank you, but about Ellen. "She, like, never appreciates anything I do. I'm the one who, like, signs all her headshots and then she complains if I do too good of a job and hides her checkbook. She calls me in the middle of the night and makes me go to the drug store to get her, like, red vines and red bull. The bitch, like, never hangs up her clothes, I gotta pick them up off the floor and take them to the dry cleaner because, she like, hates water…"

He, *like,* went on and on like this, even when his mouth was full, and finally I asked, "Why don't you just quit?"

"She won't let me quit until I can find a replacement and nobody in their right mind would want to do this job!"

That describes me to a T, *not in my right mind*—so I'll take that job now, thank you. I will be too overworked and miserable to feel sorry about my failure.

I want to text him but don't think I ever knew his name. I search my text messages for "Ellen" but there's nothing there so I must have messaged him on a gay app. But those apps don't let you search messages, just body types or top or bottom. Messages are sorted by date, so I'll have to remember *when* that was. I remember exactly how much I weighed, but not the date.

Now my thumb is cramping. I think about how this might impact my cuddling career, then laugh, sardonically. What career? What a joke. What a disappointment I am.

I am sure I will never sleep again.

I wake up the next day, half my face wet with drool. No texts. No messages.

What's that smell? Oh, it's me. I drag my sorry ass into the shower. I find a piece of pizza in my beard. It tastes good. Showering is hard. I'm tired. I fall back into bed, depressed.

THE B IS BACK

I hear my phone ping—a text message. I'm too weary to lift the phone.

But what if… No, I will not allow myself to get my hopes up. I will be "pre-disappointed" now so I can avoid it later. Even though my lack of action will ensure inevitable disappointment, I'm already so disappointed that what's a little more? Ah, that familiar, comfortingly uncomfortable feeling.

The snippet on my lock screen says, "Need your help."

I get instantly excited. No, no, no. I've already decided I'm a failure so if I try to do something now I'll be a failure at being a failure!

But what if it's Esme? Maybe she needs my help and I don't want to disappoint her.

I unlock my phone and read the message again. It's followed by a flashing *dot, dot, dot* meaning someone's typing on the other end. "Bastard."

Oh.

I can't help myself, I'm intrigued. Even encouraged. Somebody *needs* me. Somebody willing to say who they are! Somebody who's seen me work. Does it matter that it's *him?*

I consider my words carefully. "How can I help?" That's positive but non-committal.

Dot dot dot… "Come by and I'll tell you, B." So now he's just B? Is he too lazy to type, or trying to be cute? There's only one way to tell.

I get back in my Cashmerish which is starting to feel more like a costume than a uniform—like I'm only pretending to be professional.

I drive south on Coldwater Canyon—Oh no, the light at Mulholland turns yellow before I can get through. It'll be at least five minutes before it's green so I'll have to listen to Taylor Swift singing about yet another guy who did her wrong. I could write a hundred of those songs. Maybe it's my fault, or maybe it's just LA.

I wonder if it's time to leave LA. I've lived here my entire life. There's an entire world out there where I could live without sitting at a traffic light for five minutes. I fiddle with the car's trip computer and it tells me I've spent ten hours driving—in the past week. Where have I gone that took 10 hours. Let's see, I drove 120 miles. So I've averaged 12 miles an hour...

The car behind me honks. Asshole. I see the light's turned green but I can't move till the car in front of me moves so just fucking relax you fucking piece of fucking shit! I'm not feeling very Zen, unless it's the "Zen of Road Rage!" I could start a youtube channel about that. I could get a syndicated talk show. I *could* do a lot of things that will never, ever happen.

Then again, I didn't think the Bastard would ever call me, either. But he wasn't very nice, so why didn't I just text him something mean? Because I can't resist the idea that I might be helpful. I can't resist being needed.

Which is why I'm back on Alpine drive. It feels different than the first time I came here—the street's still the same, all these period houses that look like they were designed by movie studio art directors, because they probably were. But now it's familiar. I'm not intimidated.

What day is today? How long ago did the Madame X shit just happen? It feels like a long time ago, so long, like decades. In the past, anyway.

I'm anxious and amused. Bastard needs *my* help. Shit, I'm wearing the same outfit I wore the last time, I should really have bought this *Cashmerish* in several colors. I pull over and fire up the Amazon app and order more Cashmerish in *Tahitian Black Pearl, Alaskan Summer Salmon*, *Tokyo Indigo* and *Hilo Sunrise Gold*. Buy it now—click. Arrives tomorrow.

This is my uniform—I am a professional. I am here on a professional visit. I think. I don't know. Doesn't matter, I'm here.

I press the gate intercom. I hear Bastard, "Explain yourself."

"That's your job, Bastard."

The gate swings open and I drive up, parking carefully so I won't accidentally step in the moat. There's a breeze and I see Bastard has already opened the door. He's wearing a cashmere tracksuit—just like mine down to the color.

"Hi hi," he says, like we're old friends. I want to reply to his "Hi," with a "Ho," like one of the seven Dwarves, but in a gayer way, then again, seven men living together is as gay as it gets.

I mozy up the front steps—I don't know if I've ever mozied before but it's a conscious effort on my part to show how nonchalant I am about all this.

"Please come in..." I notice Bastard's feet are bare. "What should I call you? Sir?"

"Depends on why I'm here." For a moment he looks like a boulder that's blushing. He turns away and I follow him... into the kitchen, all black marble and dark wood.

"Please," he says, gesturing to a seat at the table. "Can I get you anything? Wine? Champagne? Tiramisu?"

"Come on now, Bastard, you asked for my help. What can I help you with? And Tiramisu, thanks."

He cuts a slice, places it in front of me on a square silver plate and sits at the chair next to me. "I tried to do what you did but Teddy said..." he swallows his words.

"It's OK, Bastard, you can..."

"Please don't call me that."

"I'm sorry, I don't know what your real name is."

"Oliver." he says, his stony exterior softening.

The theme from "Oliver, the musical" starts blaring in my head, "Oliver, Oliver, never before has a boy wanted more, he will rue the day somebody named him Oliver!" I close my eyes for a second and sweep it away.

"Call me Ollie," he says, softly.

"OK, Ollie. You have to understand you weren't very nice to me when I was here the first time, and then you kissed me, so I don't understand what's going on."

He lowers his head, "Sorry 'about that, mate. I gotta lotta defenses. I was a defensive lineman."

I take a bite of cake, it's cold and light and sweet. I slide the plate and fork in front of... Ollie.

"Eat this, you'll feel better," I say like I imagine a Jewish mother would.

He picks up the entire slice with his fingers and slides it into his mouth at once. To be fair, it wasn't that big a piece, but still, he manages to do it without getting any frosting on his face—impressive.

"Do you want to cuddle, is that why you messaged me?" He nods, stands, takes my hand in his big paw (surprisingly soft hands!) and leads me to the living room where there's a black leather sofa the size of my living room. It's like an adult playpen with seating on three sides and extra pieces in the middle.

"Please," I say, pointing for him to lie down. I lay behind him and immediately feel his outfit is *real* cashmere. He smells like plums. His body is hard, both from muscles and tension. I never thought I'd feel sorry for a big muscular guy, but in this moment I do.

I'm glad this is happening—it feels like a do-over. I focus my energy on him, sending joy with every breath —I am actually grateful I can breathe, I don't take it for granted, inhaling the energy of the world and exhaling it with good energy towards his ear. He sighs. Yes!

I can do this. I *am doing* this. I am good at this because I want to be here, I want to be sending this person good energy, I want to help. I know I can't do much about this frustrating, frightening world, but I *can* do this. *I am doing this.*

"Can I talk?" he mumbles.

"If that's what you feel like doing."

He shifts his big body around. Face to face. Studying him up close I can see his pores. His eyelashes. His light blue eyes. His humanity.

At first, his breath on my face makes me feel like I'm going to suffocate. I have a flashback to being a baby lying between my parents. It didn't matter which way I turned, I could only breathe their breath and it scared me.

I close my eyes and take a deep breath—I know there is enough air in this big room for the both of us. Thus armed with oxygen, I reach around and stroke the back of his head—his hair slightly prickly from product. "Tell me," I say.

"I've always been big—so people expected me to be strong. *Mean*, actually. They wanted to *use me* to be mean—know what I mean?"

I could imagine it but nobody ever expected me to be mean, much less strong. I didn't know that was even a possibility. But the past few weeks I've felt strong. Not powerful, that's bullshit, but strong, like I can take care of myself, and I can help take care of other people. "I understand. It sounds like it was hard for you."

"It was. It is. Teddy..." he stops. I hold him tighter. "Teddy's a good mate. He was my first boyfriend so long ago. Not a good one—too wrapped up in himself. But a good friend, always. When I blew out my knee and was released from the team, he hired me as his bodyguard—that's what he called me... so I had to keep acting mean, especially when Teddy came out but I couldn't..."

I inspect his face. In the past I've been so fooled by how people look—like this guy—a horizontal slash of eyebrows, angular nose, nothing soft. But I can see that inside he's got as much crap as I do, his body is just better designed to hide it.

God, I *love* doing this. I love everybody right now— underneath all their shit and defenses, I love them. It doesn't matter how they receive me, or don't, if they love me back, or not—I can still love. "You're OK, Ollie. People who know you love you. You can *let* more people love you."

He squints in disbelief. "Do you really mean that?"

"Yes. But it also doesn't matter what I think. Just what *you* think—and *feel*."

"I feel like kissing you," he says, his lips moving towards mine.

I move my hand to his cheek and gently hold him back. "Not not during this. This is a special time and we need to respect that, OK?"

He nods, "Sorry, I'm sorry..."

"It's OK, you don't have to be sorry. Thank you for telling me. Is that what you needed help with?"

"Yes. And no. And yes. But no. But a bit. I watched the video I shot of you and I tried to cuddle with Teddy, not romantically, I wanted to... I wanted..." his eyes search for the right word.

"Connect?"

"Yeah, exactly, right. I've spent years taking care of Teddy in impersonal ways, like bodyguarding, scheduling and accounting. I wanted to do something meaningful, like what you do."

"That's kind, thank you."

"But he said he couldn't feel it like he did with you."

"It's like sports, I guess, you have to practice," I say, knowing nothing about sports.

His eyes darken. "You know what I did after you left?" I shake my head. "I tried to call my mum to tell 'er I love 'er."

"That's..." I want to say "good" but I can't.

He gets quiet, "She threw me out when I was 16 and called me a faggot. I sent her presents every Christmas but I was always too scared to try to talk to her."

"Did you talk to her?" I ask.

"Naw." He sighs. "Some guy told me she'd died three months ago... Too late... so sad... got hammered and fell into the pool. Sank to the bottom. Let all the air out of my lungs and waited. Then it was like I felt her hand reach down and pull me up to the surface."

I realize I've been holding my breath.

He sniffs, "I'm crazy."

"You're human." I whisper. I felt such sadness and such joy at the same time I was lost for words. I just looked into his eyes, trying to see through the back of them into his brain and all the electrons flying around, making connections, branching off making new ones like lightning.

"I forget that," he says, his eyes moist.

I pull him closer. "Thank you. You're already getting good at this—you helped save me today, too."

"I did? How?"

"I had... a very painful experience. I couldn't connect. You are so open I feel received."

"I'm glad. That's what I want to do. Can you teach me more?"

"It would be my pleasure."

"Can we fuck, too?" he asks, tentatively, "Because I dig your energy."

"Let's finish our session professionally, Then maybe we can go to dinner and get to know each other."

"Good—though I already told you stuff I've never told anybody," he says, like a puppy dog.

"I look forward to learning a lot more about you, Ollie."

He closes his eyes, puts his head against my chest and snores quietly. So cute. So weird. So great.

THE POOL

I fall asleep. No dreams. I wake up to see him watching me, which oddly doesn't feel creepy.

"I like your nose," he says. I've never been a big fan of my own nose. It's fine, straight on, but in profile it feels off—too rounded. But not enough to get it changed. Not to mention my nose is so often stuffed up from allergies… I'm missing the point here.

"Thank you. I've grown attached to it," I joke because I don't know what else to say. I'm better at taking insults than compliments.

"Can we have dinner tonight?" he asks sweetly. I am confused, but happily so.

I feel myself smiling. "OK."

"I'll make dinner, I'm a good cook. Teddy's away so we'll have the whole house to ourselves."

"I'd love to go skinny dipping," I tell him.

He jumps up, grabs my hand and pulls me towards the pool, tearing off his clothes along the way. He's got a body like one of those greek statues of Neptune— carved from the solid muscle I see rippling under his skin. I must have muscles somewhere but I could never see them.

He lets go of my hand, launches himself into the air and does a graceful swan dive into the sparkling blue water, reminding me of a Hockney painting.

In the past I'd have been self-conscious about taking off my clothes but somehow it doesn't matter now. I feel a connection with Ollie—maybe romantic—maybe not, but man to man—male bonding, and being naked feels right.

I shed my clothes and dive in—the water is warm and soft, it holds me. Ollie pops up from the depths and puts his arms around me. His body is solid and slippery, like the dolphin I got to touch at SeaWorld. I love dolphins. I want to be one in my next life. I remember reading that dolphins have gay sex with their penises and blow holes.

I feel Ollie's hard cock pressing against my stomach. I kiss him, playfully but deep. Aggressively, but as an equal. I pull back, hold his head in my hands and look into his eyes. "I'm glad I get to know you, Ollie."

He kisses me now, aggressively, his stubble against my skin. He holds me tight—like we're twins in the womb. I let go of everything that happened the past few days—let go of the swirling galaxy of memories that otherwise flood my brain—let go of being me. I surrender. For the moment, I am part of us. Together. A new entity. Reborn.

Occasionally I'm aware of how massive his body is, how hard against mine—but it's not about body parts, it's about forgetting them, forgetting ourselves, dissolving into this union of skin and spit, moans and chuckles—playful, fun, passionate, pleasure, relief, connection, bonding, release.

I'm so happy I could cry. I stop myself until I see his tears. It feels like we've both been baptized—purified by the fire of our passion and the water around us. I don't know what to say, so I say nothing.

After a long silence he says, "I love you."

At first I'm shocked—but why? Love is the energy I've been giving out and he's giving it back to me. Maybe it hasn't been about being received by someone else—but being able to receive those feelings myself.

"I love you, too," I say, purely. For a moment I wonder if this will lead to tears in the future. But the past and future bring tears of regret or fear. In this moment I can share tears of joy.

Time has lost its meaning. The sun is setting.

Ollie and I separate back into ourselves. He rises from the water and comes back with a rainbow towel as large as a blanket and wraps it around me. I marvel at how someone who was a stranger a few hours ago is now an intimate friend. I touch his face. "You're beautiful."

He tugs my beard playfully, "You are, too." He leans down and kisses me. I'd forgotten that on land he's so much taller than I am. "Do you like eggs?"

I'm temporarily confused as to why he's asking that, then I remember dinner. "Yes, Ollie." I like saying his name.

"I make a mean omelet!" he announces, proudly, then reconsiders, "I didn't mean *mean*... I meant jolly good."

"Can I help?" I ask, actually wanting to help.

"You good at chopping?" he asks and suddenly I envision myself as a woodsman in a plaid shirt, chopping wood.

"Not really, but I'd like to cook *with* you."

"Bonza, babe!" he laughs. I follow him to the kitchen. He's still naked, and, given how he looks there's really no reason he should wear clothes—ever. I wear the towel like a poncho, but it's getting in the way so I toss it over a chair. I don't need to hide.

He spreads a selection of cheese, salami, and mushrooms across the marble countertop. He hands me a chef's knife and goes to butter a skillet. I don't really want to chop, I just want to watch him and enjoy the feeling of *having feelings* for another person. I'm not sure what those feelings are, exactly, other than a general, "Isn't he nice?" but that's enough.

He turns around, catches me watching him and winks. This is ridiculous. This is insane. This is impossible. It's too much—part of me longs to retreat into the safe warm genie-bottle of my brain.

I snap back when he gently takes the knife from my hand, quickly chops some cheese, salami and mushroom and tosses them in the one pan by themselves, while the eggs are cooking in another.

"I like to cook 'em separate so everything's all melty and merged... like we were," he reaches over and squeezes my ass.

I don't get this. I don't get this at all. And it doesn't matter as I watch him deftly flip the omelet, then slide it gracefully onto a platter. "Come on," he says, leading me to the table where he cuts it in half and plates it.

As I sit on the rattan seat of the chair, I think I really should be wearing pants—the rattan will press a pattern on my ass when I get up.

Then I take a bite of the omelet—salty, smooth, tangy, creamy, sweet. All words I could also use for Ollie. But all I say is, "Yum."

"You, too," he says with his mouth full—something we'll have to work on.

After all the eating, the clanking of forks and plates and drinking glasses against the table, I'm silent and full, so relaxed I'm not sure I'll be able to stand up.

"Sleep over?" Ollie asks.

"I don't know if I'm ready for a relationship," I tell him earnestly.

"I'm not asking you to marry me yet," he laughs. Yet? "Just spend the night."

I can do that. "OK."

We crawl into his king-size bed, cuddle non-professionally (a lot more casual), and watch *Fire Island*, a very gay movie based on *Pride and Prejudice*. I feel happy to be gay. Happy to be here. Happy to be me.

THE SLEEPOVER

It's been so long since I shared a bed with anybody that it might have been a problem if the bed hadn't been the size of Rhode Island. It's so wide I temporarily forget there's somebody else here. I remember and crawl across the expanse to sleep in his arms.

I lie there, my eyes open, taking it all in. I try to understand, then let that go. I don't need to understand —just feel. I feel warmth from him, coolness from the silent air conditioning breeze.

I like looking at his sleeping face—he looks boyish, as if all the crap of life slid away, revealing the real person inside. I always imagined that if I ended up with someone it would be a petite effete Latino artist who made collages mixing Renaissance imagery with cutouts of naked men and sold them at gay street fairs while wearing short shorts.

Ollie couldn't be further from that. He didn't want to be an artist (I asked). But he did appreciate art, and had, in fact, made the large painting over the bed. He told me the story of how he was painting a bathroom and the dropcloth was covered with drips, like a Pollack. He covered himself with the different colors of paint and rolled around on the canvas now over the headboard. "I just wanted to make my mark," he told me.

He has a good heart—even though he was born with a defective valve. Luckily since medical care is socialized in Australia it cost nothing for him to have corrective surgery. He still has a little scar on his chest which I trace with my finger—trying to imagine him as a baby, as a kid, a teenager, a football player... combining all the different versions of him into a single being inside this body.

I feel such warmth towards him I want to stay awake to enjoy it, but I fall asleep.

PING! Damn, I forgot to put my phone on silent—and it's at the other side of the bed. I ignore it. PING, it demands. The room is still dark but I can see light around the edges of the room-darkening blinds.

Ollie rolls over away from the sound and I crawl across the bed towards it. I pick up the phone then put it back down. I don't want to look.

PING! "I MUST SEE YOU" shows up on the lock screen. All caps. I hate all caps. Unless war has broken out there's no need for that. I turn the phone over and set it, face down, on the dresser and start to crawl back to Ollie when the phone goes PING! PING! PING! PING! PING! PING! PING! PING!

Now, even if war has broken out, I don't see what I can do about it, short of cuddling the generals in charge, so I'm not going to look.

"You should check your messages, Chaz, sounds important," Ollie says, sleepily. He called me *Chaz!*

I crawl back to the phone and feel anxious. I turn on the phone.

"I MUST SEE YOU AGAIN!" Oh no. Why didn't I block her?

"I AM SORRY ABOUT BEFORE." Sorry don't cut it, lady.

"THAT WAS THOUGHTLESS OF ME BUT I'M DYING." I don't care. OK, I do care but I don't want to.

"WE CAN MEET AT MY SIERRA TOWERS SUITE AND I WILL TELL YOU WHO I AM!" Somehow that's even more terrifying.

My heart must be pounding so loud that Ollie can hear it, "Are you all right babe?" He reaches across the bed and pulls me to him.

"No." I exhale.

"Did I do something wrong?" he asks.

"No, not you, you're wonderful. It's this," I show him the texts, "From the woman I told you about."

"Sounds like she needs you, boo." He kisses my cheek, his stubble like tiny pins. He gets out of bed and I admire his backside as he saunters to the bathroom.

Shit, he's right. She does need me. But I must have boundaries.

"No," I text her. There. Done.

PING! "PLEASE!"

"No," I reply.

PING! PING! PING! "PLEASE" "PLEASE" "I BEG OF YOU!"

Fuck.

I call Buck. "How're you feeling today, Chazbo?" she asks with genuine concern.

"I *was* fine until your crazy lady client texted me again insisting she has to see me."

"Oh, no. That must be upsetting."

"She says she'll tell me who she is." Buck is silent. "Buck? You still there?"

"Yeah, uh..." a long pause.

Ollie comes in, sees I'm on the phone, waves, then ambles into the hallway. I just like watching him walk.

"Buck!" I suddenly feel like other people must feel trying to get me back from my day dreams.

"Yeah, I'm here, just thinking... it could be important for you to go."

"Why?"

"I can't tell you, Chazbo, but it'll be clear. You can come see me right after so we can talk through it."

I feel nauseous. "Is this going to hurt me?" I ask.

"Hurt... and help... I hope." Buck says quietly. I trust Buck. Because if I have a nervous breakdown she'll be responsible and must know the best private mental hospitals the crazy lady's money can buy. "I will take care of you if you need it. But I can feel how you've gotten stronger."

"I don't want to, Buck," I tell her. "I'm afraid because my wall is gone," I say with a catch in my voice, scared *and* happy at the same time.

"Chip," Esme takes the phone. "I will drive you and be there for you."

"Do you know what this is about, Esme?"

"No, Buck still can't tell me, she's annoyingly ethical that way. But she wouldn't steer you wrong, partly because she's such a good person and partly because she knows I'm good with knives."

PING! "I WILL GIVE YOU ANYTHING YOU WANT."

"Oh, my God, she just texted again and said she'd give me anything I want!"

"What do you want, Chip?" Esme asks.

I frown because I don't know. It used to be easy when I only wanted *things*. "I want a Bentley," or "I want a Patek Philippe platinum minute repeater," or, most often without any good reason why, "I want a Hermes Birkin bag." I didn't even like the way those bags looked! I only wanted it because other people wanted it —now I don't care at all!

"Chip?"

"I'm thinking, I'm thinking!" I say. "No, I'm feeling, I'm feeling!"

OK, so I still wanted a mid-century modern house in the hills, like Rober's. Would she give me a house? That seemed like a lot to ask for but she's both wealthy and dying so it's not like she's gonna miss it. Wait, she mentioned *Sierra Towers*, that celebrity packed condo building just off Sunset. My neighbors would be Elton John and Cher! I could ask for *that*.

I start an angry reply to her demanding her condo, then backspace over it. I don't want to ask for that. That's crazy. That's greedy. That's unnecessary.

"I want to help," I say, surprising even myself. I text, "I want to help." Then I add, "And I want you to recommend me to your friends," I add in a stroke of—not selfishness but self-care—and self-knowledge. What I want is to make my cuddling calling real. To take care of myself—and others. That's what I want.

"You're very kind," she texts back, having rediscovered lowercase letters. "Kinder than I deserve, I know."

I manage to avoid saying, "You're right," and instead type, "See you tomorrow at 2pm."

"Make it 11am. Suite 2222. THANK YOU!" I don't mind that she used all caps at the end—but I still sigh because 11am? I'll have to wake up at the crack of 9!

"You still there, Chip?" Esme asks.

"Yes, sorry, I didn't go off into my head, I was texting her back. Now I have to pee really bad. I'll text you the deets. Love you."

"You can do this... whatever it is, I believe in you." Esme ends with a kiss.

Ollie enters, takes my hand and leads me to the bathroom. "I ran a bubble bath for you, babe." I sink into a cloud of citrus-scented bubbles. "I'll go make breakfast," he kisses me, then ambles off.

I let my worries melt into the warm water and orange bubbles. It's so soothing I have to fight from falling asleep—I don't want to drown now that I have so much to live for!

Ollie enters, "I'll rinse then dry you off," he offers.

"I'm not a baby, Ollie." I protest gently.

"You're *my* baby," he smiles, rinsing me with the hand-held shower head, then drying me with a fluffy white towel monogrammed in orange with *TT*. As if to prove his point, he picks me up like a baby and carries me to the bed. I'm gobsmacked. "I toasted some bagels, from Nate 'n Al's, with cream cheese and put lox on the side in case you don't like it." He leans down and kisses me.

I'm almost speechless, "Oh. Wow. Uh... Thank you, Ollie."

He gets in bed, balances the tray on his legs and hands me an everything bagel with a lot more than a schmear. I do love a good everything bagel because then I don't have to choose. I'm baffled by how normal it feels to be naked in this big bed with this beautiful man and a bagel in my mouth.

We enjoy a long, leisurely breakfast until it's interrupted by PING! PING! PING! PING! Oh, no, is she still at it? I look at the phone and there are texts from three different numbers.

"My darling Daffy just told me you're a miracle worker, please do let me know when you have an opening! Hot, Paris." Paris? Hilton? What the fuck? Daffy? Who's that? Is that the mysterious Madam X? No wonder she didn't want to use her real name.

Another text: "Sir, if you are half as good as Daf insists then you must schedule me for your treatment ASAP. Conscious regards. Gweneth." Goop Paltrow? Daf must be Daffy. I google "Daffy socialite" but get Daffy duck in drag—and Daphne Guinness of Guinness beer fame. She's known for being skinny and wearing avant garde clothes, so maybe it's her!

Another text: "Mr. Cooperman. Daphne says you changed her life and if you can change that bitch then I gotta see you ASAP—Kendall J." Is somebody playing a joke on me? I don't like the Kardashians but if I cuddle Kendall I'll be in all the tabloids and have no end of clients.

I'm literally frozen. The mysterious Daphne has already done what I asked her, sent me not just her friends but some of the most famous women in the world. I hand the phone to Ollie. "This is too much, Oll. I don't know how to deal with all this."

Ollie scrolls through the messages. "I met these ladies when they were here for parties. Paris has great manners. I got Gwenny to eat gluten. Kendall accidentally locked herself in the loo. They're just people."

His reassuring manner sparks an idea, "Maybe you could help me?" I can't read his expression. "No, sorry, that's too much to ask..."

His face blooms into a smile, "I wanna help! I'm good at scheduling, accounts, and have Teddy's publicist on speed dial—I'll call her and get some PR going."

I feel like there's a tsunami at my back, pushing me forward—hopefully I won't drown. But I let go of the fear and know that I'll either fly or I'll fall—either way I will have escaped gravity for a while. "Why would you help me like this, Ollie?"

"Because I need to help—we have that in common."

A thought crosses my mind that it's dangerous to mix business with pleasure... but maybe business *can* be a pleasure. "Let's give it a try!"

He places half a bagel on my head like a crown and bows to me. "My liege," he says, solemnly.

I knight him on both shoulders with the cream cheese knife.

THE (oo

"I'll set up a shared Google calendar for scheduling, and have patients pay directly to your Venmo account so you don't have to deal with dirty cash that has to be laundered."

"Money laundering?" I ask, incredulously.

"Cash is filthy, you don't know what people have done with it. I always wash and iron mine. A little starch is nice, too, crisps them up." Ollie announces as he gets in the shower with me.

I try to hold that image, but there he is, distractingly naked and beautiful. I close my eyes to get back to the subject at hand, "I need to pay you for all this, Ollie."

"You can pay me in kisses!" he says and I catch myself almost rolling my eyes because it's too ridiculously sweet. He must have noticed something on my face, because he gives me a look I recognize from when he was still *Bastard*. I'd thought it was a judgemental look, but maybe he was just confused. "What?" he asks.

"You're very sweet but I want to keep this professional."

"You don't want to kiss me?" he asks, soaping my balls which tickles.

"Yes, I do, but you're helping me and I want to help you," I explain.

"OK, we'll trade—help me learn how to do what you do," he says.

"Of course. I know you have the energy for it." He tickles under my arms until I'm in a soapy squirm. I look up and see his wide, toothy smile and am reminded that I didn't find him remotely attractive when we first met, but now that I like him, he's handsome.

A nice while later... he towels me dry. I could get used to this. Then he sets up the shared calendar and emails me, signing, *"Oliver, assistant to Mr. Cooperman."*

"Next time, sign it 'Oliver, C.O.O.'" I suggest. "Chief Operating Officer. And use your last name. I don't even know your last name!"

"Van Quince."

"Oh, my God, that's so good. You *have* to use it!"

"Oliver Van Quince, C.O.O.—yeah, I like the sound of that!"

For a moment I have to check myself. Is this really happening or am I just imagining it? Does it matter? Maybe not in the past, but now it does. "Bite me!" I demand. He does—hard on my upper arm—it hurts and leaves a mark. Feels real enough to me.

"Tasty!" Ollie smiles. "Now I'll make you a real Ozzie brekkie." When I get to the kitchen the food is already on the table. "Avo smash with vegemite."

I try not to show my disgust at hearing the word "vegemite." Esme had me try it once and it tasted like bitter beefy concentrated salt. But I will say it looks beautiful, as he's made the tomato look like a rose. I take a bite... actually good. "Delicious!"

"I guessed you wouldn't like vegemite, most Yanks don't, so I went easy on you. And I made Parisian-style hot chocolate in case you needed to clear your palate."

The hot chocolate is thick and rich, "You're very sweet," I say, leaning over and giving him a chocolatey kiss.

"Business question: How many cuddle sessions can you do in a day, do you suppose?" he asks between bites.

"I don't know, I've only ever done one in a day."

"Very exclusive—they'll love that. Gotta charge more, too, which they'll also love."

"$500 isn't enough?" I wonder.

Ollie laughs, "Pocket change. Teddy almost didn't hire you because you sounded cheap but Buck said it was a special introductory rate. I'd say $5,000 for the first session, $4,500 thereafter." I choke on the hot chocolate and it comes out my nose which is both embarrassing and fantastically fragrant. He cleans me up with his napkin. "That's like $50 to you or me."

"OK, but if I'm charging that much you need to get 25%" I insist.

"15% — that's what agents take. I already have a job, I live here, I have no expenses. You're my side hustle."

"And your side piece."

"My main course," he says, refilling my hot chocolate.

THE "WHAT iF?"

Ollie wanted me to stay the night again which was very sweet—but I needed to go home and prepare for whatever Daphne, the mystery woman had in store. I Googled but there were an awful lot of skinny rich women named Daphne so it was more confusing than anything.

Ollie. Great fun, but what if, to quote Cole Porter, "it was just one of those things?" I worry that, as the lyrics continue, *"If we'd thought a bit of the end of it, when we started painting the town, we'd have been aware that our love affair was too hot, not to cool down."* I don't want to hurt him. I don't want to get hurt. I don't know what to do.

My new *Cashmerish* tracksuits are waiting at the door with a note from Becky, "Sorry it's open, they delivered the box to our door and Gramma got it. I had to pry them out of her clutches and explain that men have always worn cashmere-ish. Love the colors. Let me know if you need me to smell you—Becks." I'm definitely going to hire that girl for something.

These tracksuits are all I need (and my summer jinbei for when it's hot). I shall shed myself of everything else—like a caterpillar becoming a butterfly!

I look around my room at the detritus of my life. Clothes I wanted but have never worn and now can't imagine wearing. DayGlo and Faux fur. Shiny sparkly "look at me" clothes that never got looked at. Why didn't I enjoy all this crap? Why was I saving it for a special occasion that never came? Now half this stuff either doesn't fit my body or my life.

I grab a box of trash bags—one for the thrift store so someone else can love it. One for the trash because nobody should be forced to look at the crap ever again.

No, wait, *everything must go!* I pull masses of shirts out of the closest and stuff them into a trash bag without even going through them. I will start over—all new designer clothes befitting my station!

That's stupid. I put shirts I actually wear on the bed. They're the things I look good and feel comfortable in. The one with a map of the Bahamas—I know that map by heart—I will go someday. The one that looks like I had a run in with an embroidered dragon and a bottle of bleach—love that. My favorite, which looks like psychedelic sushi.

Besides, I'll need a few long sleeve shirts, like the one with a celestial map (OK, so I have a thing for maps, if I ever get lost in one of those shirts I'll be able to find my way!). Pretty soon, half my shirts are back in the closet. The rest—how I wanted them at the time—but now's not the time. Into the bag they go.

I do the same thing for my pants and hats and start on the shoes... but no, I can't get rid of the painful pewter patent leather Doc Martens. Or the blue shoes printed with white clouds which are fine as long as I'm mostly sitting. I will need interesting shoes for working with women as they always notice a man's shoes.

I drag three surprisingly heavy trash bags downstairs and into the trunk of my car. I feel lighter already. I might even have a salad for dinner—except I have no cabbage and I refuse to eat lettuce, so it was a nice idea whose time hasn't come.

I turn on the mood lamp in the corner that scrolls through a rainbow of colors. When I'm antsy and agitated I stare at the changing colors and am reminded that "this too, shall pass." The red will give way to the orange, yellow, green, blue, purple, then back through blue, green, yellow, orange and red.

All the colors are beautiful. I try to tell myself that *all* my feelings are beautiful, too: joy, sadness, fear, anger... I know this is true but still don't believe it and if I had my way I would only feel the joy. But those other fucking emotions have work to do. As Pema Chodron says, they're disassembling my armor, piece-by-piece and painfully softening my heart in an effort to transform me.

Ah, back to my inner caterpillar transforming into a butterfly. I imagine emerging, colorful, and flying away, effortlessly. But I never thought about what it must be like in that chrysalis—the metamorphosis has to be terribly painful! All those legs falling off, sprouting wings piercing the back.

Going from who I was to who I want to be requires letting old parts disintegrate so integration is possible.

Good things are starting to happen—why am I so sad? Orange, yellow, green, blue, purple.

I text Ollie, "I'm scared."

Dot, dot, dot... "I'm here when you need me."

I get choked up. Do I deserve this nice guy? Am I willing to love, or fated to be like my mother and break a good man's heart, breaking my own in the process?

Why is there no word for being happy and sad at the same time? Bittersweet only really works for chocolate. Maybe chocolate would help. I eat a piece, then another, breaking my cardinal rule of "no chewing!" then remember and let it melt in my mouth.

Food isn't helping—I have no idea what to do. Ah, yes, sleep. Except I can't. I'm too anxious. My mind, which lately had started to feel quiet, is spinning again.

What if this woman is... so many possibilities. What if she's a witch? What's she gonna do, turn me into a squirrel? Would that be so bad? I don't want to be a donkey, but a squirrel might be fun.

What if she's a mass murderess? Naw, if she'd wanted to murder me she could have done it already at the private club where they're undoubtedly good at cleaning up such messes.

Cannibal? Really? I'm going there? She's too skinny. Still, I remember reading a book about those poor people who crashed in the Andes. Naw, I'm too fatty to be carpaccio.

Alien? Yes—that's a better fear... but nope, not going to think about the anal probe which, while not a bottom, I'm not afraid of.

So what the fuck am I worried about? I can't think of anything that's actually bad. She's Kaitlin Jenner? OK, not good only because she's Republican and stupid. But still, I might have an interesting conversation with her, and as a teenager I used to jerk off thinking about Bruce... who she's not anymore, I know... Now I feel bad about being un-PC.

But what if... what if... What if she's just a rich old woman who hasn't been touched in decades? No wonder she was uncomfortable and scared. What if... I can do something good for her before she dies?

I like feeling useful, but I'm not quite ready to let go of my catastrophizing. What if she's toxic! That's it. Completely general toxicity that will... that will... poison me! She already did that, undermining my confidence. I felt better because of Buck and Esme and Ollie—but what if she poisons my mind again, and this time the others can't help me—this time I sink into my own personal black hole of doubt?

There we go! Something real to worry about! But why does that make me feel better? Because it was the worst thing I could think of, and is *doubt* really all that bad? It's certainly nothing new for me. Like disappointment, I'm used to it!

I can always take that personal assistant job to Ellen, I won't starve, I'll just be miserable! Been there, done that, got the extra weight from eating cookies. I can handle misery!

I hear myself breathing—the air coming in from the world to my lungs, bringing oxygen into my bloodstream, exhaling carbon dioxide out, which plants need. I remember dad telling me every time I exhaled I was helping a plant—it made me feel part of his world, part of the circle of life.

Whatever happens tomorrow is all part of that circle. I might change her. She might change me—and that's OK. Change is what got me this far. Change might take me farther. I might have another setback, but like the first time with her, it didn't set me all the way back, did it? And that step back might have been just what I needed to move forward.

What do I know? This particular doubt feels good, letting go of certainty and jumping into the unknown! Whee!

I miss my dad. I miss believing that he knew everything. It made me feel safe. No wonder so many gays are looking for a daddy. Ollie felt a little bit like a daddy, taking care of me. I wonder what I feel like to him.

I wonder if we can take turns being stronger when our weaknesses kick in? I like that idea, repeating it in my head until I fall asleep.

THE MORNING OF...

My alarm shrieks trumpet *Reveille* from the Marine Corps Marching Band. I find it simultaneously rousing and revolting, a theme song for the patriarchy. Gone are the days when I could unplug my clock radio, or throw it across the room, now it's my phone and I can't take my early-bird aggressions out on it. I can, however, snooze it. And again. And again.

It's 9:30 before I decide this isn't a wise move. I need to leave by 10:30. I Googled and there's validated parking in the building. One should always take parking into consideration. I jump in the shower without actually jumping as that would be foolhardy. I concentrate on soap and suds and singing, "I'm gonna wash that gal right outta my hair!" an informal variation on the normal recipe from the musical, *South Pacific*.

I've made a conscious decision that no matter what this woman does, or doesn't do, I will survive, so now the song in my head morphs into the unofficial gay national anthem, *"I Will Survive!"*

"At first I was afraid, I was petrified… Oh no, I will survive, as long as I know how to love, I know I'll stay alive!"

It actually makes me feel better. I towel off but decide to have breakfast naked. Why not? The windows all have blinds and I think about how freeing it felt with Ollie. I send him a text, "Good morning…" what do I call him? "Ollie Berry?" No, what am I thinking? "You sexy C.O.O!" that's good. Send. Smile.

"You got this, Chaz!" he replies. He's more sure than I am, but I'm glad somebody is. I'm glad *he* is.

I have plain yogurt with ginger jam. I love the contrast between the creamy smoothness of the yogurt and the bite of the ginger heat. I'm relaxed, which makes me worry. Why am I relaxed? Because Ollie's already booked sessions for Paris and Gweneth and Kendall. What's Daphne going to do if she doesn't like me—text them all and tell them to cancel? Oh, my God, she could do that!

Or… I can steal her phone! OK, not *steal* it, but certainly *hide it*. In the back of the freezer. It'll be a whole *Gaslight* thing! What a terrible thought—I love it! I'll ask her to get me a drink, then say I have to go to the commode and secret her phone away behind the ice cream, except she's too skinny to have ice cream, maybe just the ice trays, but I heard her ice tinkling the last time so she'll find it… I'll figure it out when I get there!

10am. Which color *Cashmerish?* It was so much simpler when I only had *Sonoran Silver.* Now I have to choose between the *Tokyo Indigo* which feels darkly refined, and *Alaskan Summer Salmon* which kind of screams, "I feel pretty and I don't give a fuck what you think!"

I experiment with the Indigo pants and Salmon top and immediately regret it, feeling like two scoops of different flavor ice creams. Ice cream. I could stop at *Pops Artisanal Creamery* and get some Mango/Cream Cheese... but it's out of the way and I don't have time. If things go horribly wrong I'll get it on the way back. If they go terribly right I might, too.

I decide on the *Alaskan Summer Salmon*. I like the attitude and it makes my skin look rosy. I look in the mirror. I am not a bad looking man. I am an OK looking man. I am a good-looking man (though I can't help but think "good-looking is in the eye of the beholder.") That's OK—I just have to find the right beholders—like Ollie.

My ears are pinging. My hands are wringing. My phone is singing—It's Esme!

"Park in Buck's driveway and I'll drive you to the mystery woman." Her voice is so calming—like fresh sourdough bread.

"Thank you, my love, but I want to handle this on my own."

"Are you sure?" she asks, *not* sounding like she doubts me.

"51%" I say, doubting myself.

"You're a big boy now?"

"I have a feeling it's important for me to deal with it myself." I explain, now 52% sure.

"I'll wait at Buck's in case you need us."

"I will always need you, and always love you."

"Kisses!" she says. I let her love sink in for a moment before tapping the red hangup button.

I feel like I'm on a very, very, very, very high-diving board—like that guy who jumped from space. I take a deep breath. Lock my front door. Get in the car. Crank up the AC and Gloria Gaynor—*I will survive!*

THE DAPHNE
AND THE DEAD

Traffic is heavy down the Sunset strip—the famous, if not that scenic boulevard—lined with billboards for TV shows and movies— people doing something with their lives. I used to envy them. Now I'm doing something with my life. Maybe I should take out a billboard, too! No—not exclusive enough.

I see the *Sierra Towers* up ahead. I've always liked this building—perched on the edge of the green Beverly Hills—the wide white balconies making it look like it's floating. I turn into the valet parking and say, "I'm here to see Daphne..." yet as soon as the words come out of my mouth I realize I don't know her last name and wonder if there's more than one! Then I remember, "Suite 2222."

The cute I'm-only-doing-this-to-be-discovered young valet opens my door, "Of course sir."

The lobby is a sea of marble and mid-century modern. The concierge, in a simple black suit, approaches, "May I help you, sir?"

"Yes, I'm here for Daphne, Suite..."

"Twenty two, twenty two, yes, she's expecting you. I'll show you up." He slides his key card into a slot and the bronze elevator doors open revealing more marble and bronze inside. He gestures for me to enter, follows me, presses "22" and looks silently ahead as we're whisked up. The doors open on 22. "Down the hall to the right, sir," he says.

"Thank you." did he come all this way up with me just to make sure that I didn't wander off and bother Elton or Cher? I walk down the long hall's cream carpeting. Who puts cream carpeting in a communal hall? Yet it's spotless and so deep my shoes sink a bit as I walk.

I get to 2222 and the door is open. Oh, God—what happened with her the last time hits me like a YouTube video unexpectedly playing at full volume in the background. I can do this. I will do this. *I will survive!*

I peek inside and everything is glossy white from the marble floor to the lacquered ceiling. It's like walking into a kaleidoscope with the view of Los Angeles reflected vertiginously from floor to ceiling windows.

What I don't see is Daphne. I knock on the door and say "hello" and hear a faint voice saying "come in."

Another threshold. I try not to be distracted by my reflection above and below, or the stunning if slightly smoggy view from Beverly Hills to the ocean.

In front of me I see the back of a small, severely quaffed head of silver hair sitting on a white satin sofa. I approach it gingerly.

"Stop right there." The voice says, quiet but commanding. I stop. My shoes, the blue ones with a pattern of clouds, making a squeaking sound against the glossy marble.

"You said you needed to see me and I came." I say "I'm here to help."

I hear a cough and throat clearing.

"Could you just stand right there for a bit until I am ready?" she says, not moving. What's she getting ready for?

"Sure," I say, having a hard time finding my equilibrium, much less my equanimity.

She clears her throat and coughs again. I smell that perfume from the last time and start to feel overwhelmed. I lean against a shiny white bookcase and am confronted with a collection of Hermes Birkin bags arranged in a rainbow of colors. My eye stops at a green alligator bag—so *she* was the woman in Buck's office.

The back of my brain tries to take over and start spinning stories of danger and destruction. The front part of my brain wants my feet to escape towards the door. My heart tells me I have to stay.

Another cough, "You may come closer." she says.

I'm simultaneously eager to know the wizard behind the curtain and to run the other way. I take a step forward, inspecting her perfect, helmet-like silver hair. Closer still, and I see the telltale signs of age and plastic surgery combined into a taut, glossy, pallid complexion that looks like someone who used to look like someone familiar.

Then it strikes me—literally strikes me—if I wasn't holding into the bookcase I would fall over.

I recognize this face. It's not the face I knew—it's the face she constructed over the past 42 years. It's the face I've seen when I morosely Googled her at midnight to see pictures of her at some gala wearing a light dress and heavy jewelry.

I hold tight to the bookshelf as she slowly turns her face towards me.

"Hello Charles."

I say the only words I can choke out, "Hello, Mother." I frantically try to reassemble my inner wall from the rubble—Daphne, Daffy, Daffodil... Narcissa—fuck her! I need my wall high and impenetrable.

"I'm sorry about what happened," she intones flatly, reaching out with a glass of champagne as casually as if what happened was that she'd used the wrong fork.

I take the glass, careful not to touch her. I'm no longer scared at what *she* might do to me—but what *I* might do to her as anger rises within me.

She sits with perfect posture and crosses her skinny legs. Everything in the room is white, except for red pillows, flowers and Hermes bags. It's almost oppressively perfect, as if a real human couldn't possibly live like this.

I stand behind a curvy white sofa, keeping it between her and me. I inspect her as if she's a stranger, which she really is, isn't she? The song *Momma Who Bore Me* from Spring Awakening plays in my head until I pinch my leg. Now all I hear is the traffic on Sunset and her strained wheezing.

I swallow hard and take a deep breath to keep from fainting. I want air in my lungs to shout through my vocal cords—but I have nothing to say. All those years of practicing the conversation I'd have if I ever met her in person, all those fantasies of yelling and screaming and cursing and crying. But oh—Now I can't think of a word to say. I can't even remember what she just said to me.

The inside of my head is simultaneously a tornado and a vacuum. I yawn to clear my ears. "What did you just say?" I ask her.

"I'm sorry about yesterday, Charles."

Suddenly anger pours down on me like a waterfall of lava. I feel like I'm going to vomit and scream at the same time—but what comes out is a kind of feral growl. "I'm sorry for what you did 42 years ago." The words *I'm sorry* were never part of my fantasy. But I am sorry. I'm heartbroken.

"Your *Chihuahua West* Cashmere suits you," she says as if this was some casual cocktail party. I study her stillness, surgery, and slight shaking of her champagne flute.

It's all I can do to keep breathing while my mind reels. I put the champagne glass down on the white lacquer bookcase behind me without a coaster—I don't care if it leaves a ring! I need the next thing I say to hurt her, even knock her out. "You killed my father" is easier to say than *you killed me*.

I turn away from her and hear her heels clicking towards me but am unable to move away. "I didn't kill him, Charles. I set him free. You, too."

I still can't turn around and look at her. "Am I supposed to thank you? Do you honestly think that's what I wanted as a three-year-old—to be *set free* by my own mother? Abandoned and unloved by you?" I say the words as if they're a sword I can cut her heart out with—if she has a heart.

"Are you finished trying to hurt me?" She asks, putting her hand on my shoulder—making me shiver.

"I don't think I'll ever be done with that," I say, shaking her hand off.

"That's too bad. It's a heavy burden to carry. I've carried it, too and it's worn me down."

I spin around and face her, "What've you ever carried for yourself other than your Birkin bag?" I hiss.

She suddenly looks quite old, the plastic surgery and botox and filler unable to hide her emotion. She says, softly, "I hated my mother, too. I thought I could spare you that."

"You were wrong." I back away into the wall of glass. For a moment I can imagine falling backwards down 22 stories, but I don't need to hit the ground, I'm already shattered.

"What would you have me say?"

I don't have an answer. In my fantasy reunions I did all the talking, screaming, crying and blaming. She just nodded and handed me Birkin bags, keys to a Bentley convertible and her mansion. But I don't care about that shit anymore. "I want you to say it was the biggest mistake of your life to leave me. I want you to say you might have been rich but your life has been poor from not knowing me."

She looks away, then back at me, making eye contact that feels like an assault. "But it wasn't a mistake."

I stumble over to the green Birkin bag, pull it off the shelf and throw up in it. My hands are shaking so hard that the bag drops and my green puke splashes out onto the white marble and satin.

She hasn't moved. Or been moved. "It was the kindest thing I could do for you."

I swallow hard, bile in my mouth, "I hate you."

"That's too bad. I'd rather hoped you'd forget me."

I look at her in disbelief, "Yes, because it's so easy to forget my mother deserted me."

"You're right, that was insensitive."

"*That* was insensitive? I've spent years making lists of the insensitive, thoughtless, terrible things you've done. You never reached out to me after dad died. You let the bank repossess his farm. I was left to fend for myself while you lived just a few miles away in Bel Air. You never called or wrote. You never offered any kind of help—financial or emotional! I mean, what the fuck lady? You weren't just insensitive, you actively didn't give a shit!"

"I'm a selfish bitch. Is that what you want me to say?" she intones without any detectable emotion.

"That's a start!" I'm exhausted and perch on the arm of the sofa. "But it doesn't change anything."

She reaches into her white tweed pocket edged in black, pulls out a cigarette and a gold lighter. "But it changed you—for the better."

"Now you want me to thank you for your neglect? And what the fuck do you know about how I turned out?"

She exhales smoke, then coughs, "You turned out better than I did—and better than you would have if I'd been around. "

"Fuck you."

She doesn't look at me. "I've been fucked for a long time, darling." She sits in a big white swivel chair and turns to face me, "Does that make you happy?"

It does—the most caustic happiness that starts burning down my throat. I close my eyes to feel it, to savor it, but it just hurts. I fear if it keeps moving down it'll burn my heart away. I can't hold onto that feeling anymore. I shake my head, turn away from her and head for the front door.

Her voice is breathy but ceaseless, "It's better that you hate me than become like me. You were better off with your father, a loving man. He was a disappointment to me but I knew he wouldn't be to you."

I stop but don't turn around. "Disappointment? Do you even know what that means? I loved *you* more than anybody, even Dad. But you didn't love me. And if *you* couldn't love me then *nobody* else could. You can't even imagine my disappointment."

There's a long pause. I'm ready to leave when I hear her, gasping for breath, "Sadly, I can. I have never loved anyone. Including myself. Maybe I don't know how. Maybe I never allowed myself. I watched love kill everyone it touched. Including your father. You need to know this: He didn't want to be a landscape architect. He liked to fiddle with flowers—he wanted to be a florist—and probably gay, too. But he got me pregnant. He adored you—and by extension, me. So he got a real job. Love—that's what killed him."

I spin around to face her, "Shut up! You don't know what you're talking about."

"Yes, I do. I knew what I wanted, too. He couldn't give it to me: Money. Society. Envy. All so much easier to deal with than love. So I married Kenneth. I didn't love him so it didn't matter that he didn't love me, either. He got what he wanted, a beautiful wife who knew how to impress his friends and ignore his mistresses. I didn't care. About anything. Even when he found a young version of me."

"I don't give a shit about your cliche trophy wife story, you harpy!"

She makes a choking, cackling sound. "Harpy! I love that."

Fuck. I can't help but laugh. She thinks I'm laughing with her.

"I'm glad you see the humor in it. I was greedy but not as smart as I thought I was. All I got in the divorce was this condo and just enough money to get by."

"Boo hoo," I say, horribly. "All I got from you was nothing!"

"You're 45, let it go already," she says like it's no big deal.

"You're, what, 100? *You* let it go."

"You're still such a child. It's cute now, Charles, but won't be when you're 50."

"How can you remember that long ago?" I say, viciously.

"The same way you can remember 42 years ago, kiddo." Her calling me *kiddo* makes me shrink. Like it or not, I am this woman's spawn. Like it or not, half my DNA is hers. I can blame her for *half* my bad decisions, but the other half are still mine.

She continues, matter-of-factly, "You'll be happy to know I'm leaving you this condo and whatever money I have left."

"How do you know what will make me happy, *Daphne*," I don't want to call her *mother*.

"I wanted you to forget me—so you think I forgot you. But I followed what you were doing. Yes, I saw you struggle, but I also saw you grow."

"So you were spying on me my entire life? You knew I needed help, yet..."

"You didn't need help. You helped yourself. That was the most valuable gift I could give you." She blinks and swallows. "I wanted to see you for now for completely selfish reasons: To make it clear I don't consider what I did a mistake. I'm relieved you turned out well, like your father. Not like me."

I'm too stunned to cry. "Do you feel better now? Good, that's my job. This visit is on the house. There won't be another one."

She shakes her head, sadly, "The apple didn't fall far..."

"I didn't fall—I was torn off! Then I finally find my way and you show up to ruin my life—again. But not this time. I'm fine forgiving you or forgetting you. I'm a big boy, momma. Big enough to take care of myself and leave." I stop and take a breath. "I pity you."

I get to the front door and hear her cough. Do I really want this to be the last thing I say to her? To replay this scene over and over in my mind for the rest of my life, imagining what I *should* have said? I'm better than that now.

I turn around. "I'm grateful you didn't raise me. You fucked me up by leaving but you would have fucked me up far worse if you'd taught me I couldn't love. Because even now—I can still love *you*."

I start crying, angry, sad, a deafening cacophony of inner voices: my three-year-old crying as mother peeled me off her to leave, my four and five and six year-old self crying at every birthday. At 20, and 30, and even 40 wondering what I did wrong to make her go. And now, because she isn't the person I wanted her to be. I steady myself against the doorframe.

Then I feel it—

—under my anger—

—*sadness*—so old—so deep—

—that it's still at the core of my being.

I close my eyes and feel it. Ollie and his mother flash in my head—I can't leave like this. I turn and walk slowly back to her.

Our eyes meet. She has my green eyes. Or I have hers. My mind goes silent.

Suddenly, *her* sadness is as clear as mine—but older and deeper. We have that in common— probably more.

I finally *see her*—under her Chanel suit she's just a frail old woman.

But *I* will survive. *As long as I know how to love, I know I'll stay alive.*

My wall crumbles. I collapse onto the sofa, my hands covering my face with fingers spread just enough to still watch her. She dabs her eyes with a monogrammed hanky. She briefly notices the mascara stain on her white Chanel jacket, but she keeps looking at me as I take slow, deep breaths.

My anger is gone—now there's nothing to hide the deep lake of sadness that laps at my heart. I close my eyes and have to fight falling asleep to escape. I must stay awake—float on this lake and row across it until I reach the other side.

I am surviving.

I take my hands off my face and open my eyes. Now adding to my sadness is what I'll lose when she dies. *Shit!*

If we'd never met, I would have rejoiced when she died. I would have sung, *Ding Dong the Witch is Dead*. Now I'm going to have to sing Sara McLaughlin's, *I Will Remember You*, which always makes me cry.

Fuck! I'm going to lose her *again*. I'm back to thinking about myself, which feels better—until it feels narcissistic—but that's *her* fault. Can I keep blaming her after she dies? Should I stop blaming her now?

Woah! I feel love welling up inside me. Not just the professional love I can give to strangers but love for the only person alive who's shared the same blood with me.

Love for the person who lives on in me.

And love for the person I have finally become.

I look at her tiny body slouched in the big white chair. I kneel next to her—putting my arms around her.

She feels weak. I feel strong.

I rest my head on her shoulder—her floral perfume reaching up into my nose and sparking memories I finally understand—of yesterday—of 42 years ago and how I loved the way mama smelled.

I hold her and send all the love I've been learning to feel and yearning to give. The pain, too—without the wall—all of it. Purple, blue, green, yellow, orange, red... I send it in the hope that she can feel what it's like to be alive before she dies.

I breathe her air. She breathes mine.

The timer on my phone goes off. It's been 50 minutes. I shut it off as fast as I can.

"Do you need to go?" She whispers.

"No."

She pats my head, "You hungry?"

"I could eat. But how can *you* be that skinny and eat?"

She looks at me like she's going to impart some earth-mother wisdom of the ages, "I mostly drink. Though now I eat chocolate cake, too, because why the fuck not?"

"Why the fuck not!" I agree. I don't know what to do with all these feelings. Loss and love and, surprisingly, pride.

Her fridge is empty but for six bottles of Dom Perignon and three elegant chocolate cakes from The Ritz in Paris.

I remove a cake from its box. Fancy lettering on the frosting reads, "Happy Birthday, Daphne." I didn't know.

I run a knife under hot water then let the blade melt its way through the cake, making a fat slice topped by the word "happy."

This is how a world ends. Not with a bang, but a birthday.

THE FUTURE

We ate cake and drank champagne. It was a celebration. An ending. A beginning. *A wake while we could still enjoy it.*

Together we met with Buck who, I have to say, is very wise.

I'm glad I got to spend three months with Daphne before she passed. I learned a lot about myself from what I saw in her. Her last words were, "I love you."

Then she smiled and let go. I still cry when I think about it.

We have the perfect relationship now that she's dead.

Her famous friends and their friends became regular clients. Under all that money and genuine cashmere even rich people are just people—they need to be held, too. The nice thing is they don't mind being *held up*.

Their money let me start the *Embraceable Foundation*. We teach poor and sick kids how to cuddle for their emotional health, as a community service (cuddling people in hospice and hospitals), and as a career at our affordable offshoot, *Embraceable You, Too*. Disney kept trying to buy it but I turned it into a nonprofit which Ollie runs—out of New York City.

Ollie always wanted to live in NYC. I could have figured out a way to make him stay—if I hadn't loved him. But I did. I do—so I wanted the best for him. In that way, maybe Daphne knew how to love but just didn't recognize it.

I want him to have what he needs, even when it's not me. I go to NYC to see him, he comes here to see me. We use our time apart to keep seeing who we are. Maybe in a few years we'll grow up and settle down. Or maybe we won't need to. In the meantime, we're open—to anything. That feels right.

I tried living in the condo Daphne left me. Great view. Cool neighbors even with Elton's loud late-night piano playing. But it never felt like home to me. It did to Rober, who fell in love with the place—white furniture, loud piano and all.

So we traded houses. Cher finds Rober charming (they have similar appetites for food and footwear) and he promised *not* to manage money for his neighbors.

I'm living in Rober's former house, seeing select clients in the pool for what I've branded *rebirthing*.

Esme and I have a son together, Calix Cooperman-Collins. Thankfully he's got Esme's forehead and my sense of style.

He also has two loving mothers and fathers who give him all our love. We feel it shining back to us. Cal's a character—we're a captive/captivated audience for his many musical extravaganzas, the latest being *Dancing Dinosaurs: T. Rex got rhythm*.

I do a lot of pro-bono cuddling: for sick kids, like Ollie was; and old people, like Daphne was. The kids are so serene I feel like I should be paying them—so I subsidize their medical care. The old women mistake me for their late husbands or lovers or both—everybody has a story to tell.

I give them love—joyful that I know what love is and get to give it away.

The rich people pay me royally to leave. The poor and sick don't have to pay me anything to stay.

Am I a whore or a saint? I'm good both ways.

Don't make life "either/or," when it can be "and…"

DANIEL
WILL-HARRIS

Daniel Will-Harris is a best-selling author of four plays and novels.

MoMA has called Daniel's work "truly unique."

He's developed plays with the Kennedy Center Playwriting Intensive, Naked Angels Theater, and The Actor's Centre in London. His plays are distinctly theatrical to engage with the audience in ways they can't experience with electronic mediums.

His 8 books have sold over 300,000 copies. He has three produced feature film screenplays to his credit and has written over 600 short stories currently featured in his popular story podcast.

To learn his writing practice, called "Write in the Now," go to *www.WriteInTheNow.com*

He's also an award-winning designer of wristwatches. You can see all his work and contact him here:

www.will-harris.com